All Who Dream

Letting Go Series
Book Three

By Nicole Deese

All Who Dream is dedicated to my baby sister,
Aimee Brooke Thomas.
(July 26, 1987 to November 25, 2013.)

**Aimee loved beyond limit, laughed without restraint, and
believed that every dream was a gift from above. You were our
gift, Aimee. I love you.**

"May the God of hope fill you with all joy and peace as you trust in
Him, so that you may overflow with hope…"
Romans 15:13

Prelude

All Who Dream

There's a time and place for dreaming

A melody within life's meaning

You search and seek and pray and pine

Yet in the end its hope you'll find

Some days are bleak while others bare

Some feel rooted in deep despair

But don't lose faith and don't lose sight

For dreams will come to those who fight

If chance is slim and risk is great

Remember the reward at stake

The test is found in how you fail

For joy itself cannot turn stale

This truth and hope act as a team

They light a path for all who dream

Prologue

Since the day I found out I was pregnant, there was one prayer that never strayed far from my lips.

Just. One. Prayer.

"God, please protect my son."

It was a typical Tuesday night. I had locked down the house, closed the curtains, and rearranged the leftovers in the fridge, when I noticed my brother's wallet on the countertop. Shaking my head, I slid the heap of worn leather into the top drawer, and flicked off the kitchen lights. Briggs might be a fireman by trade, but his reputation for misplacing personal belongings predated that superhero status by two decades. I texted him to let him know.

Padding through the quiet house and down the hall, I pushed away my nausea with a cleansing breath. I hated the darkness of night, especially without the security of my brother nearby.

Though I'd escaped the hand of Dirk Luterra two years ago, the prison of paranoia that held me now was almost as bad. *Almost.*

Trailing my fingers across Cody's door as I passed, I whispered, *"We are safe here, son."* But even as I said it, I knew safety was only an illusion—a vapor easily diffused.

Just before the thick haze of sleep lured me deeper beneath my comforter, I *heard* it.

The heavy scrape of boots plodding up the porch steps.

One did not forget the sound of terror.

A scream keened in my head, but an invisible band gripped my throat and refused to let the sound leave my lungs. The same band seemed to wrap my entire body. I couldn't move, couldn't breathe . . . *Cody!*

As if shot from a catapult, I lunged from the bed and snatched my cell off the side table. Phone clutched in my fist, I raced for the nursery. Chills clawed up my legs as my bare feet slapped the wood floor in sync with my heartbeat.

Darting into Cody's room I slammed the door behind me. At the sharp sound, a whimpery gasp came from the crib. A crash of wood splintering erupted from the living room, turning my knees to gelatin. I sagged, leaning the weight of my body against the closed door.

Arm shaking, I lifted my phone and punched in 9-1-1. My breathing rasped in my ears as the call went through. A brisk voice answered, requesting the nature of my emergency.

"Please help us—"

A heavy weight rammed the door panel, and I was flung across the room, phone slipping from my hand and skittering under the rocking chair.

Dirk.

I sprang to my feet and ran toward Cody, to throw myself on top of him—to shield him. But Dirk was quicker. His fingers gripped my arms, and I imagined my bones snapping within his grasp.

"Found you, Angela." The moonlight that peeked through the curtain revealed the familiar hollowness of addiction in his eyes, and the soulless timbre of his voice sent prickles up my spine.

He slammed me into the wall again, my head throbbing and blurring my vision as a metallic substance coated my tongue. The world tilted; I fought to stay alert.

He leaned over the crib and ice seized my chest. Cody whimpered at the rough awakening. Grabbed at the waist, Cody was flung over Dirk's shoulder like a sack of garbage. He stalked out of the bedroom, heading toward the fractured front door.

I staggered to my feet despite the aching in my skull. "You can't take him!"

Dizzily, I stumbled after him, tripping down the porch as a familiar warmth oozed down my neck. He yanked open his truck door, ignoring my pleas and tossed my toddler inside. Cody shrieked with arms outstretched.

I lunged at Dirk.

He fisted my hair and crushed my back to his chest. While his arm tightened around my throat, I blinked rapidly, refusing the pull of unconsciousness as long as possible.

"Angie!"

A voice called my name in the distance—a voice so familiar I wanted to weep at the sound. *Briggs! I'm here!* I dug my nails deeper into Dirk's forearm, begging God for Cody's life as something sharp pierced my side. Hot agony speared through me.

Chaos ravaged my mind and body as I slumped to the ground. But as quickly as the pain came, it was gone.

A quiet assurance pulsated in its wake.

I'm going to die.

I forced my lips to move as the darkness descended over me like a heavy quilt.

"God, please protect my son."

Chapter One

-Six Years Later-

I don't belong here.

With each clipped step I took across the marble floors of Pinkerton Press, I believed this more and more. Straightening my thrift-shop skirt for the millionth time, I stepped inside the elevator and pressed the button for the twentieth floor. Closing my eyes, I wished my phobia of plunging to my death while inside an elevator shaft could take a rain-check today. My mind was far too pre-occupied to think about that right now. *Besides, there are worse ways to die…*

I fought to regulate my breathing as the mirrored coffin rose, but suddenly my stomach—which had been left on the first floor—caught up with the rest of my body, twisting into a sick knot when the doors opened. I touched the pendant at my neck and walked toward the receptionist's desk. A woman with the reddest hair I'd ever seen sat fiddling with a computer on the opposite side.

"May I help you?" she asked.

"Yes, thank you. I have an appointment to see Mrs. Bradford."

"Oh, you must be Angela Flores. You are even prettier in person! You certainly don't look like you could have an eight-year old son." She smiled wide. "Just a sec…I'll see if Dee is ready for you." The redhead picked up the phone and hit a series of buttons.

"Oh, uh…thank you." I gulped my anxiety back down.

The past couple of weeks had been interesting, to say the least. Winning a radio contest I didn't enter—compliments of my best friend, Rosie—for my single parenting blog had come as quite a surprise. But even more than that, the popularity that seemed to spread overnight was beyond dumbfounding. I had stopped looking at the number of followers after the first few days. The figures made my palms sweat so badly I could hardly type a fresh entry.

And being recognized at the grocery store by a stranger who read my blog? That was beyond strange.

At twenty-nine, I didn't exactly feel old, but if age was measured by life experience alone, I'd be an antique by now. Self-consciously, I lifted a hand to my blonde hair, smoothing back the flyaway strands that had surely sprouted during the windy walk through the parking lot.

"Right this way, Miss Flores."

I followed the receptionist down the hall where she stopped in front of a swanky office. I hauled in a long, shaky breath. An explosion of wealth and success lay just beyond this portal. My heart knocked hard against my ribs as the receptionist ushered me inside.

"Miss Flores, please come in," said a striking woman I assumed was Dee Bradford. "Thank you, Sylvia. You may go."

The soft click of the door behind me propelled me forward.

"I'm Dee Bradford, but you may call me Dee." Dee extended her manicured hand for me to shake.

"It's nice to meet you, Dee, and thank you," I said.

"Please have a seat, we have much to discuss."

Dee's hair was white as the clouds and wafted around her wrinkle-free face in artfully arranged waves, she had to be well into her 60s. Yet, nothing about her seemed "old." She was a classy sort of beautiful, slender figure wrapped in a navy skirt suit that branded her both professional and stylish. Her makeup was understated and impeccable. I hoped I could age *half* as gracefully at that.

I eased into the leather chair across from her desk and took in the view through windows that lined three-quarters of her office. Dallas was not known for its scenic charm, yet from this elevation, the skyline was breathtaking. Dee cleared her throat, and I brought my attention back to her face. She smiled at me, and my cheeks grew warm.

"It's a unique view of Dallas from up here, isn't it?"

"Quite. I'm not much of a city gal, but if I saw this kind of view every day I think I could be easily converted."

Dee laughed and leaned back in her chair to cross her legs.

"I'm sure you're wondering why I called you, Miss Flores—may I call you Angela?"

"Angie will be just fine, thank you."

Indeed I *was* wondering why she had called me to meet with her.

"I am quite connected when it comes to the voices in this city, Angie. It's my job to know the latest trends and movements, as you could imagine. Many well-known authors have sat in that very chair you occupy now."

I nodded hesitantly. How else could I respond when I couldn't yet make heads or tails of where this conversation was going?

"A good friend and old colleague of mine is the owner of *The Edge 102.5,*" she continued. "He insisted I read your blog. He claimed what I would find within your entries was a rare and deeply connected portrayal of a single mother. And while I hesitate to call your writing addictive, I will say we want you, Angie.

"We are launching a campaign this summer—one focused primarily on families. Not only does Pinkerton Press have interest in publishing your blog into book format, we also want you to represent this generation of single moms."

She paused, gaze wide and focused, as if she could see my head spinning right off my shoulders.

"*Excuse me?*" I rasped, my heart making strenuous efforts to beat right out of my chest.

Smiling, she rose and moved to perch onto the edge of her desk.

"We would like you to join our publicity tour in New York City, as well as several other locations on the East Coast, this summer. Though we would put a rush on the publication of your book, it wouldn't hit bookstores until late fall. So in the meantime, you would be meeting, representing, speaking, and interviewing as a contracted author with Pinkerton. You have what we're looking for, Angie."

I shook my head. "But my son—"

"We've planned on you bringing him. This may be *unusual* protocol for us, but I am almost never wrong about people. What I'm offering you is a six-week, all expenses paid opportunity to connect with other mothers who desperately need what you possess. And if that's not enough…we'd like to offer you a ten thousand dollar advance."

My eyelids nearly fluttered off my face. Surely, I hadn't heard what I thought I heard.

"I can give you until Friday to decide," Dee went on. "We can go over contract terms and specifics if and when you decide to proceed. I can assure you I will personally see to your arrangements while on tour." She stood up. "Please don't hesitate to call me with any questions."

Questions? I could hardly think through the haze of dollar signs in my mind. Ten thousand dollars was a third of what I made all year. I could catch up on a lot of bills…pay rent ahead of schedule…afford for Cody to attend soccer camp in July.

But this is crazy. I can't be a spokesperson for single moms!

I swallowed. "I…I'll call you by Friday. Thank you, Dee."

I wavered to my feet and allowed her to walk me to the door.

Her gentle tone purred as she turned toward me, eyes locking with mine. "I was a single mom for nearly ten years. Don't underestimate what your voice could do for others. I surely don't."

****

For being five-foot nothing and less than a hundred pounds, my best friend, Rosie, gave hugs that could double as a chiropractic adjustment.

"You made a decision yet?" Rosie unwrapped her arms from my waist and immediately began straightening chairs for tonight's meeting in the community room at Hope Church.

I followed suit in the row behind her. "No, I haven't, just like I've told you for the last two days," I replied.

She huffed. "Well, I don't see what you're waiting for. This is the best thing ever to happen to you, Ang. I mean, *hello*, Briggs and Charlie even offered to fly to New York to bring Cody back home for his soccer camp. And Carol told you she would give you whatever time off you needed at the flower shop. You have no excuses. Nada."

"I'm not trying to come up with excuses, Rosie-"

She whirled around, hands gesturing as wildly as her little Latina mouth could speak. "Yes you are. Every time I call you, you give me a new reason why leaving is a bad idea. Be honest with yourself Angie, you're scared. And I can understand that. You have a lot to consider when it comes to you and Cody, but you know what my mother always said?"

Rosie loved to quote people. I shook my head.

"God never wastes an opportunity."

****

An hour later, I peered out into a sea of faces, some I recognized, but many I did not.

Over the last several years the numbers had gone from a mere twenty to upwards of two hundred on any given Wednesday night. It was humbling; it was beautiful.

I walked to the center of the small stage and opened my journal, my stomach knotting as I prepared to share. No matter how many times I spoke on a Wednesday night, this part never got easier.

I cleared my throat. "Welcome to The Refuge. My name is Angela Flores and I'm a survivor of domestic abuse. If you're new here tonight, please know that all of us have had a *first* time and that you're in a safe place. Five years ago I took a seat in the back, wishing my life had turned out differently. I was hurting, and broken, and very confused. But I found hope here…and healing, though sometimes old mindsets die hard." I looked into Rosie's face in the crowd. She winked at me. "Tonight is your chance to start over, to reclaim peace and freedom in your life. I wrote a poem several years ago I would like to share with you. It's called, *The Last Time.*

The Last Time

"When the last time is the last time, you'll know it in your heart.

You'll know the dream that crumbles when your world's been torn apart.

When the last time is the last time, you'll feel it in your soul.

You'll deny the pull of darkness for a light that makes you whole.

When the last time is the last time, you'll run for safety's haven.

You'll run from all the pain and loss, and for the life worth saving.

When the last time is the last time, you'll let out a victor's cry.

You'll hear redemption call your name, and peace no more shall die."

I handed the microphone off to the next speaker and made my way down the steps. This was not a place for clapping and carrying on, but of silent affirmation. Heads nodded around me. As I made my way toward the back of the room, several hands reached out and clasped mine.

At the end of the evening, I talked with Jenny—a woman Rosie brought to me. My heart broke for her. At the age of twenty, she had been exposed to more heartache than most would know in a lifetime. Growing up with a violent father, she lived now with an abusive boyfriend. It was a recipe for destruction, but tonight she had taken the first steps toward healing her past and reclaiming her future—one free of violence. I cried with her as she told me her story, and our conversation ended the same way I ended every conversation with a first-time visitor, I handed her a card with my phone number on it, along with explicit instructions to call me day or night as needed.

As I drove home to pick Cody up from his friend's house, my thoughts lingered on Jenny. Her story pulled me back to the memories of my past, reminding me of the voices I had ignored for so long.

I packed carelessly, stuffing a third pair of sandals into the large, black duffel bag on my bed. My bedroom door flew open with a bang, and I staggered back.

Briggs, my younger brother by a year, stood in the entryway, his legs planted wide. "Tell me it's not true."

"What do you mean?" I asked, staring a hole into my duffle bag. Why couldn't I disappear into it?

"You know exactly what I'm talking about. It's all over school, Ang."

My eyes darted toward his, my stomach hallowing as our gazes connected. This close to graduation I'd hoped the rumor mill would've been busy with other gossip, but apparently I'd been wrong.

"I love him, Briggs." The statement came out weaker than I had intended.

He wrapped his fists in his hair. "No, you don't…and Dirk Luterra sure as heck doesn't love you, Angela!"

"And what makes you such an expert on love? You have a new girlfriend every week!" He wasn't the only one who could yell in this family.

"You don't know him." He dropped his hands to his sides and took a step forward. "You might think you do, but I see how he is when you're not around. He's a lazy deadbeat." Briggs grabbed my wrist, eyes pleading as he looked from me to the duffle bag. "Please call this off. I'm begging you, please."

"I'm marrying him, Briggs."

He released my hand as quiet commanded the room. Minutes twisted into a long braid of silence. We were at an impasse—our first.

My brother's stare brimmed with a potent mix of hurt, fury, and disappointment. But my desperate need to be loved was stronger than the deepest dregs of his opposition.

As he walked toward the door without another word, panic swelled in my chest.

"Wait—are you making me choose?" I blurted.

Briggs turned around slowly. Our eyes met, and a dull pain burned in the back of my throat.

"There is no choice, Ang. You're my sister; you'll always have me. I'm just afraid I won't have you anymore."

I lifted up a silent prayer for Jenny, that she would break the cycle now. That she would never have to know the pain and betrayal of a husband who would vow to love and protect her and then do the total opposite.

Betrayal tainted love's purity.

And tainted love changed one's view of humanity.

****

After helping Cody with his second grade math homework and saying bedtime prayers, I logged into my blog, *A Lone Joy*. I read the counter at the bottom and nearly fell out of my chair. *That's impossible!*

My most recent post had been on the topic of *Fear: A Parent's Deadliest Pitfall*—a subject I knew all too well. My heart thumped hard as I read through the comments.

"…I never thought anyone would understand my struggle as a single parent…until I read your blog."

"I used to cry at night after my daughter was born, I felt so isolated and alone…and afraid. A friend suggested your blog recently and it's given me hope. I can do this."

"Your posts make me laugh, cry, and feel connected. Thank you, Angie."

Pushing back against my chair, a new warmth radiated within my chest.

"God never wastes an opportunity." Rosie's voice from a few hours earlier echoed in my thoughts.

Maybe she was right. Maybe, just maybe, my simple little blog had a purpose beyond my understanding.

New York.

Who would have thought?

Chapter Two

(Six weeks later)

"Mom! Mom! Look at that!" Cody exclaimed, looking out the window of the plane and pointing as New York City came into view below us.

Cody had been like the energizer bunny ever since we stepped foot in the DFW airport in Dallas. The trip to New York was only a three-hour flight, but I was grateful to be landing. Rosie had put several of her favorite books onto my e-reader, but there was no way I could read when Cody quizzed me on every fact he'd studied about The Big Apple. My eight-year-old loved facts; he lived and breathed them. Unfortunately, I wasn't nearly as well-versed in the city's history or attractions. When he'd started making the questions multiple choice— just so I could get a few answers correct—I knew it was going to be a long, long flight.

"Did you know that the Brooklyn Bridge was the first bridge to be lit by electricity, Mom?"

"No, sweetheart, I did not."

"Did you know that there are enough restaurants in New York City for one person to eat out every night for 54 years and never visit the same place twice?"

"No, sweetheart, I did not."

As we made our way through the busy airport to baggage claim, I scanned the crowd. Dee had assured me that the assistant they were sending would be holding a sign with our names on it. Cody spotted his Transformer suitcase come down the conveyor belt. I pulled it off, and seconds later, reached for my own. At least I'd had the good sense to wear comfy clothing for the trip. But if Rosie knew I had on a pair of black capri yoga pants and a yellow fitted tee, she would probably disown me as her BFF. I liked comfort; why was that such a crime? On the fashion-plus side, I'd worn makeup. That should count for something. It wasn't like we were going anywhere other than the corporate apartment this evening, Dee had sent me the itinerary in advance.

Cody and I rolled our suitcases through the swarm of people at baggage claim, and headed through the doors to stand on the curb. Then I spotted the bright green sign with our names on it. As I approached the young Wynona Ryder lookalike holding it, she was standing on her tip-toes, scanning the crowd.

"Um…excuse me?"

"Yes?" she said in a perky tone, turning vivid green eyes on me.

"I'm Angela Flores and this is my son, Cody. Are you with Pinkerton Press?"

The young woman stared as if trying to solve a complicated math equation, mouth hanging open a tad. I touched my face, checking for leftover animal cracker crumbs.

"*You're* Ms. Flores?"

"Yes…is there a problem?" I looked down at Cody, who seemed equally confused by her reaction.

Suddenly the woman smiled—white teeth gleaming as her eyes sparkled with life.

"No! I'm sorry!" She shook her head, "You're just…*different* than what I was expecting."

What had she been expecting?

She clapped her hands together, smashing the neon-colored sign between them as she hopped in place twice—yes, hopped. The tone in which she said the word *different* wasn't insulting, but it did spark my curiosity.

"I'm Pippy! It's so nice to meet you Miss Angela Flores! And you, young sir, must be Cody!" She extended her hand to each of us after dropping the sign at her feet.

"Nice to meet you. It's *Pippy,* you said?"

You don't hear a name like that every day.

She beamed as if I had just complimented her. "Yes, my full name is Penelope, but everyone I know calls me Pippy. My twin brother came up with it when we were toddlers, and it just kind of stuck. Come on, let's get your bags into the car and we'll get you settled in at your apartment." She looked toward an older gentleman standing behind her near a shiny black town car. "This is Walt. He's Mr. Ross's personal driver."

Dee had mentioned that name several times during our meeting with the attorney three weeks ago when we finalized my contract. *What had she said about him?* I couldn't remember now. My mind had been far too preoccupied that day to retain such details, except for one, my concern for Cody's privacy.

Dee's eyebrows had shot up as I spoke my terms, and anxiety built within my chest.

"So you refuse to answer any questions regarding Cody's father?" she clarified.

"That's right," I said quietly. "Though my son doesn't remember him, I won't discuss our family history with the media."

She nodded slowly, a hint of comprehension passing over her features. "You're so young to be a widow." She exhaled. "We'll make a master list of approved questions for your interviews."

I fought back the urge to swallow. "Thank you."

And with that, an addendum was added to my contract.

I reached my hand toward the driver. "Hi Walt, it's nice to meet you."

He was an older gentleman, early sixties maybe, with grayish-white hair, dressed in slacks and a button-up shirt and tie. He loaded our bags in the truck and then opened the door to the nicest town car I'd ever seen. The black leather inside smelled new—a far cry from my old beater back home that smelled of crusty french fries and dirty socks.

Pippy scooted in next to me. Her hair was styled in the cutest pixie-cut I'd ever seen, framing her oval face perfectly. Her green eyes seemed to exude happiness when she spoke with dainty, heart-shaped lips.

Cody had already struck up a conversation with Walt, quizzing the driver on New York facts. The man seemed pleasantly amused, so I turned my attention back to Pippy.

"So here is the new itinerary." Pippy handed me a sheaf of papers. "I wanted to make sure I gave it to you today so we could go over any questions or conflicts before tomorrow. I'm sorry I didn't get it to you sooner, the work load has just buried me alive this week—not that I'm complaining—but that's also the reason I wasn't sure who I was looking for at the airport. I didn't have a chance to look at the picture Dee sent before I left for the airport."

"Oh…okay, thank you," I said, reaching for the six-week schedule. I bit my bottom lip as I counted the highlighted formal events. My two semi-formal dresses were about to get a lot of use. This was not good.

"Is something wrong?" Pippy stared at me.

"Um…I just didn't realize there would be so many formal occasions."

My hand instinctively went to my necklace, as my thoughts cast around for some kind of answer to this new dilemma. I had no idea how or where to shop in this city, or what kind of extravagant cost would be associated with such an endeavor. This was so not my element of expertise.

Pippy nodded, her smile sweet and genuine. "I can take care of anything you need, Miss Flores, just let me know."

No one had ever said such words to me before, yet even at her young age I sensed she was more than capable. I could just picture Pippy smiling at the challenge of any task asked of her—big or small. Her personality was like sunshine: bright, warm and totally addictive.

About forty-five minutes after leaving the airport, we pulled up to a large, red-bricked building with black shutters that had intricate detailing around every window. My stomach dropped to my knees. *This is really happening.* A doorman stood outside of the massive glass doors, and Cody was beside himself in child-like wonder, eyes wide. The gold-plated words scripted over the doorway read, *The T. Ross Building—Est. 1945.* A young man at the desk in the lobby took our luggage from us and allowed us to catch the elevator ahead of him. Our room was on the fourteenth floor, and I found myself thinking again about the long trip down to the bottom. Pippy handed me the room key (which was an actual key) with a tag looped through it, the numbers 1408 stamped into the metal.

When we reached our room at the end of the hall, I unlocked the door and exhaled loudly. Though the apartment was small in size, it was nice—*very* nice. Two bedrooms were attached by a central living area with a galley kitchen at the far end. It was fully furnished, with a chic sofa and chair set, a small table, and even a corner desk. Cody ran for the room on the left. I heard several loud gasps, while the sounds of paper ripping gave me pause.

"Mom! Mom! I have a big basket on my bed! It's full of toys— Mom! You won't believe it! There's an iPad in here and a card with my name on it!"

I dropped my purse to the floor in the entry way and met Cody inside his new bedroom. No bigger than a walk-in closet, Cody's room was made up of a full-size bed, small desk, chair, and closet. It was a perfect space for him. He sat on the bed, touching the loot beside him—an iPad and a basket filled with toys and books appropriate for an eight year-old boy. I was stunned—speechless.

Who did this? Dee?

Cody passed me the card as he started opening the box for his new iPad. He probably knew exactly the steps necessary to set it up. His best friend, Dillon had one, so he had seen the device in use plenty of times.

Dear Cody,

Thanks for visiting our city with your mom. We hope you will have a good time here even though there will be a lot of very boring events filled with boring people.

Hope this helps.

Jackson

Pinkerton Press

"Who's Jackson?" I asked Pippy who was standing in the doorway, smiling.

"Oh that's-"

A phone buzzed.

Pippy searched the giant bag slung over her shoulder for the vibrating device, placing several things onto the arm of the sofa outside Cody's door during her mad scramble. Finally, she found it.

"Hello? Yes…sure, okay…I'll add it. Oh? Sure, I'll be down before he's here then."

Pippy slid the phone into the front suit coat pocket, a wise choice since the entire state of Texas was in her bag.

"I have to get going…I have some things I need to attend to this evening, but there has been a change in the schedule."

I suppressed a frown that tried to surface. *Okay…so maybe this is something I need to get used to. The schedule has changed twice, and I've only been in New York for an hour.*

"You've been asked to attend a special dinner tomorrow night—you are welcome to bring Cody, of course. It's a meet and greet with the upper management at Pinkerton and some of our sponsors.

Dee thinks you should be there—she called Mr. Ross to make sure you were extended an invitation."

"Oh? Okay…" I started to sweat at the thought of my measly wardrobe. I looked at Pippy, debating. Seeing the way Pippy and Walt were dressed on a Thursday evening after a workday made me question the few things I had packed. I hoped one of the two dresses I had would be sufficient for such an event, but all of this was so out of my league. "Um…I'm sorry to ask this of you—I'm just really bad at this kind of thing. Would you mind looking at my dress options and telling me which is most appropriate for a dinner event like that?"

Pippy grinned like I had just offered her a briefcase full of cash, and followed me into my room where my suitcase lay on a luggage stand at the edge of the bed. The thin garment bag was hung in the closet. It held several blouses, slacks, a pencil skirt ensemble and two semi-formal dresses. One dress was short, fitted and black, with a shimmery overlay, while the other was a red, silky slip dress that Rosie insisted I purchase. The hem stopped just above my knee. Floor-length gowns were always a letdown as they usually fell just above my ankle—one of the curses of being tall.

As I pulled the clothes out and laid them on the bed, Pippy looked back to the garment bag as if expecting something else to come dancing out of it.

"Oh, is this it?" Her eyebrows lifted.

"Yes…until…I can figure something else out." Heat flushed my face.

"Alright, then I'd go with the red one. That will be beautiful with your blonde hair and hazel eyes."

Pippy's phone buzzed again. After reading the screen she hurried into action, hiking her purse higher up on her shoulder before heading through the living room toward the front door.

"I'm sorry—I have to leave, but tomorrow morning the car will be here at nine to pick you up for the signing at the first bookstore. I'll fill you in on everything else then, and we can talk more about the plan for tomorrow evening."

"Oh, okay, sounds good. Thank you for all your help, Pippy…it was nice to meet you." I followed her out the door of our new temporary home.

She stopped mid-stride in the hallway and turned toward me. Her smile was huge. "The pleasure is all mine, Miss Flores. See you tomorrow."

Inside our apartment I found Cody spread out on his bed, iPad instruction booklet in hand, and shook my head, laughing. I'd never see the kid during the course of the next six weeks if I didn't lay down some ground rules soon. Tonight though, I'd let him have his fun.

As I passed the couch I saw Pippy's green binder, the one that had held my most recent itinerary.

"Cody, can you stay here for a minute? I need to see if I can catch Pippy. Come lock the door behind me. I'll be right back."

"Sure, Mom." Cody walked to the door as I raced down the hallway toward the elevators.

Fidgeting, I watched each number illuminate as I made my descent down fourteen floors. Finally, the door dinged open, and I raced through the lobby toward the exit doors where Walt had parked earlier. As I trotted into the bright lights of the city, I turned my head, hearing Pippy's voice rise above the sounds of traffic. She was engaged in a focused conversation with a tall, suited figure. Though the man's broad back faced me, I could clearly see how he dwarfed Pippy.

I paused my steps as her words found me.

"...so I'm thinking I should take her shopping, but I'm not sure what kind of budget she has...her wardrobe is scarce at best."

"Pippy—I trust you can take care of it. I pay you to sort these types of things out so I don't have to," the man said, seemingly preoccupied with something in his hands—I couldn't see what, but I assumed it was a phone.

"I can expense it, then? I think she'll need quite a few items-"

"Pippy, yes, expense it—fine. I have more important things on my mind than a wardrobe crisis at the moment. What is it with all this nervous chatter of yours tonight?" His voice shifted into a growl as he looked down at her. "She's just a mom."

Until that moment, I hadn't known how that word could be used as an insult. I also hadn't realized how utterly inferior and inadequate a phrase could make me feel. It wasn't that he'd called me a *mom*; it was the word he said right before it: *just*.

A second later, Walt pulled up to the curb in the town car. Then Pippy saw me—standing like a frozen idiot on the walkway, her green binder in my hands.

"Oh—uh—Miss Flores...I didn't know you were standing there," she said, motioning to the man beside her. "This is Mr. Jackson Ross."

The man turned around, and my stomach bottomed out. He was young—much younger than I'd imagined the Mr. Ross that Dee spoke about so highly. But his youth was not what caused my breath to hitch. This guy looked like he'd been plucked right off a Hollywood movie set. He was the perfect type-cast for a rogue-assassin plotting to save mankind from the deadly grasp of evil!

Okay, maybe that was a *bit* of a stretch, but seriously, Jackson Ross was the polar-opposite of average. The deep espresso of his hair served to highlight the ocean-blue of his eyes, locking me in place where I stood. My heart skipped a beat...and then another.

His good looks were far superior to his charm, however, as his stoically handsome face remained unchanged, no apology offered in regards to his offensive comment only a second prior. Instead, he stared unabashed, his gaze washing over me. Both horribly awkward, yet undeniably magnetic, the moment had paralyzed me. I wanted to say something—*anything*—but my mind was blank.

Humiliation burned my cheeks as I remembered my *mom wardrobe*—the one I was currently wearing.

The intensity of his blue-gray eyes softened slightly as he cracked a tight smile. "Ms. Flores." He gave a curt nod of his head. "You're not what I expected."

Though his words were similar to what Pippy had said to me at the airport, his tone lacked warmth. I pawed at the pendant around my neck and searched for the words to reply to such a comment. *Or was it a compliment?* I honestly didn't know.

Pippy looked at me. "Yes, I said the same when I met her earlier this evening." She moved aside to let Walt open the back passenger door. "You'll be late for your appointment, sir."

Mr. Ross took three steps to the car, his almond-shaped eyes drinking me in—me, who stood stalk still like some sort of freak-show mime. A hint of something new crossed his rugged features, his right brow arching ever so slightly as he held my gaze a moment more. With a curt nod from Jackson, Walt closed his door, leaving me spellbound at the silence exchange.

Was it curiosity that had transfixed him? I didn't know.

But as stunning as Jackson Ross was to behold, what lurked beneath the surface he portrayed was something as dark as it was mysterious.

The hair on my arms stood at attention as I watched his car pull away.

"Hmm...that was strange." Pippy's eyes followed the town car as it pulled into the flow of traffic.

I did a double-take at the young woman. *Strange? Really? That's what she's going with?*

Pippy shrugged. "The good news is...you and I are going shopping on Saturday morning! I can't wait! I'll write it on the new schedule." She beamed.

Another schedule? Lord have mercy.

Chapter Three

The Storm

I am fragile

The wind has no discretion

It doesn't care that I fall

It doesn't care that I cry

It just keeps on blowing

I am weak

The gust has endless power

It doesn't care that I break

It doesn't care that I hurt

It just keeps on blowing

I am frail

The storm has infinite rage

It doesn't care that I fear

It doesn't care that I cower

It just keeps on blowing

I am alone

****

I stepped over the porcelain ledge of the tub and wrapped the white, fluffy bath towel around my body. Cody was still asleep, and I was certain he'd been up playing on his new gadget long after I called lights out. As the mirror defogged, I pulled my long, blonde hair over my shoulder and combed through it with my fingers. A glint of gold caught my eye in the mirror—my necklace, the one I'd worn for close to ten years.

It had belonged to my granny. Fingering it, I headed into the bedroom to dress.

We had never lived near her, but I looked forward to her visits as a child even more than I had looked forward to Christmas. She smelled of cherries and vanilla, and though she was covered in wrinkles, her skin was perpetually soft like a rose petal.

She was my mother's grandmother, and she was also the one who had named me—Angela Christine. My name meant messenger of God, or angel. She always spoke of angels. Though my parents were too busy to be bothered with faith, my granny was known for nothing else.

During her visits, I sat with her after my parents were in bed and listened to her stories for hours on end. I would lay my head on her lap as she stroked my hair. Her touch was a memory of affection I would hold near to my heart long after she passed; affection was scare in our household.

The necklace was a tiny, gold pendant: angel wings that formed a heart.

Granny passed unexpectedly two days before my high school graduation. I didn't receive the necklace, though, for almost six months. The bequest had been missed during the initial division of her estate and belongings.

I'll never forget the day Dirk tossed a padded envelope on the counter like it was nothing—like it meant nothing—though the packet had my name handwritten on the front with my granny's return address in the upper left hand corner. He knew what she had meant to me. I'd been an emotional wreck the day of my graduation—and consequently, during our elopement to Vegas the day after her memorial service.

The envelope had been stamped, but never mailed. It was to be a graduation gift, one that held unmatched significance. Though the little angel wings were tarnished, the vintage piece was invaluable. Priceless. Irreplaceable.

My granny had placed the necklace inside a delicately folded piece of stationary. In her beautiful, shaky cursive, she had written:
My Dearest Angela,
I was given this necklace on my wedding day by your granddaddy. I wish you could have known him. He was my angel in disguise. I pray this necklace provides you

with strength and courage in the same way it has for me.
"For He will order His angels to protect you wherever you go."
Psalms 91:11.
I'll love you always,
Granny

I had repaired the fragile chain twice, but other than that, I had not taken it off. The necklace was a part of me—Cody had never seen me without it.

The reflection of my necklace in the mirror brought me comfort in these new surroundings. Dressed in black slacks, heels and a sleeveless, lavender blouse, I applied my makeup with care, using brown eyeliner to accent my hazel eyes. Leaving my blonde hair to fall below my shoulders, I assessed the woman that was my reflection and decided that she was light-years ahead of the *just-a-mom* from the night prior.

I'll prove him wrong.

****

True to her word, Pippy arrived with Walt and the car at nine a.m. on the dot. The signing was to start at ten. Cody begged to sit up front next to Walt's in the driver's seat, I agreed, and was relieved to see Pippy alone in the backseat of the town car—or at least that's what I told myself. As Walt opened the back door for me, Pippy launched into a story, her hands in full animation-mode. I decided right then that

Rosie and Pippy should never meet. This world was not big enough to contain that much energy in a single space.

"Good morning! I didn't know how you liked your coffee…so I just took a stab at it. Peter—my brother—says I'm the worst at ordering coffee because I only drink it for the sugar, but I did my best at guessing what you'd like." Her long, black eyelashes fluttered excitedly as she held out the drink. Evidently, she was waiting for an assessment—or an approval—I wasn't sure which. I took a slow sip. Peter was correct. It was like drinking hot, liquid sugar with a splash of coffee flavoring.

I forced a swallow down.

"Thank you," I said.

"See…he doesn't know what he's talking about—I thought we'd have similar tastes."

I grinned.

"So, let's see," she hurried on, "today you have this signing from ten until two—we will break for thirty minutes for lunch. As I'm sure Dee told you, this publicity tour is quite unique—we have never set up a tour that has a single theme and focus like this one does."

"You mean like on parenting?" I asked, confused.

"No, I mean on family: marriage, parenting, single parenting and adoption. Pinkerton Press wants to raise the bar—provide resources for a generation who seems clueless on keeping family a priority. They have handpicked these authors—it's quite inspiring actually. There are five authors in total. You are the only one who is still unpublished, but your blog has drawn a lot of attention. That's why we're pre-selling your book. It should be out around Thanksgiving, as you already know."

"Wow, Dee mentioned that there were other authors promoting family, but this sounds phenomenal."

Pippy nodded her head. "This tour has been very well advertised; we are expecting it to do well, that's why we're taking it into several cities."

A wave of anxiety blindsided me. "Am I the only author representing single parenting?" I looked at Cody in the front seat. He was engaged in a riddle-fest with Walt.

Pippy's eyes twinkled. "Yes."

****

When we walked into the three story bookstore my head felt light and airy, like at any moment it would take off without me into the great beyond.

Four lines of ropes corralled hundreds of chatty women, children, and a few dozen men who all looked bored out of their minds. My mouth gaped at the sight.

"Look, there she is! Hi Angie—and there's Cody!"

"Angie, can I get my picture with you?"

"We love you, Angie!"

Cody pulled on my arm as we continued to walk. "Mom, do all these women know you?"

I shook my head, dumbfounded, waving and smiling as I followed Pippy, who didn't miss a beat. She stopped at a long table near the center of the first floor. There were three other tables set up around the room—two were already occupied: one by Sue Bolen who wrote *Adoption Answers* and the second by Tom and Julie Zimmerman who co-wrote, *The Reconnected Marriage.*

A picture of my face—one that I recognized from my blog— hung on a banner in front of the table displaying the title of my blog: *A Lone Joy.* A large pile of various signing materials and pre-book orders were neatly arranged on the tabletop. I swallowed hard.

"Exciting, isn't it?" Pippy nudged my arm.

"Yes…very." I ignored the ball of cotton that had sucked my throat dry of moisture.

"So I was thinking Cody can either sit here with you, or there's a special kid's corner right over there. I made sure they put this table where you could still see him. Whatever you think best is fine," Pippy said.

"Is that okay, Mom?" Cody bounced on his toes. "Can I sit over there?"

"Sure, honey." I tousled his hair. Just make sure you let me know if you plan on going anywhere else. This place is very crowded. Also, you are only to read. You will be spending enough time tonight on that iPad, so don't take it out of your backpack while we are in the store."

"Okay, Mom."

Pippy escorted him to the brightly painted kids' corner which was just forty feet away or so and looked at her watch. I looked around the room. I'd been dying to ask her about some questions about Mr. Ross, but the words wouldn't form.

I stopped my eyes from rolling at the thought of Mr. High-and-Mighty as Pippy announced it was time to begin. I took a deep breath and braced myself for the onslaught before remembering Rosie's words when she came to say goodbye.

"Embrace this, Ang. It's your destiny."

Chapter Four

By the time our lunch break started, my stomach was angry. Pippy had purchased a bag of chips for Cody a while ago, but I'd barely had a sip of water during the last three hours. With every face I saw, every hand I shook, every note I wrote…I felt inspired. I wanted to know them all: their names, their stories, their struggles. I had been in more pictures today probably than in my whole lifetime, but I smiled genuinely in each one. These women had found their way here for reasons I had yet to understand, and I wasn't about to give them anything less than my all, even if I was starving!

Cody had checked in with me several times and even added his own notes and signatures on a few of the cards and posters. The moms went crazy over him, which then drove him back to the kids' corner.

I scarfed down my turkey sandwich, chasing it with a diet soda, when I turned toward the door. A rush of ice and heat swept down my body.

Jackson Ross.

Even his name was striking. He stood near where Cody sat, leaning against a wall in his dark, rich, designer suit. He stared at his phone and typed furiously, as if his life depended on the message he was sending—maybe it did; what did I know?

I bit my bottom lip as I watched him. Though I'd never before found facial hair attractive, Jackson knew how to pull it off. His sculpted beard was trimmed and edged into a flawless outline of his firm jaw. *Rugged heartthrob meets GQ.*

I didn't know how long I watched him, but apparently it was long enough for Pippy to take notice.

Her laugh jolted me back into reality.

"You ready to go?" she asked.

"Oh, sure." I turned my head, trying to pretend I was looking at something else—or better yet, *someone* else.

Who am I kidding? I was a horrible actress.

As I bent to retrieve my bag from under the table, I was suddenly aware of the broad-shouldered man who stood behind me. My pulse quickened.

"Was the day a success?" Jackson asked.

Cody skittered past me, holding Pippy's hand as he chatted away toward the exit door. Though the room was filled with people conversing, my ears were tuned-in to his voice.

I gulped. "Yes. I'm shocked with how many women showed up." I smiled. "It was really amazing."

The corner of his mouth curled slightly, but before my stomach could react with an acrobatic flip, Jackson turned sharply, and exited the building.

I followed, feeling more like an unwanted puppy than the up and coming author Pinkerton had painted me to be.

Stepping out into the sunlight, I watched as Jackson bent and spoke to Cody. I couldn't quite make out his words, but in response, Cody let out a rapid fire of factoids.

Sue Bolan, the adoption author, tapped me on my shoulder to ask me about my signings and fans. I pried my eyes from Jackson and Cody, and gave Sue my undivided attention as we discussed the highlights of the bookstore—that is, until her ride pulled up a few minutes later.

Turning my attention toward Cody once again, I saw it—a sight that nearly caused my knees to liquefy.

A smile.

Jackson Ross was smiling at Cody. And it was exquisite.

Cody giggled as Jackson caught my eye. He sobered immediately.

"There's Walt!" Cody said.

I tore my gaze from the brooding man in front of me just in time to see Walt pull up.

"Will you be riding back with us to the apartments, Mr. Ross?" Pippy asked him.

He glanced at me before his eyes landed on Pippy once more. "No."

And that's when the thought hit me—like a brick to the chest.

Feeling like an idiot, I addressed Mr. Ross, "Oh gosh, you probably need your driver back! Cody and I are perfectly fine to take a taxi—it's no problem at all. I'm sorry for any inconvenience we may have caused you."

Pippy opened her mouth, but Mr. Ross put a hand on her shoulder, not a word escaped before he nodded toward me.

"Don't be late to dinner."

By the time I comprehended his words he'd already climbed into a yellow cab. Seconds later, he was but a blur in a sea of buttery traffic. It dawned on me then what had just taken place.

Other than issuing orders, the man had practically stared right through me! One minute he seemed to despise my very presence, while the next he seemed to not even know I was there.

For all the years that I had begged God to make me invisible, all the years I had prayed to slide under the radar by the one man to whom I had so stupidly bound my life...being ignored was the antithesis of what I wanted now. I wanted to be noticed—by Jackson Ross no less.

Why do I even care what he thinks?

I slid into the backseat of the car before I allowed myself to answer.

****

I did not enjoy primping. It was one thing to get ready for a day of book signing, but it was something else altogether to get ready for a night of introductions and first impressions at a formal dinner party. After I slipped into my red dress and heels, I took careful steps to pin my hair up and darken my makeup application by a shade—the way Rosie had shown me. I topped off preparations with red lipstick. Not fire engine red; Audrey Hepburn red.

"Whoa, Mom! You look really different!" Cody exclaimed as I walked into the living space. He sat on the couch in khaki pants and a blue button-down shirt.

I was really starting to hate the word *different*. I scrunched my face at him.

"Like *really pretty*," he said, beaming.

My heart melted into a puddle.

"Well, I'm quite lucky to be escorted by the most handsome man in New York tonight." I winked at him.

"Who? Mr. Ross?" he asked, wide-eyed.

I almost choked on the air I sucked in.

"No—you! You crazy boy." I laughed, ignoring the knot forming in my stomach.

"Oh. Right."

He took my hand as we walked out the door. I shook my head, grounding myself. If only I could escape the anxiety that was taking up residence in my core.

When Pippy called to confirm Walt would pick us up as planned, she said she had to stay back and finish up some last minute work but planned to meet us at the event a bit later.

No mention of Mr. Ross.

As the evening was young, the sky was still bright. I studied the city from my window in the car. Maybe the shopping outing tomorrow might include some sort of tour. Apart from Cody's fact drills, I knew next to nothing about New York and was anxious to see it. The sounds, the sights, the smells were all so foreign to anything I knew. Though Dallas was a major U.S. city, it was nothing like this. New York was its own unique breed.

We pulled up to a beautiful building that seemed to be inspired by French-Colonial architecture. Everything felt rich, elegant and luxurious.

We checked our names on the guest list then entered the opulent foyer. Cody linked arms with me like a gentleman, and together we walked toward the banquet hall.

Pippy had said this dinner would be full of upper management at Pinkerton, along with their affiliates. I wasn't expecting a large crowd, but again I was proven wrong. The room was swimming with bodies—all dressed to the nines. I patted Cody's linked arm, reassuring him this party was going to fine. Really, it was me who needed that reassurance.

Within thirty seconds of stepping into the extravagant space, filled with crystal chandeliers and beautifully-set tables, a tall, attractive man with dark, spikey hair approached us.

"You must be Pinkerton's secret weapon—Angela Flores, I presume? I've heard so much about you. Dee and I go way back."

I laughed softly. "Oh, I don't know about that—Mr.?"

"Vargus. Stewart Vargus. I'm the Chief Operating Officer at Pinkerton," he said, shaking my hand.

"Well it's nice to meet you Mr. Vargus. This is my son, Cody."

"It's nice to meet you, partner," he said to Cody. "Let me introduce you to some folks and then we can find your table for the evening."

I'm not sure how many people I met—but there was no earthly way I could remember all the names and faces. Mr. Vargus escorted us everywhere. He seemed friendly and eager to help me settle into the crowd—unlike another certain person who'd made my acquaintance of late. Finally, he led us to our table then kissed my hand gently before making his way back to his own.

It was then that I saw Pippy flitting across the floor in her black stilettos, holding one edge of her long, emerald gown. How the girl could move so quickly in heels that tall I had no idea. Her smile was contagious as she found me.

"Hi! Wow, you look beautiful, Angie! I was hoping someone would take you under their wing until I got here." She looked around briefly and then frowned. "Although I kinda had someone else in mind for the job." Her last words were mumbled, but I didn't miss her meaning. Her face held an unmistakable look of disappointment.

She noticed Jackson's disdain for me, too, then.

I swallowed, my face burning with fresh humiliation.

Until her statement, I was still holding onto a thread of hope that I was assuming too much—making presumptions about Jackson based on my own experiences with the opposite sex. But apparently I was spot on. Jackson Ross didn't like me. And the worst part was, he didn't even *know* me! Suddenly, I thought of the "feeling chart" we used in small group at *The Refuge*. It took me only a millisecond to identify the emotion I was currently experiencing: anger.

In my head, a full-on toddler tantrum raged. Pippy smiled apologetically. I hoped she wouldn't make excuses for him—he was a big boy. Thankfully, she pursed her lips together and turned to Cody instead.

"Cody, you will love this food—it is scrumptious," Pippy began. "Have you ever had escargot?"

"Ewww...no way. I know what that is. You can't trick me." Cody scrunched up his nose.

Pippy laughed and threw her hands up in mock-surrender, "Touché! I forgot what a smart boy your mom raised! She claimed you were very bright. I guess she doesn't lie."

"Nope. My mom *never* lies," he said, smugly.

I kissed the top of his head as my stomach rolled.

Chapter Five

Lies

I lie to keep me safe

I lie to keep me sound

I lie even when there's no one else around

I lie to make it better

I lie to make it right

I lie in the hope it won't turn into a fight

I lie when I'm scared

I lie when I'm hurt

I lie to avoid the flames though I'll still be burnt

I lie when I'm sad

I lie when I'm weak

I lie just to prove I still have a voice that speaks

I lie to be loved

I lie to protect

I lie to everyone I know yet they all suspect

****

I saw him during dinner.

Every female in the room looked up when Jackson entered. An exotic-looking woman with dark skin and even darker hair rose to greet him. She kissed him on each cheek before escorting him to her table. Something hot burned in my chest as I pulled my gaze away to glare at my cheesecake.

I *hated* cheesecake.

I took a bite, willing myself to enjoy the flavor.

I did not enjoy the flavor.

I jabbed my fork into the creamy mound and took another bite.

"Miss Flores?"

Lifting my eyes from the now massacred dessert, I found Stewart Vargus standing at my table. He looked from me to Pippy.

"Hello, Pippy," he said, nodding to her.

Pippy's gaze darted to the table that held Mr. Ross. "Hey, Mr. Vargus."

"May I have a word with you, Miss Flores?" Stewart asked and offered me his hand.

I glanced at Pippy. She seemed to be saying so much with her eyes, but I understood none of it.

"I'll stay here with Cody," she said hesitantly then turned to Cody and engaged him in conversation.

The next thing I knew, I was standing up, and Stewart's hand was on my lower back, propelling me toward the far corner of the room. People were starting to rise from their chairs and form small social circles again, but my attention was focused on the unwanted touch that was burning a hole in my spine. I took two steps to the side, and he dropped his hand immediately. I exhaled, feeling the panic rush from my body.

"Miss Flores, I was hoping we could set up a meeting at my office sometime during the next week. I can have my assistant speak with Pippy to arrange it. I know you're on a fairly tight tour schedule, but I think there are a few things we should discuss…about your book contract."

"Oh? Can you be a tad more specific Mr. Vargus?"

Before he could answer, my phone vibrated inside my clutch purse. Mr. Vargus gave a quick nod of his head, indicating I should check the caller. After a quick glance at Pippy and Cody who were still at the table looking at Cody's iPad, I slid the phone out. I knew the area code but not the number.

"May I?" I asked him.

"Certainly, I'll be in contact," Mr. Vargus said then walked away.

Slipping into the hallway I answered the phone.

"Hello?"

"Is…is this Angela?" A shaky, female voice asked on the other end.

"Yes, this is Angela. May I ask who's speaking?"

"This…this is Jenny. We met a few weeks ago at *The Refuge*."

Her face appeared instantly in my mind's eye. I had spent nearly an hour listening to her heartbreaking story last month. I remembered her well.

"Yes, hi, Jenny. How are you? Is something wrong, sweetheart?"

I walked down the hall and through a door that led to an outside exit.

"Not really—no. I left him…my boyfriend."

I breathed in deep, relief filling my soul. "Okay, and where are you now? Are you safe tonight?"

"Yes, I made my exit plan like we talked about, and I did it. I left. I'm at my Aunt's house in Oklahoma."

"Oh, Jenny, I am so proud of you. I know it was hard. I know you're feeling a lot of things right now, and not all of them feel good…but you did the *right* thing. You are worth more than staying with an abuser. I want you to hear that."

I could hear her crying on the other end. I waited, giving her time to speak.

"Thank you—I just kept replaying your words over and over in my head. You gave me the courage to do it."

"No, you had the courage…you just needed some support."

"Yes, you're right," she said.

"Promise me you'll keep me in the loop—I also want you to let either Rosie or Maggie know where you're at, okay?"

"Okay, I promise."

"I'm proud of you, Jenny."

After a few minutes more of reassuring conversation, I hung up the phone and slipped it back into my clutch.

"Problem?"

Though he had spoken less than a dozen words to me since we'd met, I *knew* that voice. What was wrong with me that I had subconsciously committed it to memory the first time I heard it? I turned around, slowly.

There stood Jackson Ross, ten feet from me, arms crossed over his broad chest, an eyebrow raised in expectation.

My pulse quickened as our eyes met. "No, just had to take a phone call."

He stared at me, his face blank of emotion. "You have no business with Stewart Vargus."

He saw me speaking with Stewart Vargus?

I shook my head. "I'm sorry—I didn't—"

"Why?" He lifted a second eyebrow in question.

"Why what?" I asked breathless.

"Why are you *sorry?* I was stating a fact, not seeking your repentance. Are you always so needlessly apologetic, Miss Flores, or is it just a bad habit of yours I should get used to?" He dropped his hands to his sides, never once breaking eye contact.

His audacity was shocking. Though it was typical of me to hold my tongue, there was *nothing* typical about this man or this conversation. Heat flashed inside me, and my fingers curled tight to my palms.

I scowled at him. "Well, are *you* always so impolite when speaking to a woman you just met, Mr. Ross, or have I done something to warrant this disdain you seem to have for me?"

My audacity was shocking as well. I had never spoken so freely...to anyone, much less a CEO dressed in a suit that was likely worth more than my car.

He smiled—a real, earth-shattering, heart-melting, need-to-brace-myself-against-a-wall kind of smile.

I hated its effect on me.

"Disdain?" He asked.

"Yes. Disdain, dislike, displeasure, disgust-" I rattled off.

The corners of his mouth ticked. "I'm quite familiar with the word, but thank you for providing such worthy synonyms."

I pursed my lips as he took a step closer, my neck suddenly boiling with heat at his nearness.

"But I'm afraid your observations are misguided, Miss. Flores. I'll see you tomorrow." He walked away, rendering me speechless. Like usual.

I hadn't the slightest clue what was going on tomorrow—or why he would be seeing me—but when Jackson Ross spoke, his word was law.

Unyielding.

Uncompromising.

Unbreakable.

****

Morning came too early. After chatting with Rosie late into the night, careful to leave my most recent interaction with Jackson out of our conversation, my sleep was fitful at best.

But today was Saturday: a.k.a shopping day, and I was determined to make the most of the opportunity, even if I was sick to my stomach about spending money on frivolous items like clothing.

I checked the schedule, which Pippy had agreed to email me since the changes were constant. There was another dinner this evening. I guessed that was the event to which Mr. Ross had been referring last night. My cheeks burned with remembrance.

"Mom, how long are we going to shop?" Cody took a bite of a blueberry muffin as we waited for Pippy to arrive. She'd texted she had a stop on the way, so we decided to grab a quick breakfast at the bakery next door to the Ross building.

"Don't talk with your mouth full, honey. And I'm not sure. I don't know what she has planned, but it might be longer than you're used to." I rubbed his head.

"Well, I have my backpack loaded and ready."

I giggled. *Goofball.*

When we walked outside minutes later, I nearly gasped. There, standing on the sidewalk in another designer suit, was Jackson Ross.

What is he doing here?

"Hey, Mr. Ross!" Cody said, giving him a high-five.

"Hey, short-stuff."

"Are you going shopping with us?" Cody asked.

"Thought you could use a man-break."

My ears perked up at the casual way he spoke to Cody.

"What's a man-break?" Cody asked.

"It's what men do while ladies shop." He shrugged.

"Oh, cool," Cody said happily.

Pippy was inside the car already—on her cell. She was pressed up against the inside of the door, absorbed in conversation. Cody jumped into the front seat without a second thought, leaving me with Jackson.

"After you." Jackson said, holding the door for me.

A rush of heat flooded my gut and my cheeks simultaneously.

"Cody, you need to offer that seat to Mr. Ross. Where are your manners?" I scolded.

"Oh...did you want to sit here, Mr. Ross?" Cody asked, turning around in his seat to stare at us both standing on the curb.

"No, thank you," he said.

I glanced up at Jackson as I heard a hint of something quite unusual in his tone—amusement.

I slid into the seat, acutely aware that I was in jeans, ballet flats, and a black tank top—apparently underdressed for the excursion. He must not have been too concerned about me contaminating his fancy suit pants though because there wasn't a spot on my leg that his leg didn't touch. I tried to scoot closer to Pippy, but my attempt made no difference. We were like peanut butter and jelly—oozing together despite the distinctly different tastes.

Hearing a low, deep chuckle escape him, the irrational fire that had filled my core last night, returned. Though I'd spend years helping women analyze the relationships in their lives, I still did not understand this man—much less, the affect he had on me.

I turned to him, my prior insecurities of speaking my mind to a man of his position and power, now completely absent. "Cody doesn't need a babysitter, you know. He is used to tagging along with me, and if I recall correctly, I thought you had more important things to do than to be bothered with shopping."

"You don't."

I took a deep breath and then gave in to the bait set before me.

"I don't what?" I stared out Pippy's window as she covered one ear with her hand, still speaking on the phone.

"Recall correctly."

I most certainly *did* recall correctly. I remembered every word that came out of his mouth during our first encounter, including his hurtful assessment of me. Me, *the just a mom.*

"You said you had more important things on your mind than a *wardrobe crisis.*" My low-voiced exclamation came out more like a hiss than a whisper.

His smile was smug, as if I hadn't just proven him wrong.

"True, but other concerns don't rule out my company today."

"Fine." I clamped my mouth shut, refusing to say more. I didn't want to play into whatever game this was.

"Fine." He took out his phone and scrolled through his emails, a slow grin working it's way on his face when he glanced at me.

I felt exhausted already, and the day had yet to begin. One thing was for certain: I wasn't going to let him have the last word *every* time.

****

I couldn't remember the last time I was in a store that only sold clothing. I did the majority of my shopping where I could get groceries, office supplies and bathroom products all within a few aisles of each other. That was not the kind of store Pippy had in mind for today, however.

Walt dropped us off near the Soho district, which Pippy had suggested. The second we walked into the cozy store I knew I was in way over my head. Back home Rosie was my shopping buddy—and though she was far more fashionable than I—this place would put her to shame. Pippy took hold of my arm, reassuring me as we browsed the *great quality* of clothing the store possessed, but all I could think about was *price point*.

Cody and Jackson found a nice comfy couch to occupy while Pippy held up multiple dresses against my skin. I looked at the price tag first, much to Pippy's dissatisfaction. The guys were sucked into their electronic devices, both intent on the screens before them.

"This is going to be like playing dress up with a real life Barbie Doll! Eeek! I'm so excited!" Pippy grabbed another gown and hooked it onto the dressing room door.

My cheeks flashed hot. Couldn't she have a little more of an *inside voice*?

"Pippy…uh, how many dresses did you put in there?" I whispered, hoping she would take the hint.

"Oh, uh…maybe twelve? You should probably start trying them on, I guess." She grabbed my wrist and pulled me toward the room.

Having a second alone with her, I whispered, "Pippy, what is Jackson really doing here?"

She shrugged, "I was as surprised as you were to see him this morning. Just roll with it, okay? I don't want to jinx our shopping day. This kind of thing is highly unusual for Pinkerton, but…." Her eyes crinkled as she grinned at me.

"But what?"

"Mr. Ross doesn't make mistakes. He does what he wants."

There were closer to twenty gowns hooked on the inside of my dressing room door. I laughed to myself as I started the process of trying them on. Pippy waited outside the door, ready to give her approval, or disapproval, along with plenty of commentary each time I stepped out. A few size exchanges had to be made between unveilings, but for the most part, Pippy had been spot on with her guesses.

Her enthusiasm never faltered; she was an endless supply of energy and optimism.

I stood in the fourth navy, floor length gown she had brought to me.

"Ooh…that is just such a great color on you! I definitely think we should get that one."

I laughed. "You have said that about every one I've put on so far. I think we should stick to three—total."

"*What?* No way. We are not leaving with only three. Mr. Ross gave me permission to expense whatever you need," she said.

Although I appreciated her help and kindness, I felt very uneasy about expensing more than what I knew I could repay. I had done the math in my head and three was the absolute maximum I could afford—if I stuck to the clearance dresses, which I planning on from the second we entered this fashion boutique.

"Well, I think *need* is a bit of a strong term. Three will be suitable. I can just rotate them."

She frowned, puckering her lips, and then put her hands on her hips.

"You aren't planning to-"

"Pippy, *three* will be just fine. Let me try on a few more, and then we can decide together which work best."

I shut the door of the dressing room and pulled out a champagne-colored gown from the mix. As I slipped into it, the dress spilled over my hips, sparkling like a chandelier in a ballroom. The gown's tiny, spaghetti straps were barely visible, but they were the perfect set-up to the sweet-heart neckline. There was no doubt about it, this gown was the most gorgeous piece of attire I'd ever seen, much less, worn. Swaying in the mirror, the tag flipped over, revealing a number that caused me to gasp. *Twenty-two hundred dollars!*

Pippy knocked with what I was sure was another load of options in her arms. With one hand holding my hair off my neck, I used the other to push open the door. But Pippy was no longer her cute, Pixie-like self, instead she had transformed into a wickedly-handsome man.

Jackson's eyes roamed the length of my dress, slowly making their way up to rest on my face. I dropped my hand from the loose up-do I was holding on top of my head. My hair spilled down my back and around my shoulders in one quick sweeping motion. Every cell in my body was aware of his presence, begging silently for his approval. He placed a hand at the back of his neck and looked away—briefly.

He cleared his throat. "Pippy—uh, Pippy said there's a problem?"

"What? No…not that I know of." I felt for the pendant at my neck and rubbed it gently between my fingers. He looked back again, watching my hand with interest.

"She said you aren't comfortable getting more than three dresses…Is there a reason?"

He studied my face as if all my thoughts were written on display for him.

"I don't need more than that."

"Well, she seems to think otherwise."

He crossed his arms as if anchoring his position. Several ladies walked by us, throwing glances our way—*his way* in particular.

"You probably shouldn't be back here," I whispered.

"There are doors. They'll live," he mock-whispered back.

His eyes challenged me to continue.

I swallowed hard. "I can't afford more than that."

He sighed. "There is nothing to afford. You're not paying for them—I thought she explained that to you."

"I don't feel right about the company paying for my formal wear—it's not their fault I didn't pack the right attire. I just need a short-term loan, and then I will repay it, three is what I can afford."

He opened his mouth twice before he spoke again, "So you're saying you have a *moral issue* with the company expensing your dresses without repayment?"

"Yes."

He chuckled once and shook his head, "Okay...well, there's a first time for everything, I suppose. Make your selections, Miss Flores. I'll speak with Pippy."

He turned to leave and then stopped, turning back to me as his eyes roamed my figure unabashed. My throat went dry.

"You should get that one."

I shut myself inside the dressing room and bit my lip as a pink blush crept up my neck and into my cheeks. His statement wasn't quite a compliment, but I'd seen something in his eyes just now...something that no longer could be concluded as disdain.

Pippy and I had narrowed the selection down to ten, and from there I picked my favorites, and by favorites, I meant the least expensive. As an associate came over to carry the precious cargo up to the counter, my heart nearly beat out of my chest. I never spent this kind of my money on myself. Ever.

Pippy looped her arm through mine. "Hey, let's go grab some lunch. It sounds like the guys are hungry."

"Oh, okay. Don't I need to get my bags?" I asked, peeking around her to the counter where my selections lay.

"Uh, Walt is gonna swing by and pick them up so you don't have to carry them into every store we go in today."

"Oh, alright. That's nice of him." I smiled, and so did she.

Cody got his "New York hotdog" and was happy as could be. The rest of us preferred a sandwich, so we found a sub shop and sat at an outside patio table. The weather was warm, but not too warm. What a difference from the heat of Dallas. I enjoyed the fresh air immensely. Jackson was leaning back in his seat, scrolling through his emails and texts when I turned my head toward our social coordinator.

"Tell me about your brother, Pippy?" I asked her.

"Oh—Peter. You will probably meet him soon, he works for my, uh—Mr. Ross as well," she said looking from Jackson to me and smiling. "He works as a liaison for our different publishing houses."

"Oh? So you spend a lot of time with him?" I asked.

"Yeah. He's my best friend."

The way she said it broke something loose inside my chest. Briggs and I were close like that, although things had changed a bit since he'd gotten married. But I had expected as much.

"I'm very close with my brother, too. That's a rarity."

"It is, yes. I couldn't imagine not having him in my life. We are two peas in a pod—speaking of, he will just love Cody! He may be twenty, but I swear he never grew up. I'm sure he'd love to show Cody around and play some soccer with him at the park one day."

"Really? Your brother plays soccer?" Cody asked, invested in the conversation for the first time.

"He sure does, and I hate it…so I'm sure he'd love to play with you!"

"When can I meet him?"

"I'll find out. I'm sure he will be at one of the dinners next week, or maybe he can come by at a signing and meet you then."

Cody chomped on a big bite of hot dog, "Cool."

Pippy giggled and I echoed. Jackson looked up from his phone, his eyes regarding me curiously as a bolt of lightning charged through my core.

Six weeks with Jackson Ross would be my undoing.

Chapter Six

Pulling Cody into the backseat with me on the ride home, I made sure the front was wide-open for a certain sexy bachelor. I could only handle so much Jackson in a day.

Jackson hadn't said much to me since our showdown in the dressing room, other than to ask if he could take Cody for ice cream. The request had actually come at the perfect time since Pippy had wandered inside a discount shoe store.

Our lack of conversation was fine by me. I wasn't up for another battle of wits with him. I needed to save my mental energy for dinner. Pippy said the gathering would be small—just the authors on tour and a few editors. I was actually looking forward to the event.

After we parked in front of the T. Ross Building, Walt assured me he'd have my purchases brought up to the apartment. I started to argue, but his sweet smile melted my heart.

"Well, thank you," I said.

Jackson was on his phone, avoiding eye contact when I said goodbye to Pippy.

Inside our room, I checked my phone messages. Rosie had called several times. While Cody rested on the couch watching Disney Channel, I logged in my daily chat time with Rose.

"Hey! How are you?" she said.

"Good—tired," I admitted.

"Tell me everything! I'm dying to know what it's like…when you texted me that you were going shopping I just about passed out from jealousy!"

I laughed. "It's been good day so far—shopping in New York City is pretty fun if you have the cash to spend. Mr. Ross's assistant is a great gal; she helped me pick out some evening dresses. You wouldn't believe how many formal events these people put on over here."

"So what's *he* like?"

"Who? Mr. Ross?"

"Don't be coy with me. I Googled him! He's a hottie!"

Oy. "He's…insufferable."

She laughed—hard. "No way! God doesn't make packages that pretty for them to be rotten inside."

"Well, he might not be rotten, but he certainly isn't ripe. He's…I don't know. He's a mystery."

"Oooh, mysterious, huh? I don't know…I think you're holding something back." Her tone lowered as if she was about to share a secret. "I would absolutely *love* to know what he thinks about you, though. I read he was a bachelor—a very rich bachelor. And I bet he was pretty surprised when he met you for the first time."

"Why do you say that?" I snapped, remembering that introduction with vivid clarity.

"Because that picture on your blog is awful, Angie. It looks nothing like you! I told you to change it months ago."

"Hey! I *like* that picture. Cody had just won his first soccer game; it was a proud moment." I huffed into the phone, furrowing my eyebrows.

"Okay, sure…it was a good moment. But it was also ninety-five degrees outside and your hair was in a ponytail, not to mention it only shows half your face…the other half is of a soccer field! *A soccer field!*" she repeated. "All I'm saying is I would have loved to have seen his face when he met you. I bet you're the most gorgeous author he's ever had work with his company."

Now it was my turn to laugh heartily. If only the truth of our meeting wasn't so humiliating, I would retell that shining moment in my history. But it was too embarrassing to recount, even to Rosie.

"Well, keep on dreaming, sister. You didn't miss anything. And I can assure you that Jackson Ross doesn't think anything about me—not in the way you're insinuating anyway.

It was nice to catch up with Rosie. She was my connection to home—and real life. I filled her in on my phone call with Jenny and made sure she would follow up with her. She agreed. After our call ended, I closed my eyes. I just needed a few minutes… what could it hurt?

I awoke with a start to my phone buzzing beside me. A glance at the bedside clock sent my pulse into overdrive. *Oh, my gosh! I've been asleep for over an hour!*

The phone kept buzzing and I answered. It was Pippy.

"Hey, I just wanted you to know I won't be there tonight. I have to fix a scheduling crisis with a couple of the interviews for Monday."

"Oh." I had only known Pippy for a couple days, but already she felt like my safety blanket in this world of unknowns. I was disappointed…and nervous to go without her.

"Don't worry—you'll do great. It's purely recreational tonight. Just get to know the others and have a great time."

I wanted to ask her if Jackson would be attending—the question was on the tip of my tongue during our entire conversation, but I refused to indulge my demented curiosity.

"I'll see you tomorrow afternoon at the signing."

"Oh, on a Sunday?" I asked.

"Yes, the tour doesn't allow for many breaks—sorry."

"Okay…thanks for calling, Pippy. See you tomorrow."

We had an hour before Walt would be here to get us for dinner, and—*wait, where are the dresses?* I stumbled into the front room, and saw several large garment bags sitting on the couch next to Cody, who was playing on his new best pal, Mr. iPad.

"Did you answer the door while I was sleeping, Cody?"

"Uh, I looked through the peephole first, mom. I promise." Cody glanced up and me quickly before returning to the wonder of his gaming device.

Before I could unleash a mom-lecture, my eyes drifted to the bags again, mouth going dry.

This isn't right…there are too many. One, two, three…six! Six bags!

Scooping them up in my arms, I laid the selections on my bad and then paced my floor as I tried to understand how this mistake could have been made. As I got up the nerve to open each bag, my stomach dropped to my knees.

"No." My voice was a shaky whisper as I pulled out the beautiful champagne-colored gown from one of the garment bags.

All I could think about was the price of this one gown, one gown which could have paid my rent for nearly three months. Searching every last corner of each garment bag for the receipt I had specifically asked Pippy to supply me with, I turned up empty handed.

I texted Pippy about the error, asking her to call me as soon as she could.

No reply.

The clock was ticking, and I had to get ready for dinner. I exhaled, envisioning the fancy boutique rejecting my request to return the items without a receipt. Tears pressed behind my eyes as I calculated the cost of such a mistake. I'd be paying Pinkerton Press back for a very long time.

I was never frivolous. I'd lived lean for long enough to know that squandering money on temporary pleasures only resulted in the sacrifice of essentials: groceries, gas, utilities. Instead of pre-paying our rent and catching up on past-due bills with the advance money I'd received, now I had a closet full of silk to show for it.

My chest ached.

By the time Cody and I got into the car, my mind was so far down a rabbit trail of worry that I was in no mood to keep anyone company. Clothed in a money-sucking, plum-colored ensemble, I had just single-handedly thrown away more money than I had seen in years.

I followed Cody through the dimly lit Italian restaurant, a symphony of swoony romance music dominating the atmosphere. I loved it immediately.

We were the last to arrive. Two agents, three editors and four authors sat staring at their menus—but Jackson was not present.

Formal introductions were made around the table before our waiter came by to get our drink orders.

"Mom, do they have spaghetti here?" Cody whispered in my ear.

"Yes, sweetheart, probably the best you've ever eaten." I glanced at the prices on the menu and sucked in a breath. I'd never seen a dish of noodles cost so much.

"May I sit here?"

I looked up to see Jackson Ross peering down at me.

My stomach flipped like a gymnast on a trampoline. Every molecule of moisture in my mouth was sucked into a black hole.

"Sure." I leaned into Cody while he sat down next to me.

"I didn't think you were coming." Though I made the comment under my breath, I stared ahead at my glass of water.

"I have a strict policy not to disappoint women, Miss Flores." His voice was low and smooth, no detectable emotion behind it.

I gulped a quick swig of my drink. "Somehow I find that hard to believe."

A crooked smile danced on his lips. "Try me."

I looked away immediately, mouth as dry as the Sahara once again.

A deep rumble shook his chest while I tried to focus my attention on the Zimmerman's agent—Carly Grant. She was telling a story about when she traveled to Denmark to meet a client a few years ago. People were laughing, but the humor escaped me. I was too busy trying to forget that Jackson sat next to me.

The night carried on as Cody worked to finish a bowl of spaghetti the size of New Jersey. He had been asked a lot of questions and was included in a great deal of the evening's discussions. Their kindness toward my son blessed me. Many times in my life as a single mom I had been on the receiving end of eye rolls and whispers for bringing my son with me to places when most people would have hired a babysitter. This situation was one of the topics I had written about in a blog post, actually—a relatable topic for many in single parenting. Nights like this—nights where we could be treated like everyone else— were a rare, sweet gift.

At the end of the meal I found myself worrying less about my dress-debacle and thoroughly engaged in the company of this group. If not for *The Refuge* or the walk-in customers at the flower shop, I would be a social shut-in. As it was, Rosie already thought me one.

I enjoyed meeting people though—I loved hearing people's life stories. They reminded me that not everyone faced tragedy and heartache to the degree I had known it. That fact gave me hope—for Cody.

I smiled at him and reminded him softly to wipe his mouth with the napkin on his lap. He nodded.

Surprisingly, Mr. Ross pulled my chair out as the guests at the table stood to say their goodbyes.

We walked to the curb and waited for Walt to bring the car around.

"If you don't mind, I'll catch a ride back with you tonight."

I stared at him, leery of this new, seemingly well-mannered Jackson Ross.

"Sure, of course," I said.

Inside the car, he checked his phone. Cody sat in the front like usual.

"Tonight was nice," I ventured.

"Indeed." He scrolled his thumb over the screen.

"Do you go there often?" I asked.

He glanced up at me, a tiny smirk on his face, "Yes. That is one of my regulars. Pane Di Vita is a great place—as is the owner."

"Oh." I shifted in my seat, his close proximity causing me to sweat.

I stared out the window and watched the lights of the city blur past. This city was a different kind of beautiful—New York. Loud, busy, crazy, chaotic…but I could find an appreciation for it, even if my heart did yearn for the quiet of country living. That dream would most likely stay just that—a dream.

"I trust you have what you need now for the events on the tour schedule?"

I jumped at the sound of his voice. He studied me, a gaze of his I'd grown used to.

"Yes, thank you for asking…and for coming along today. Cody had a good time."

A cold chill invaded my gut as I thought about the huge debt I owed.

"It's a part of the job."

I nodded. *Of course…I am his job. Remember that, Angie.*

The car stopped outside of the T. Ross Building and I stepped out. I realized then that Pippy had never texted me back about the missing receipt. It took every shred of courage for me to ask him, but I needed to know the final number—the damage.

Turning back toward the car as Cody walked into the lobby, I indicated for Jackson to roll his window down. He did, tilting his head to the side, brows raised.

"Is there something wrong, Miss Flores?"

"Uh—not exactly, I just couldn't find the receipt for the purchases today…and I need to know the total."

His head tilted to the side as he seemed to ponder some deep, philosophical query. I was about to restate my question when he finally opened his mouth.

"You have no total. Your *moral issue* has been resolved."

"I—what do you mean, exactly? I thought we had an understanding that I only wanted *a loan*. I am going to repay every penny, as I indicated to you earlier." My frustration grew exponentially as he leaned back into his seat and crossed his arms, amusement dancing on his lips.

I opened my mouth, no sound coming out.

"You had a moral issue with the company expensing more than three dresses because that is all you could afford? Correct?"

My brows furrowed. "Yes, that is what I said."

"Great. Well, your purchases today were *not* expensed. They are a gift. And after careful deliberation with my own moral compass, I hope you will come to the same conclusion as I have: a gift cannot be repaid."

I gawked at him. *He cannot be serious.*

"No…" I shook my head. "There are *six* dresses in my room right now." I pointed to the building as if he could see them with some magical x-ray vision. "That's an extraordinary amount of money! I cannot accept any gift that large—not from the company."

He was quiet for a beat too long as I tried to ignore what I was reading in his eyes.

"It's not from the company."

Flames engulfed my neck and face. "I cannot accept a gift of that magnitude, Mr. Ross."

"I assure you I expect nothing in return. No need to jump to any ridiculous conclusions. They are only pieces of cloth, Miss Flores. Not a dowry."

I was beyond mortified. If only I could die. Right here. On the sidewalk.

"I—I—"

"Goodnight, Miss Flores."

He rolled his window up as I stared after the black town car driving away.

Despite my resolve to have the last word...tonight would not be *that* night.

Chapter Seven

Three interviews spread between NYC and Philadelphia, along with five bookstore signings and a whole lot of eating out later, there was one glaringly obvious common denominator: no Jackson.

I had begun to think he'd given all responsibility over to Pippy when he suddenly showed up Thursday morning at a radio interview in Rochester. Cody was waiting with Pippy just outside the studio, watching us through the glass. I had my headphones on, as did Sue Bolan who was representing our Publisher's tour with me today. I knew the drill by now. They usually asked around six to eight questions, all of which I had read and approved beforehand.

Though I'd taken my own precautions by changing my last name from Luterra to Flores after the attack six years ago, I couldn't be too cautious—not when it came to Cody. His name was innocent of his father's sins. And I'd do anything for it to stay that way.

I smiled at the host, feeling confident about the interview…until I saw Jackson standing in the control room with headphones on, staring at me.

"…you have one son, and you have raised him entirely on your own?" Brian Marks—the radio DJ asked me.

"That's correct. It's just been Cody and me since his birth, although I've had wonderful support from my brother and some good friends."

"So it does take a village then—to raise a child?" he asked.

"Oh, absolutely. I think one wrong assumption that is made about single parenting is that we have to be both mom and dad—and that is simply not possible. Responsible parenting involves creating a world in which there are multiple healthy influences pouring into your child's life. We are connected to a church that has really helped me with that challenge. I think that is one of the most important aspects of parenting—whether single or married."

"I think you make a great point, Angela," Brian said. "A well-rounded child is one that is connected to the world around them. You certainly seem like you're a good mom, and I'll tell you folks, her picture on her blog, *A Lone Joy*, does little justice to the beautiful woman that sits before me now. Let me be the first to say, you don't have a face for radio."

He winked at me as I blushed, fingering my necklace. "Well, thank you. I do try to be a good mom, but behind every good mom there's a mom that is afraid she's failed."

"And what's your advice to those mothers—single moms in particular?" he asked.

"Not to give up. To look at each day with fresh eyes, no matter how hard things were the day before. To remember the reasons why your heart sings when you see your child succeed in something, or when you watch them make a choice for the benefit of another person. To stop comparing yourself to the mom down the street that has, does, and is everything that you are not. At the end of the day, if your child knows that you love them…let that be enough. And let tomorrow be a clean slate."

"Well said." Brian grinned at me. "Smart, talented and gorgeous. I have a feeling you won't be single for long Miss Angela Flores. NYC, you'll want to meet this pretty lady. Her tour dates and schedule are located on our website. Check them out…and we'll be back in a moment to talk with Sue Bolan about her book *Adoption Answers*—what are the questions and answers you need to know?"

Brian hit two buttons in sequence then took off his headphones and stared at me.

He pushed long blonde hair out of his eyes and reached his hand out for mine as I stood. "Wow, you were awesome—a pro! If being a big time author doesn't pan out, you should look me up. I'll hire you, though I was serious about your face not being made for radio. You shouldn't be held up in some dark hole like me."

I shook his hand as heat rushed my face. "Well, thank you, you made it easy."

He was handsome, in his own way. Blue eyes, fair skin, and a couple tattoos on his right bicep. His face wasn't made to be in radio either, but I wouldn't dare say that aloud.

"Here…" He handed me his card. "If you ever want a tour guide while you're here, I've grown up in New York. I can show you an insider's tour."

"Oh, well…thanks. I have Cody, so I doubt I'll have a free evening."

He shrugged. "I like kids. Bring him with you. I gotta get back on the air, but call, anytime. I mean it."

"Thank you again, Brian."

I left the studio just as Sue began drumming a nervous rhythm with her fingernails on the table in front of her, headphone on, eyes closed. She hated radio interviews; she had told me so earlier, which was why I had gone first.

Cody opened the studio door and rushed to hug me. "You did so great, Mom! Pippy said it was your best one yet."

Pippy nodded in confirmation as I saw Jackson step out of the control room—face tight, pensive. As he walked past us, I fought the urge to ask what he thought.

Hot. Cold. Hot. Cold.

The man was a broken water heater.

Keeping my eyes on Jackson—who was ten steps ahead of us—I asked, "So what else is on the agenda today?"

"Well, I promised Cody he could meet my brother today. What do you think about getting a little tour through Pinkerton Press?"

"Oh that sounds great…how far away is the office building?"

"About an hour from here, give or take, with traffic. It's only a few blocks down from where you're staying." She smiled and shrugged, stopping in the hallway as Cody ran to catch up with Mr. Ross.

"Aren't you coming?" I asked her.

"Oh, didn't I mention I have to stay until Sue is finished?" She smiled at me sweetly.

"Uh…no. Do you want us to wait with you, then?"

"No, absolutely not. Mr. Ross is going to take you. He's agreed to give you the tour—thinks it will be fun, actually. I'll just meet up with you there."

"Are you serious? I highly doubt Mr. Ross wants to be our *tour guide*. He barely wants to say hello to me. I think I'd rather wait for you."

Now she was laughing, full-on Pippy-laughing.

"What? I'm serious. The guy is like a dark rain cloud who keeps the sun away *on purpose*! Does he even know what *fun* is?" I planted my hands on my hips, battling a smile that kept trying to sneak across my lips.

"I promise…he's not usually…like that—" Pippy was laughing so hard she could barely speak.

"Pippy, I am an expert in the art of denial, and you've got it, bad."

Her laughing slowed as she shook her head. "It isn't like that. I've known him a very long time…he's one of the best people this world has to offer. He's just going through an rough season-"

"Yeah, I've said that line myself. I know all about 'rough seasons'. Believe me."

I stared as her face sobered almost immediately. *What was her loyalty to this guy?*

Suddenly I remembered all the times she'd come to his defense. And when I saw her straighten his tie before dinner last week. How she brings him a morning coffee without being asked, and laughs when no one else finds him funny.

She was a sweet-natured girl, but could it be more?

Could Pippy be in love with Jackson?

She may have been close to ten years his junior, but that wasn't beyond the realm of possibility…was it? Pressure built in my chest, almost to the point of explosion. I opened my mouth to—

"Are you coming, Miss Flores? Cody and Mr. Ross are waiting in the car for you." It was Walt. Good old, sweet Walt who had probably put up with years of ego-driven demands from Jackson Ross.

I narrowed my eyes at Pippy. "We are not done with this conversation. There is a lot more I feel I need to say to you."

Her eyebrows rose. "Oh…okay, sure."

Her face had guilt written all over it.

I shook my head, heart reeling at the results of my detective work.

Chapter Eight

"You know, if your brow was any more furrowed, I believe steam would be coming out your ears." Jackson glanced at me for the millionth time since I got into the car.

I ignored him again.

The longer I sat on the knowledge I'd uncovered, the more anxious I became. I cared about Pippy—a lot. I felt a sort of loyalty toward her that caused my inner-mama bear to awaken. I wanted to protect her, her heart especially. Though I had never sensed any physical danger from Mr. Ross, his personality type was dominant, one that could easily overpower her sweet spirit and optimism for life—and her innocence.

I couldn't sit back and watch that play out. I wouldn't. My fingers curled into fists.

"Mom, do you have the grumpies?" Cody turned around in his seat.

"What? No," I said quickly.

"It looks like you do. You've had a lot of think time, and you still look grumpy."

I shook my head, "No, Cody—"

Jackson leaned forward and grinned at Cody. "Hmm…what's this about curing the grumpies, Cody?"

"It's what mom and I do when one of us is having a bad day. I just need to find the right music…"

"Cody," I warned through my teeth.

"Sorry, Mom, but you always say we don't make good decisions when we're grumpy. Mr. Walt, can I search for the right station on your radio?"

"Certainly, Mr. Cody. Be my guest." Walt laughed.

I closed my eyes. *This is not happening!*

Soon the car was filled with a beat that could have roused the dead. Cody began his signature car dance in his seat, and a deep laugh boomed from Mr. Ross. Soon Walt was grooving, also. I bit the corners of my cheeks to halt my smile from filling out my face, but soon lost the battle. When Mr. Ross joined in the hip-hop with a roll of his shoulders, I had to surrender.

A giggle spluttered from my lips. My whole body quaked with chuckles that demanded release. Mr. Ross turned his head toward me and raised his eyebrows.

"It really works then, huh? The cure?"

"For the moment."

"Ah, yes. That does seem to be the way of a woman." He shook his head and looked down at his phone.

"What is that supposed to mean?" I raised my voice to compensate for the music. Walt and Cody were still dancing in the front seat.

"It means you women never know what you're feeling. One moment up, the next moment down...pick one."

"At least I have more than *one* mood to choose from!" I hissed.

He glared at me, searching my face.

"Good to know."

"What's good to know?" I balked.

"What you think of me."

"I...I don't think of you in any way...I don't think of you at all." I was digging a slow grave.

A crooked smile painted his mouth. "Well, you might consider thinking about me a little bit more the next time you accept a date while on the clock—a clock I help provide payroll for."

What? What was he talking about?

He held my gaze, pushing me to remember a memory that I didn't have. I never accepted a date...wait...

"You mean with Brian? That's not—"

"Please keep your personal agendas from interfering with company time."

"Unbelievable," I murmured under my breath.

"What is?" He said, leaning toward me.

"Your attention to *personal detail* within this company is quite limited if you ask me, yet no one is willing to step in to protect the virtue of a young woman who's in way over her head."

He furrowed his eyebrows as his mouth turned down. "Excuse me?"

I leaned in closer and spewed the words. "You know *exactly* what I am talking about."

The car lurched to a stop. Cody opened his door and stared up at the skyscraper in front of us. I was much too distracted by the intensity of the man sitting beside me to shift gears.

"I'm afraid I have no earthly idea what you're referring to, Miss Flores."

"Pippy! She's in love with you! And you treat her like a groupie in your fan club, leading her on without a care in the world."

His mouth opened.

Closed.

Opened.

Closed.

Then . . .he laughed.

Tears poured from his eyes. It was the first light-hearted laugh from him I'd heard. I refused to let my body warm and relax the way it wanted to at the mellow sound. Instead, my cheeks heated at the nerve of this man—this man to whom I was so physically attracted it was almost painful.

Bolting from the car, I grabbed Cody's hand and stalked to the building's main entrance.

At least for once, I'd had the last word—sort of. If you didn't count the laugh of an evil villain as a word.

****

I heard Jackson—Mr.Ross—behind us. He was still cackling as he walked into the building. He laughed in the elevator, and all the way down the hall, composing himself only when we reached the doorway to Peter's small office.

"Hey, there!" A masculine version of Pippy stood before me: charming, slim, handsome. He shook my hand and waved us inside, greeting Cody with a fist bump.

"You must be Angela Flores," Peter said. "Pippy has told me so much about you—she really likes working with you."

"Well, I have really loved working with your sister as well. She's a special girl." I glanced behind me at Mr. Ross, who had started laughing again.

"Tell…tell Peter your diagnosis of Pippy," Mr. Ross said.

"What?" I scowled at him.

"What diagnosis?" Peter's lighthearted attitude showed through his question. He was just like his sister, smiling like the world was made of gumdrops and mint patties.

"Mrs. Flores has just informed me that Pippy is *in love with me*. Weren't those your words?" His gaze gleamed amusement.

Peter gaped at me and then scratched his head, cheeks reddening. I was so confused. *What is going on here?*

"Uh, that's not possible." Peter's face quickly went from embarrassment to pure pity.

"Why's that?" I asked softly, already feeling the weight of my body pressing against my knees. I wasn't stable. This wasn't going to end well. I braced my hand against the wall.

"Mr. Ross is our Uncle."

Oh Gosh…Oh Gosh…Oh Gosh…

I'm an idiot…I'm an idiot…I'm an idiot…

"It's okay…he's only ten years older than us, so I could see how…well, maybe…" Peter started then his voice trailed off.

He was trying to make me feel better—very Pippy-style—but it wasn't going over well. If I could melt and slither away between the seams of the wood paneling, I'd jump at the chance.

"No, I'm so sorry. Gosh, I'm so very sorry." The lame words stuttered from my lips. "Is there a restroom nearby?"

"Sure, right down the hall next to the elevator. Want to meet us on the second floor in the café? It'll get too busy if we don't secure a table soon. Pippy is on her way."

At the sound of her name I wanted to vaporize. Why—oh, why—couldn't I control my thoughts and mouth around Jackson Ross?

"Sure. Cody, stay right here with Peter."

"I will, Mom."

My black slacks swished around my legs and ankles as I rushed to a stall in the restroom and closed my eyes.

"Stupid, stupid, stupid…" I chanted to myself under my breath. "This is why you shouldn't make assumptions!"

I went to the sink and ran the cold water over my hands in an attempt to bring down my body temperature, which seemed to be roughly the same as molten lava.

I cannot face him again—ever.

I opened the door to the restroom and turned in the direction of the elevator, took a step, and smacked right into the fancy dress shirt of one Mr. Jackson Ross.

"There you are."

I glanced up at his face, and then immediately wanted to die. Again.

Shaking my head, I searched for the words to make this right. "I...can we...I'm so sorry—"

"Ah, and there it is. I had a bet going with myself that I would hear one of your famous apologies."

I took a deep breath, no anger left within a hundred miles of me. I was far too ashamed of myself to feel angry. "Well, I mean it. I was wrong to make an assumption like that. I feel so stupid."

The atmosphere shifted, almost like there was a physical charge in the air around us.

"You aren't stupid. The idea that my niece could have feelings like that is fairly disturbing and downright comical, but you aren't stupid."

Though the inflection in his voice was unchanged, his overall demeanor seemed…softer.

"I don't know why I've felt it my place to be so outspoken with you, but you have my word that it will stop. I am not usually like this—that's a lame excuse, I know, but it's true. I hope we can move on. I can be professional. I *will* be professional."

He stared at me, and a sensation like fizz bubbles floated throughout my body.

"Please, don't," he said, softly.

"Don't what?"

"Don't stop. No one ever tells me what they really think anymore. I like your thoughts, and I like your words—even if they're not always accurate." A lopsided grin teased at the corners of his mouth, and in that moment, I wanted nothing more than to feel those lips pressed against my own.

My heartbeat went staccato as my eyelids blinked in echoing pattern. He stepped closer.

"That's…surprising," I said, his minty breath wafting in the narrow space between us. I bit the insides of my cheeks.

"What's surprising?" he asked.

"I didn't think you noticed much of what I said or did."

His gaze roamed my face intently as I swallowed. "I notice everything, Miss Flores."

At the simple, heartfelt tone of those words, the bottom dropped out of my stomach like the elevator had just shot upward a dozen floors.

Chapter Nine

Pinkerton Press in NYC was a mirrored replica of the branch in Dallas that I had visited a month earlier when I met with Dee Bradford. The only difference was, this time, I was walking next to Jackson. People seemed to stop what they were doing to greet him. Why was a man who didn't seem interested in the pleasantries of life so popular amongst this crowd, but it was as if the Prom King himself had just made his entrance into the café.

His facial expression had changed a tad since we entered—it was softer, and for the first time I could see how much he cared about these people. This company. I watched the transformation, intrigued. The café was buzzing with people, tables full of lunch trays with a large variety of food to choose from: Chinese, American, Indian, Greek. Several chefs along with a gourmet salad bar were stationed at the far end.

Cody and Peter were laughing when we reached their table near a window. I had a million questions running through my mind about Jackson, but none seemed appropriate to ask in public. Given my most recent lack of restraint, I decided it was best to do as Rosie did— Google him. I was already planning a date with my laptop as soon as I got back to my apartment.

Pippy joined us about thirty minutes later and filled us in on the adoption interview. Sue had almost passed out from nerves, but Brian had coached her through it. As soon as Pippy said Brian's name, Jackson looked at me, as if waiting for me to announce an engagement.

I did not oblige him. I picked at my salad, instead.

"Mom, Peter said he would practice some soccer with me in Central Park."

"Oh, that's sounds great. You could use some good exercise other than the sports games you play on that iPad—speaking of, I never thanked you for that basket—"

Jackson looked at his plate. "No need."

"Well…it was a very nice thing to do for Cody."

He nodded and picked up his hamburger. Discussion apparently over.

Pippy beamed at me, her eyes sparking like the noonday sun. The girl was positively giddy just to be alive.

I took in the three of them now: Peter, Pippy and Jackson. Their family resemblance was remarkable. Again, I found myself wanting to ask more questions in regard to my recent discovery but chickened out. The lines were all blurred now. I didn't know my place—or my level of access to such personal information.

Was the family relationship supposed to be a secret? Or were they just trying to maintain professionalism within the workplace and not discuss it with outsiders? I suspected the latter. If only I had picked up on that tid-bit-o-information say… last week.

Hindsight always mocked me.

Just as I stood up to dump our trash from our lunch, a woman with long, dark hair, dark skin, and legs that seemed endless, approached our table. I plopped down with a thud. It was *her*—the woman who had so openly kissed Jackson on the cheek at the dinner last weekend and pulled him to her table.

"Hello, Jackson." Her voice sounded like a recording from one of those risqué perfume commercials where every model spoke French and wore an eight-inch piece of lace. I almost laughed at the less-than-subtle nature of her voice, but I was far too busy staring at the red silk blouse plunged to the middle of her chest, unbuttoned. I diverted Cody's eyes, handing him my phone to text an update to his Uncle Briggs.

"Hello, Divina." Jackson turned toward the woman. "What brings you here, today?"

I stared at Jackson's face, trying to pick his closed expression like a lock. *Nada.* The bolts were impenetrable.

"Oh, you know." She laughed breathily. "A little of this, a little of that. Always working to get on top." She winked at him and smiled. Her long black lashes teased as they opened and closed slowly, her lips forming a permanent pout.

I decided I'd rather be elbows deep in a trash can then stay for this brazen attempt at seduction. I stood and gathered our plates, catching Jackson's eye in the process.

He cleared his throat. "Divina, have you met our newest addition to the family tour?"

Her gaze swept over me as if she could identify each cheap thread used to make my second-hand clothing.

She extended her perfectly manicured hand toward me—bright, red polish on her nails. I put the plates down, and shook the slender cold fingers, not missing the way she positioned her hand in mine: as if she was the Queen of Sheba, and I the lowly servant.

"It's nice to meet you, Divina." I forced my tone to sound kind, but saccharine never could pass for the real thing.

"Yes. I have heard so little about you, but it looks like that will change soon enough. I will be interviewing you in two weeks." Her tone took on an irritated edge as her narrowed eyes traveled from me to Jackson and back again.

"Oh, are you in radio?" I asked.

She threw her head back as if I had just slapped her flawless face.

"No," she spat. "I'm an anchor on The Eastman Morning show."

My face flamed at the look she gave me, one that screamed disdain for my ignorance like a siren.

"Oh…I'm sorry. I'm not from around here."

"Yes, obviously. It's quite alright." Divina looked me up and down again, smirking.

Working to steady my quivering insides, I cleared the table. Cleaning was a good excuse to leave that woman's company—Divina: exotic goddess of television.

"It really is in your DNA code, isn't it?"

"I'm sorry—what is?" I asked Jackson. He stood over me as I dipped a napkin into a water glass and began wiping the crumbs off the tabletop where we had sat—once a mom, always a mom.

Peter and Pippy were getting a drink refill with Cody.

He laughed. "You don't even realize how often you say it, do you?"

My face reddened, I *had* said it to Divina. *Dang.* "Okay…so I have manners when I speak to people." I let my tone suggest that he didn't. He laughed again.

"No, you have a *compulsion* when you speak to people." His eyes twinkled at me like stars in a desert.

I glared at him. "There are worse things than saying *sorry*, Mr. Ross."

"I disagree. The travesty is not in the words, Angela, but in the mindset behind them."

A cold, chill washed down my arms as I heard my name spoken from his lips, goose bumps left in its wake.

"And what mindset is that?"

He shook his head. "That's a question you must ask yourself."

I sighed as he strode away toward Cody and the twins at the drink machine. Meanwhile, I was still bent over the café table starring into my own version of *Cinderella: The Mom Edition*.

I threw the wet napkin away and followed behind the family-tour-parade, pondering his question.

****

Later that evening, after Cody showered, talked with Uncle Briggs and Auntie Charlie via phone, and said his evening prayers…it was time for my Google-snooping to commence. Pushing my guilty conscience aside, I scrolled through articles and pictures like a history timeline.

Rosie does this all the time; it's not wrong.

And then I stopped, hovering over an article link with my cursor.

Click.

Jackson Ross—prodigal son—steps into CEO position at Pinkerton Press.

After four generations of Ross men filling the seat of CEO at Pinkerton Press, the baton has been passed yet again. This time to Jackson Ross: the younger of two sons in the Ross family legacy. He is described as a prodigy in his own right, with a quiet, yet defiant nature. However, at twenty-eight, his past remains almost as much a mystery as his claim to bachelorhood.

Ross is said to be well-traveled and well-versed in the publishing world. After his father, William Ross passed away nearly eight years ago, the position of CEO fell to the eldest Ross brother—Jacob Ross. It is rumored that the elder brother has stepped down due to a serious illness. There are no updates on his current condition.

"Transition should be motivating. If it doesn't create an atmosphere of unity—one that pulls people together—then the issue is not in the company's change of command, it's in the morale," Jackson Ross said at the press conference last Friday, May 6th, 2011. He says he is determined to take the company onward and upward and follow in the footsteps of the "wise men that have gone before him."

"Wow…" I said aloud.

So Jackson Ross became a CEO two years ago at the age of twenty-eight, graduated with honors from NYU, and was now a smart, sexy, successful bachelor. I could think of a thousand worse resumes than that one. I gulped, closing my laptop lid and laughed out loud. Mine was at the top of that list.

Here I was: a single-mom at 29. No college degree to my name, no shining career to claim. My only note-worthy accolade was a blog.

I called Rosie. And though I tried at first to divert the conversation away from Jackson, it went there anyway, talking at length about our recent conversations along with my own Google "research" findings. The girl had a one-track mind, and apparently so did I. As soon as we ended the call, I grabbed my black journal and wrote an entry.

****

My hands shook as I made my way onto the stage at the Anthem church in Philadelphia. I'd been invited as a guest speaker to join a small panel of mothers discussing parenting questions and concerns. Pippy stayed back at the apartment with Cody to watch movies and eat Pizza, while Walt drove me to the church in the town car.

I sat on a stool, a microphone wired to my blouse, as Mrs. Dyson, the Pastor's wife, spoke to the large gathering of women, introducing the panel while I looked around the spacious room, wishing Rosie's face would suddenly appear in the crowd. I could use a friend right now.

"And this is Angela Flores. She's a single mother of an eight-year-old son, and currently on a family tour with Pinkerton Press. Her blog, *A Lone Joy*, has just been picked up for publication, releasing this fall. Let's give her a warm welcome. Thank you for coming tonight, Miss Flores."

"It's my privilege. Thank you for having me," I replied.

The audience applauded as Mrs. Dyson went down the line, introducing each of the four panelists on stage.

Question after question was asked from the note cards provided to each attendee as they entered the church, and so far, my responses were similar to the ones I'd given during radio interviews.

"This question's for you again, Miss Flores." Mrs. Dyson read the notecard. "I'm a divorcee with two school-age children. I've recently started dating a bit and I'm wondering what your advice would be on talking to my kids? Do you tell your son about every date you go on, and if so, have you prepared him about the possibility of marriage in the future?"

My heart beat wildly in my chest as the panelists and host turned to me for an answer. Was it just me, or had the temperature risen to about a thousand degrees in the last thirty seconds?

I cleared my throat and took a sip from my water bottle. Plastering a smile on my face, I peered out into the crowd. "Although I'm an advocate of open communication with children, this is one category I'm afraid I don't have a lot of experience in. I haven't dated since I've been a single mom, but that's not to say I have a stand against it, I don't. It simply hasn't felt like the right timing for me, personally." I glanced around the room, straining to see the faces in the audience as the lights blinded me from above. "However, I think if there's ever a time when a man comes into my life who changes that..." I nearly gasped when I saw a figure I recognized leaning against the sidewall. Though I couldn't make out his expression, I *knew* him. A second or two passed before I was able to continue, recovering the best I could. "My advice...would be to give a new relationship a bit of time before talking about possible future scenarios with your children, but it might be wise overall to share your desire for remarriage—to open the lines of communication."

Mrs. Dyson nodded and then opened the question up to the other panelists. My gaze shifted once again to the man who made my pulse race and my cheeks burn. A man who had singlehandedly reminded me that I was a woman with desires, wants, and maybe even needs.

Jackson was here.

The rest of the evening was a bit of a blur as I remained hyper-aware of his presence. I answered questions on a variety of topics, most having to do with discipline, school activities, and schedules, but Jackson was never far from my thoughts.

As the audience clapped, signifying the close of the evening, I followed the three panelists off the stage. A small group of women found me immediately afterward, hugging me and asking for pictures and autographs. The group soon swelled into a mass of faces, and I feared I'd lost Jackson in my attempt to be polite to each woman who handed me a notecard to sign.

But then Jackson was there, at my side.

I glanced at him, the voices muffling around me when our gazes locked. There was something new in his eyes as he watched me. And though heat sparked in my core, his gaze seemed to calm my anxiety instantly. As his hand pressed my lower back, he whispered in my ear, "When you're ready to leave just give me a nod. I'll stay right here beside you."

"I'll stay right here beside you."

His words flitted in and out of my head as I worked my way through the crowd. And when I finally did give the nod, Jackson's warm hand found my lower back again, his touch sending flurries of delight up my spine.

Ducking into the town car, Jackson slid in beside me. Walt closed the door after him.

Jackson was the first to speak, "You have a natural stage presence, Miss Flores."

Walt signaled and turned onto the highway.

I straightened my blouse. "I didn't know you were coming tonight. I figured I was on my own."

Jackson turned to me, arching an eyebrow. "Is that what you prefer—to be on your own?"

The question took me by surprise. "No, I...I like people."

"You just don't like men?" Jackson asked, one side of his mouth lifting into a lopsided grin.

I tucked my hair behind my ear. "I never said that."

He chuckled. "We say so many things without ever using words."

My throat went dry. "I would have to agree with that, I suppose."

His smile dipped as the car went silent.

"Is it true what you said tonight? You haven't dated since Cody was a baby?" Jackson asked.

My stomach tightened. Jackson didn't usually ask personal questions. He didn't usually ask many questions to me at all, actually. "Yes, that's true."

Jackson's gaze roamed my face and then the car lurched to a stop, jerking our bodies forward as the squeal of tires and horns erupted all around us. I gasped, clutching the seat in front of me as Jackson's hands reached for me.

Walt apologized profusely, claiming a driver had just cut across two lanes of traffic, which had nearly caused an accident in the lane to our left. Jackson looked me over, the concern in his eyes nearly doubling my already increased heart rate. He gently pushed the hair from my face, and tucked it once again behind my ear.

"Are you alright?" He asked softly.

No. "Yes," I rasped.

As Walt started to pull the car into traffic again, Jackson's hand was slow to move off my shoulder.

Leaning back against the seat in an effort to calm my frazzled nerves, I glanced at him. "Thank you for coming tonight."

His eyes captured me once again. "You're welcome, Angela."

And in that moment, I wondered about the words he hadn't spoken, the ones trapped in his gaze, his voice, and in his posture. Because sitting beside me now, was not a man full of image-driven mysteries, but a man who felt deeper and understood more than I ever dared to realize.

Chapter Ten

All That Remains

I hear it like a whisper, calling out my name

Singing ever softly, to quiet down my shame

It beckons me to come, to leave the old behind

To choose the narrow path, not stumble like the blind

This pull is always constant, never has it strayed

Even death's dark shadow, cannot force it to the grave

Something stirs within me, a lonely desperate plea

Begging truth to show me, how I might be free

I answer it in secret, fear choking me so tight

I pray that I can choose, the way I know is right

The promise I hear back, is the opposite of blame

It's a hope that surges through me, to all that still remains

****

(Three years into marriage)

The night was calm, much unlike the war that raged within me. Once I spoke the words there would be no going back. The plan would be set in motion. There were no brakes that could stop this choice once it was decided..

Sometimes, even when you know the right thing to do, doubt still creeps in, twisting and turning until it's voice is stronger, louder, and bolder than the truth ever was.

That was my whole life story: one time had turned into two, which had turned into ten, which had turned into normal. My normal was wandering around in a maze of lies, and there was no way out. My escape was only a mirage in the distance; no substance to cling to, no shelter to hide under, no truth to be found.

But everything was different now. Two words had changed me forever.

I had to find the strength.

I had to find the girl inside that used to hope in something more...

I stood at his apartment door and took a deep breath. He opened it on the second knock; his face ashen with concern when he saw me. I never sought him out anymore. I never asked for his help. And now I was here, standing in front of him.

He waited for me to speak.
"I'm ready," I said.
With a stiff nod, he closed his eyes briefly, as if in a prayer. His consent was the assurance I needed. I relaxed as he pulled me into a hug. He'd always been my safe place—the only one I'd ever known.

"When can we leave?" Briggs braced my arms with his hands as he pushed me away from his chest .

"I need a week. I have some paperwork to file, and I need to put some cash away."

He exhaled hard.

"Okay. One week. Not a second longer."

I nodded in agreement. It would be hard for him to wait, but I couldn't afford to be hasty. There was too much at stake now. His eyes narrowed as he searched my face for the missing piece, for the link between the truth and the lies, for the reason behind my newfound courage.

It had been so long since I had cried, but the tears fell anyway, undeterred.

"I'm pregnant."

****

I'd lost count of how many restaurants we had been to, but there were many. I never thought I'd tire of gourmet food. But I was wrong.

So very, very wrong.

I longed for a snack-dinner; the kind made of crackers, cheese, apple slices and summer sausage, or even a nice, home-cooked, breakfast-for-dinner option. After seventeen days of being in New

York, I was *over* the romanticism of eating out. The one interesting development was that Jackson had been accompanying us for dinner more and more, and when he showed up, he always pulled my chair out for me and took a seat at my right.

I liked this new routine more than I cared to let myself believe.

What amount of work must he be delegating to others in order to spend so much time with Cody and me? I dared not ask the question aloud. If there was one thing I tended to do often with Jackson, it was sticking my nose where it didn't belong.

We sat now with the men Jackson referred to as "the borings". In reality, they were six older gentlemen who were current shareholders in the company, as well as board members. The seventh member, whose name I didn't hear, was not present. Jackson seemed more than okay with that fact. Along with the six of them, sat Peter (for the sake of Cody) and four other clients and editors. I knew none of them, as they were not on the *family tour*. I wasn't quite sure why we'd been invited, but I never questioned dinner plans anymore.

We looked at our menus. Thai was the pick of the night—not my pick, but I smiled and went along with the flow. I was *not* a spice-fan. To be honest, I was the biggest baby about hot food, and as such, I usually avoided anything that resembled noodle dishes from the orient, but Jackson insisted I let him choose one for me. I gave him the honor and asked the waitress for an extra glass of ice water.

Jackson laughed at my dramatics—although I wasn't that big on drama. I was simply a realist. I knew I would drink every last drop of cool moisture.

We sat at the far end of the table while several men debated over current stock-trading. Peter and Cody were still talking about the latest in sports, and Pippy was on a date. She had been swooning over a boy named Caleb for the past week. He had finally asked her out—today. Jackson had given her a hard time about skipping out on such an *important dinner*, but I saw him smile as soon as she skipped away, happy to have the night off.

"So what do you think?" Jackson asked me as I leaned over the steamy plate of noodles covered in spicy peanut sauce.

"Pretty good." I pasted on a smile.

He smirked. "You are a terrible liar."

"No, it is. Thank you. Good pick." I twirled up a forkful and forced it down. Five seconds later, hot, steaming coals burned their way back up through my esophagus. I gulped water.

"You don't have to finish it, Angie," he said.

Something in the way he said my name made me smile.

I was wearing one of my new dresses, a navy one that Pippy had selected. But even in stylish attire, I felt like an impostor next to this man in his expensive suit. Everything about Jackson seemed affluent, including his attitude in life. What I had first seen as cocky arrogance, I now envied. He was confident, collected, and self-assured—always. There was no second-guessing, no indecisiveness, and no uncertainty lurking under the surface.

He just was. Jackson.

"I will eat every last bite." I lifted my chin.

The corners of his eyes crinkled. "I'll bet you five hundred dollars you won't."

He chuckled as my eyes rounded in shock.

"I don't-"

"If you win, you get five hundred cash, but if I win, I get to order your next five meals for you," he clarified with a lop-sided grin.

I bit my bottom lip, thinking the proposition over as my stomach churned. "Deal."

He smiled that crooked, sinister smile of his and echoed, "Deal."

****

I didn't speak on the car ride home. My stomach hurt way too bad for talking—no, instead, I held my head high and waved goodbye to Jackson and Peter, *five* one-hundred-dollar bills in my hand. Cody pressed the elevator buttons, and my stomach heaved, but I bravely battled the nausea down. On the way up, I closed my eyes and leaned my head back against the wall.

As soon as I was through the door of my bedroom, I tore off the skin-tight dress and slipped into my yoga pants, hoping the elastic waist would bring some comfort—even if just placebo comfort.

Cody was laying on his bed reading, so I made my way to the couch with my little black journal and applied all my will-power to calming the storm that thundered inside my belly.

I opened the journal and flipped through the pages, landing on an entry I'd forgotten.

I had only been sitting on the couch for five minutes when the first horrendous cramp gripped my body. The wicked vice of pain was like the onslaught of labor; only a sweet newborn baby wasn't going to be the grand finale of this ordeal. Before I could utter a word to Cody, I was running to the bathroom, Thai food revolting in my gut, ready to reveal itself a second time.

And it did.

The violent attack had a mind of its own, forcing me into slavery with the porcelain bowl.

"Mom? Mom, are you alright?"

I could hardly turn my head to see Cody standing in the bathroom that linked to my tiny bedroom.

"I'm sick, Code."

"What do I need to do?" he asked.

My hands shook as a cold sweat broke out all over my body.

"Call Pippy…cancel tomorrow's plans."

"Okay. I'll get your phone."

He was gone, and a second later I heard him talking faintly in the other room. Then another round of porcelain worship came for me. Cody returned to the bathroom and draped a cold, wet washrag on the back of my neck the way I always did for him.

"Thanks," I rasped.

"Do you think dinner made you sick?"

Just the thought of Thai noodles drew a graphic answer from my stomach.

Five-hundred dollars was not worth this.

"I'll be okay, Cody. You should go to bed…"

I didn't want him to see me like this. It was bad enough for me to have to deal with illness, but there was nothing more that he could do for me.

"Okay…are you sure, Mom?"

I nodded.

I lay on the cool, tile floor, drifting in and out of consciousness, waiting for the nausea to wear off so I could go to bed. Then I heard something: a voice? My ears perked up, but a second later, I decided I must be delusional.

I had no reference for time, just endless cycles of puke and sleep.

As I closed my eyes I heard the voice again, this time clearer...closer...here.

"You look awful."

I snapped my head up. Too fast. I gripped my skull with both hands as a sharp pain splintered my brain. Peeking with only one eye, my living, breathing, nightmare stood on display before me. I squeezed my eyes shut. I had to be hallucinating. *Please, God, let me be hallucinating.* But someone nudged my foot as he knelt beside me.

I squinted up again.

Yep. This was it: my most humiliating life moment to date.

"Why are you here? Who let you in?" I groaned, unmoving.

"Because you look like death. And your son, who else?" Jackson said.

"How did—why did—"

Speaking hurt too much. I couldn't ask questions. I didn't care about the answers anyway. I was too sick to worry about anything other than *not* vomiting on Jackson Ross. That was pretty much my only priority at the moment.

"Pippy called me. She was worried, but she's still out with what's-his-face."

"Caleb."

He laughed. "Of course, you remember that."

He picked up the washrag that had fallen on the floor next to me and ran cool water over it, then wrung it out in the sink and handed it to me. Then he sat down. On the bathroom floor. Across from me. *Me!* Throw-up girl!

I closed my eyes. "Thanks, but you should leave."

"You should stick to being nice. Bossy doesn't become you."

I shook my head, trying to sit up, slowly. He reached toward me, but I waved him off. I wouldn't let him touch me. I should be quarantined, not assisted by a handsome, rich CEO.

And then I noticed what he was wearing.

It was the first time I'd seen Jackson in anything other than a suit. He was dressed in jeans and a black t-shirt. *And, my word, does he look good.* I shut my eyes, suddenly hyper-aware of how *not-good* I looked.

"So, I think Thai food can be eliminated from our food options in the future," he said.

"Urgh…can you not mention food for a while, please."

"Sure. Do you need some water?"

"I should probably wait a bit, but I think the worst has finally passed."

"Good. Do you want to move to your bed?"

I looked at him and shook my head. There was only so much humiliation a girl could take in a single evening.

He leaned his back against the wall and crossed his ankles. "Okay…so we'll just sit here then."

"Okay." I said, resting against the tub. "Is Cody in bed?"

"Yes. He was reading when I knocked on the door. He told me you were in here, but that you had sent him to bed 'cause you didn't want him to see you sick."

Smart kid.

"That's true," I said.

He gave me a look I couldn't quite identify and sighed deeply. "I had food poisoning once. I'll never look at eggs benedict the same way again."

"You're talking about food again. Can we *please* switch topics?"

"Oh, right." He chuckled. "Uh, what do you think of New York?"

I pursed my lips, a laugh rising up through my nausea. This had to be the most ironic moment in history.

"So this is what it takes to get you to converse with me? I look and smell like the after party at a fraternity house, and you choose *now* to make small talk?"

He shrugged. "Guess so."

I undid my ponytail and combed through my hair with my fingers then put it back up. I was still shaky, but strength was slowly returning to my weakened body.

"I haven't really seen much of the city. I mean, I see a lot of traffic and a lot of restaurants, but I'm sure there's more to The Big Apple than that."

"There is, although…" he shook his head as his words trailed off.

"What?"

His gaze swept across my face, taking me in before continuing. "I used to think New York had some sort of magical power about it. I did a lot of traveling after college, and I always thought this would be home, that I would feel the same kind of energy forever, but I haven't felt it for a long time. Sometimes I don't know why I'm still here."

His gaze dropped away and I stilled. Those words were the most personal thing he had ever shared with me, and I didn't want this moment to end. I didn't want to interrupt him, not even with my quiet breaths.

"Have you ever felt that way about a place?" he asked. "Do you feel that way about Dallas?"

"No," I said quietly. "I've never really had a place I called home. I do feel that way about a few people in my life though. But not about a place…maybe someday."

He nodded slowly. "I think what you have is the better of the two definitions. Finding home in relationships is much more challenging than finding it in a location."

"Yeah, but someday I'd love to have a place of my own. On some land…surrounded by trees and hills-"

His eyes crinkled. "So you're not a big city girl."

"Nah, but, it's okay. I'm where I'm supposed to be for now." I had nothing but warm feelings for my charming rental home in Texas. Bringing my knees up to my chest, I crossed my ankles and rested my head on my arms.

"Must be some special people you have—back in Dallas?"

I managed a weak smile. "Briggs—my brother. He's my rock. And Rosie, my best friend. I don't think I would be here if not for them."

He pursed his lips, questions clearly forming in his mind, but before he could ask any I cut him off. "I think I'm going to take a shower now. Thank you, Jackson ... for checking on me."

"Is that your send off?" He raised an eyebrow.

"Well...uh...I'm sure you have better things to do with your Friday night."

He seemed to consider the statement as he stood up. "I'm going to grab you some saltines and ginger ale from downstairs. You'll need them to settle your stomach in a bit. Where's your key card so I can drop them back off?"

"Oh, uh, sure. It's on the coffee table."

"Okay."

I shut the bathroom door and heard the door to my bedroom close a second later. Bracing myself on the vanity, I glanced in the mirror.

Yikes!

I was right. I shouldn't have looked.

Chapter Eleven

I Once Believed

I once believed you loved me…even when

Your voice didn't sooth

Your hands didn't comfort

Your heart didn't reach

I once believed you loved me…even when

Your footsteps instilled terror

Your face instilled pain

Your presence instilled sorrow

I once believed you loved me…even when

Your intentions lacked honor

Your words lacked truth

Your actions lacked conscience

I once believed you loved me…but when

Your rage smothered me

Your deception smothered you

Your addiction smothered us

...I stopped believing.

****

I stood in the shower for a long time, letting its warmth revive me. By the time I got out, I felt considerably better. At least I wasn't suffering from a virus that might be contagious—that was the glass-half-full in this situation. I brushed my teeth for an entire five minutes and gathered my hair into a wet bun then dressed in a clean pair of comfy pants and shirt. A glance at the clock said it was just after 12:30 a.m. I had taken so long trying to wash off the smell and look of death that I was sure Jackson was long gone.

I walked into the living area, and the room transformed into a vacuum, sucking every last ounce of oxygen inside of it.

The second before he saw me, he was bent over the coffee table...reading...my black journal. He stood slowly as I blinked in rapid succession, trying desperately to process the mental image of him violating my privacy.

No one spoke.

Space and time were obsolete.

A thousand emotions surged through me at once. The invasion was incomprehensible, the exposure unparalleled. Yet his face held no trace of guilt or regret.

"Were you just reading my—"

"Did you write all of these poems, Angie?" He lifted the journal from the table.

I nodded as he stared, assessing me as if for the first time. My blood pumped cold within my veins, leaving a feeling of prickly pins and needles with each pulse. There was a bold look in his eyes that seemed to diffuse me, leaving me spellbound instead of furious. He took several steps toward me, stopping at arm's length.

"You're a victim of domestic violence?"

"No." I squared my shoulders. "I'm a survivor."

This was always the part I hated most.

I'd said that phrase hundreds of times at *The Refuge*, yet it never got easier, especially outside of that safe bubble. There were too many stereotypes to break through, too many tainted TV shows and fictional characters that had defined the "role of a victim".

The pity and detachment that always followed such a confession was nearly impossible to avoid or divert.

But the truth was, there were many more stories out there than what the average person cared to realize—stories of sisters, mothers, aunts and daughters. The cycle of living in secret had been perpetuated by the shame of such confessions. And as much as I hated the pity, I hated the shame even more. Exposure of truth killed shame.

Jackson had just read *my* truth.

I waited to see the pity…to see the revulsion on his face…to see the awkward roaming of his eyes…but the reaction never came.

"I saw the book lying on the table and didn't know what it was at first…but then when I realized what it was, I didn't stop. Maybe I couldn't stop. Your words…I've never read anything like them."

I swallowed hard, dragging my eyes up to meet his again. His gaze held, igniting a fire in me.

"You had no right to read my poems." I forced myself to speak when all I wanted to do was run.

"I know…"

"No one has ever read that journal. It's private, Jackson! You had to know it was wrong to keep reading it!" Heat burned my cheeks as snippets of entries flashed through my might with lightning speed.

"You have every right to be angry with me," he said.

I shook my head. "I don't even know what to say to you right now. How would you feel if this situation were reversed?"

He said nothing, the intensity of his stare breaking something in me.

"This," I said, taking the journal from his hand, "is not the property of Pinkerton Press."

His features changed then. Instead of his usual look of indifference—the one I had come to expect—a pained look passed over his face. The expression was so brief I almost missed it.

"Despite what you may think, I'm not some leech-sucking business man, Angie. I would never exploit you—*ever.*" The sincerity of his words shocked my brain. There was not a trace of anger to be found in them.

My heart beat hard and fast, knocking against my ribcage. His eyes were locked onto mine and in them I uncovered the truth, one that could have dropped me to my knees: I *wanted* him to know me. The *real* me—almost as much as I wanted to know the real Jackson.

I took a deep breath. "I believe you."

"It's the truth," he said.

I nodded again, refusing to break eye contact. "I should probably take this opportunity to tell you I've done some snooping of my own."

He groaned. "Google?"

I scrunched my nose up in embarrassed confirmation.

"And the Internet is such a *reliable* source of information."

"Well, next time I'll just look for your journal lying around…"

"Touché."

Jackson reached for my arm, his touch stirring something deep inside me.

"Will you forgive me?" he asked.

I studied his face. His determined eyes, his firm jaw, his exquisite mouth…I swallowed. "You won't invade my privacy again without permission?"

"Never."

And then my face was crushed to his chest, his hands strong against my back as they held me against him. I melted, my heart thumping hard. I hadn't been embraced by a man—outside of my brother—in more years than I could remember.

This hug gave more than comfort; it gave hope.

"Will saltine crackers and ginger ale suffice as a peace offering?" he whispered into my hair.

Smiling into his t-shirt, I replied, "Yes. Thank you, Jackson."

For more than you could ever know.

****

"I heard you were sick…do you need anything?" Dee Bradford said on the phone at nine the next morning. She had called several times in the past few weeks to check in.

"No, I'm feeling much better today, thank you. My dinner didn't agree with me last night, I guess."

"Okay, well, I hope you recover soon."

"Thank you, Dee. We're doing great here."

"Glad to hear it. I'll check in with you next week."

I was feeling almost a hundred-percent as I sat next to Cody on the sofa, reading on my Kindle. Cody was big into the *Choose Your Own Adventure* books, and it was nice to have a day that wasn't planned from start to finish. Pippy had cancelled my commitments for the next twenty-four hours; texting that she would take care of rescheduling. She also texted that she would have an updated schedule for me by the end of the day—I didn't doubt she would.

Cody flipped through pages to the back of his book.

"What ending did you choose?" I asked him.

"I think Marcie should go to her Uncle's Alligator farm in Florida rather than that stupid band camp."

"Oh…yeah? I think that sounds a bit more exciting, too."

"Yep."

I laughed.

There was a knock at the door.

"I'll get it." Cody jumped up with the book still in his hand.

"Look through the peep-hole first, Cody."

"I know, Mom. You always say that."

I smiled. At least he listened.

"It's Mr. Ross!"

My stomach flipped. Cody opened the door for him. Jackson entered, smiling.

"How's the sickie today?" he asked Cody.

"She's better...no more throwing-up."

I groaned, remembering the state I was in last night, the state Jackson had *seen* me in last night.

"Well, that's good. I hate throw-up." He smirked at me, the rat! He must know I wanted to crawl into a hole and never come out. "I thought maybe we should go somewhere today—if your mom's up for it."

Cody jumped in excitement and Jackson laughed, shrugging at me with a question in his eyes.

"Um…what did you have in mind?" I narrowed my eyes at him.

"You up for a trip to the zoo?"

"Yes!" Cody yelled.

"I guess so." I laughed.

"We can stop for lunch on the way if you haven't eaten."

"Is Walt outside waiting?"

"No. I drove."

"You know how to drive?" Cody gaped.

Jackson roared with laughter, slapping his thigh, while Cody's brow puckered. I smiled and escaped into the bedroom to change. If only I could calm my heart rate, but it was a lost cause.

A Saturday afternoon spent with Jackson—*when did my life become so interesting?*

Chapter Twelve

It was a warm day—very warm. I was glad I had chosen to wear shorts, so had Jackson. Seeing him in something other than his daily suits made him seem more human—less CEO, and more average guy (although Jackson Ross could never be average). It was like seeing a picture of the President playing with his dog, or out for a jog—there was a connection to *normal* society with such photos.

The Bronx Zoo was gorgeous, like walking through a colorful, well-maintained garden. I loved the plants and scenery almost as much as I loved watching Cody's face light up at each exhibit. He loved animal facts, so we couldn't pass a sign without him stopping to read it. I watched Jackson, checking for indications of impatience as these fact-interruptions were continuous, but he seemed legitimately interested in the things Cody discovered.

Cody had the map in his hand and led the way as we strolled behind him. So far we had seen: bears, tigers, elephants, zebras, giraffes and gorillas. We had also watched the penguin feeding show, which was my favorite event so far. Cody though, was most looking forward to the Madagascar exhibit. I sipped on a large ice water as Cody ate his way through a giant blue puff of cotton candy. I had turned down lunch for fear of a recurring episode of last night's humiliation, but I regretted that decision now.

A massive headache was brewing in the back corner of my brain as we strolled through the paths leading to *Madagascar*. As usual, Jackson was overly observant.

"You're not feeling well again." Jackson scrutinized me.

"I'm fine…it's just a headache."

"Give me your hand."

"What?"

He furrowed his brows, "Just give me your hand…*please.*"

My face heated. "Okay?"

Cody had stopped a few feet ahead and was reading a sign on the Madagascan Tree Boa as Jackson took my hand in his. My stomach knotted at his touch. He laid my hand flat on top of his, and with his other hand pressed a spot between my pointer finger and thumb. The relief in my head was nearly instant.

"Oh, my gosh…that's amazing."

He continued to press firmly as we started to walk again, following Cody. How long it had been since a man held my hand…

He's only helping my headache, not holding my hand! Get a grip.

"It's a pressure point."

"Huh…how long are you supposed to do it for?" Was it too much to hope he'd say an hour?

"One minute increments. The pressure usually cures after a couple of times."

A minute passed and he let go. I prayed the disappointment wouldn't show on my face.

"Better?"

"Much. Thank you."

"You should probably eat something soon. Figure out where you want to go for dinner... I think we've seen pretty much everything here."

The air in my lungs went buoyant. At least our dinner routine was still on, even though our day had been drastically detoured.

After the Nile Crocodiles, we headed for the exit trail, but Cody stopped abruptly and searched the map in his hand.

"Mom? Can we see one last thing before we go?"

"Sure...is it on our way out?" I asked.

"Yeah, it's right there...the butterfly garden."

"Um-"

Cody smirked at me and peered up at Jackson. "Do you want to come with me, Mr. Ross?"

"Sure. Aren't you coming?" Jackson asked me.

"I—um-"

"She doesn't like butterflies."

Jackson's eyebrows shot up as he looked from me to Cody.

"It's true," I said.

"How is that even possible? Who doesn't like butterflies?" The corners of Jackson's mouth lifted. His gaze was incredulous.

I bit my cheeks and shifted uncomfortably, hoping Cody wouldn't say more.

No. Such. Luck.

"She's afraid of them."

"What? No—you're joking. No one has butterfly-phobia." Jackson's mouth gaped.

"Well, technically, it's not just butterflies. It's all flying insects. Aviophobia is the correct term."

Jackson's expression froze, and then he cracked up. His laugh was deep, loud and uncontrolled. *Can a woman fall in love with a sound?* Even though the reaction was at my expense, I couldn't help but laugh with Jackson, nor could Cody.

"*Aviophobia?* That is best thing I've heard in months," Jackson said, "Come on Cody, let's go before your mom decides she's afraid of grass…or air."

"Hey! It's a real thing!" I called after them.

Jackson's laugh tickled my ears even after he was out of sight. I hugged myself, grinning like one of the local hyenas.

I just made Jackson Ross laugh.

That sound had secured a place in my top-ten favorite sounds of all time...maybe even in my top three. I had to hear it again.

I was growing quite fond of New York.

****

Jackson's small black sports car was very different than the car we'd been traveling around in for the last couple of weeks with Walt. I didn't know anything about cars, but I definitely hadn't been *inside* a car like this before. Everything was shiny, sleek, and compact and...shiny.

"So, where to?"

I looked at the clock. It was just after five. I tapped the pendant at my neck. The idea of going out to a restaurant was nauseating—literally, but I was starting to feel very hungry. Jackson eyed me, waiting.

"Do you have a kitchen?" I ventured in a small voice. .

"What kind of a question is that? Where do you think I live—a cardboard box?"

I laughed—hard.

"I'm thinking I'd like to *make* dinner...but my tiny kitchen doesn't really accommodate such a task."

"Are you inviting yourself over?" His smile was devilish.

I rolled my eyes and nodded toward Cody. "I'm asking if I can make us all dinner."

He stared at me, lips pursed. "I think that sounds…nice."

"Mom's a great cook," Cody piped up from the backseat. "Do you have any movies Mr. Ross?

"Hmm…not really. I don't watch a lot of TV. I usually read if I have free time."

"I love to read, too!" Cody said.

"Yeah? What are your favorites?" Jackson pulled out of the zoo parking lot into the flow of traffic.

"I love *Choose Your Own Adventure* books," Cody said.

"Oh, I used to read those…it's nice to feel in control of a storyline, isn't it?"

"Yeah."

I glanced at Jackson and smiled, he caught my eye and smiled back. Goosebumps washed over my body like an ocean wave.

"I'll need to stop at a store and pick up some things," I said.

"There's one very close to where I live. Cody can pick out a movie at the Redbox if he wants."

I looked back at Cody who had been quiet for a while, only to find he had passed out—asleep. I laughed as I told Jackson.

"So...can I ask you?"

"Ask me what?" he said.

"About my Google discoveries?"

He raised an eyebrow at me which set off a rapid increase in my heart rate.

"Oh. That," he groaned. "Okay..."

I waited for him to say more—to give me parameters or limitations—but he said nothing else. I took his silence as a *free-for-all.*

"Your family started Pinkerton Press back in the 1940's?"

"True."

I smiled. *So this was his game. True or False.*

"Your great-grandfather was the founder?"

"True. Teddy Ross."

"Oh? Is that a relation to the building I'm staying at? The T. Ross?"

"Yep...he had a gift in real-estate as well."

"You have one brother? Jacob? He's older?"

"True."

"Is he Pippy and Peter's dad?"

"True."

"So…he's…"

"Twelve years older—he's my half-brother."

"Oh! Wow…more than a one word answer. I feel quite privileged."

He grunted, but I saw a corner of his mouth creep upward.

Bingo.

"Okay…so…back to it then. Um…you became the CEO two years ago after your brother became ill?"

His face tightened, and immediately wanted to retract my insensitive question. I opened my mouth to-

"Don't you say it." He dropped his hand on my knee.

I froze and looked up at him.

How did he know I was about to apologize?

"If there were restrictions on the questions you could ask, I would have said so. And that one…is true."

I exhaled as he removed his hand. "But it wasn't what you wanted to do—work for the family company I mean?

I hadn't read that online, but there was something on his face that indicated such.

"It wasn't my plan, no."

"You said you'd traveled a lot after college...what were you doing?"

"Living my dreams...or so I thought."

I wanted to ask him more, to find out what the mysterious Jackson Ross was doing prior to becoming a corporate man, but I didn't.

"Are you close with your brother?"

He smiled at me, as if grateful for the diversion.

"We've had our issues, but yes. He's a very good man. Tell me about yours," he added.

I nodded. Warmth spread through me that he had remembered our conversation last night when I mentioned Briggs.

"I could write a book about Briggs. He's quite the character. A reformed bad-boy by the world's standards, but even through his rough seasons, he's always had the most loyal heart. He's funny, spontaneous, strong-willed... and he loves Cody as if he were his own.

He just married an incredible girl, too. She's tamed him quite a bit." I smiled, thinking of Charlie. "I've never seen him happier."

Jackson went quiet, then, and so did I. I gazed out the window, watching the crowded sidewalks slide behind us. Life here was so different from what I knew; yet as I glanced at Jackson, I realized *different* had many definitions.

And sometimes different was exactly what was needed.

****

Whatever notions I had convinced myself about earlier in regard to Jackson being a normal man in camo shorts slid to wayside the second we pulled into his condo's garage. I was far from well-versed in New York real estate, but it didn't take a genius to figure out that Jackson's condo was…expensive. With several grocery bags in hand, and a movie rental for Cody, we walked through a lobby that made the corporate apartment building I'd been staying at look like a second-hand store. We rode the elevator up to the twenty-third floor— to which I didn't cringe or imagine myself tragically plummeting to my death—and entered the French doors to Jackson's home.

My jaw needed to be shoveled off the floor. I couldn't stop Cody's observations or "oohs and ahhs" because I couldn't speak.

I followed Jackson past the living area to the kitchen that reflected our images every which way we turned. Everything was stainless, black and smooth….and *shiny*.

There was a definite theme going on here.

"Here we are," Jackson said, placing the bags on the black granite countertop.

The place made me feel inconspicuous. Everything was perfect. There wasn't a single spec of dirt, or even a physical sign that someone actually *lived* in this stunning residence. It was like looking through the windows of my old Barbie Dream Mansion…only nothing here was made of plastic, and nothing was hot pink.

Jackson waved his hand over my eyes as if attempting to wake me from a trance. "It's just a place to sleep."

I gaped at his casual tone. *Uh, hardly.*

"Right…" I pulled several items out of the grocery bag as Cody took his backpack over to the couch and laid back, relaxed. I smiled. The kid could adapt to anything quickly: even a plush condo in Manhattan.

"So…put me to work," Jackson said, washing his hands in the fanciest faucet I'd ever seen.

"Oh? Okay…um…" I glanced at the ingredients surrounding me.

"You're not so good at delegating are you?" He lifted an eyebrow.

I frowned as he chuckled, "It's been a long time since I've had a helper in the kitchen that could use knives or work on the stovetop." I looked over at Cody who was busy playing on his iPad.

"Well, you have one now. Tell me what you need, Angie."

My stomach tightened at his words—their effect on me, daunting. Despite my usual resistance toward male relationships, I had just invited Jackson to cross the line, without him ever knowing one existed. It was the line that separated me from *being fine* and *not being fine*. The line that divided *safe* from *exposed*. And *necessity* from *want*.

The colorless hue that abuse paints onto the canvas of life acts as a thief, robbing its victims from ever knowing the joy found from simple pleasures. Abuse dulls the art of dreaming and dampens the passion of desire. Abuse smudges and blurs the colors until one day the damage overtakes the original completely...leaving it bland and lifeless.

But within Jackson's short phrase, *my* canvas, the one that held neutral pigments of ash and gray, had unexpectedly been splashed with the unfamiliar. Bright colors of emotion—hope, joy, laughter . . . and desire. Intense desire, but for what I couldn't afford to dream of having. Maybe the colorless canvas was better. Safer.

Jackson brushed my hair away from my shoulder, "You okay?"

I nodded as his touch heated my skin and seared into my soul.

The touch of the only man to ever show me *color*.

Chapter Thirteen

Several internal self-pep talks later, I managed to cook alongside Jackson without having to use my escape plan—the restroom down the hall—if things became too intense for me. Every cliché about *heat in the kitchen* flooded my mind. But seriously, brushing up against Jackson was enough to boil my insides.

Tonight we were having breakfast for dinner: banana-nut pancakes, bacon, hash browns and fruit salad with yogurt. The menu was Cody's favorite, and one I thought I could stomach—minus the bacon. Jackson had peeled the potatoes and chopped some fruit, glancing at me every few minutes.

"You enjoy cooking?" he asked.

"Yes, although it's tricky when it's just Cody and me. Most recipes are meant for a much larger family size than ours, but I have some girlfriends I cook for, too. Rosie is usually over a few times a week. She is a fabulous cook, so we take turns in the kitchen."

"Rosie—she's the other person you named last night, besides your brother. How did you meet her?" He cut into the pineapple with ease.

Do I tell him?

I pondered the question. Should I filter my answer or not?

"We lead together in a group for women called, *The Refuge*. We met there six years ago…our lives looked very different then, but we both have a passion to give back to others what was given to us."

He stopped cutting. "And what was that?"

"Hope."

The look on his face matched the look from last night when he had held my journal in his hand.

"You're a strong woman, Angie."

My throat thickened with emotion, as I turned toward the batter I was stirring.

"I wasn't for a long time," I whispered.

"True strength doesn't just appear out of nowhere—it may develop during seasons which are unseen, unheard and almost always unrewarded…but that doesn't mean it didn't exist."

I had to remind myself to inhale. Why did he keep saying things that took my breath away?

A buzzing on the counter pulled me out of my trance—my phone.

I dug the phone from my purse, but didn't recognize the caller's number. "Hello."

"Hello…is this Angie?" The somewhat-familiar voice asked.

"Yes, this is she."

Jackson shot me a questioning look.

"This is Brian, from the radio station. I hope this isn't too weird, but I called and got your number from Pippy."

"Oh…uh, hi." I turned away from Jackson.

"Hey, so I was wondering if you'd like to take me up on my offer to show you around the city…maybe next weekend? You can bring your son along, too, of course."

I closed my eyes.

Worst. Timing. Ever.

I heard rather than saw Jackson shuffle up next to me.

"I so appreciate the offer—really, I do, but the tour keeps me pretty busy. I'll have to check my schedule and get back to you."

"Okay, well, I'd love the chance to get to know you better, Angie. Call me if you're free."

"I will, thank you," I said, careful not to say his name aloud. "Bye."

I hung up and quickly went back to the mixing bowl to scoop batter onto the skillet. Jackson's eyes were on my face, arms crossed in front of his chest, but I didn't dare look at him. I kept right on scooping.

"Brian, I presume?"

I shrugged.

He laughed humorlessly and shook his head.

"What's your problem with him, Jackson? He's a nice guy," I said defensively.

"A nice guy," he repeated. "Is that all it takes?" His eyes challenged me.

How quickly this man could start a fire in my veins.

"What is that supposed to mean? 'Takes to what' exactly?"

He shook his head and went for the spatula, flipping the pancakes over one by one.

"Can I put the movie on now?" Cody walked into the kitchen.

"Sure."

"No."

I stared at Jackson. We had answered at the same time. Cody and Jackson looked at me in surprise.

Why did I say no?

"I mean…that's fine. Dinner will be ready in a minute, so be prepared to pause it," I corrected.

"We can eat on the couches—as long as it's okay with your mom," Jackson said.

Cody watched me, as if waiting for a rebuttal, but I nodded in agreement instead.

"Cool!" He grabbed the movie off the counter and trotted back into the living room.

"I'll show you how to set it up, Code." Jackson wiped his hands on a towel and following Cody.

My momentary frustration toward Jackson turned to warm appreciation the second he said my son's nickname. Flipping the last of the pancakes and bacon, I watched as the two of them got the movie set up. The scene in front of me warmed me to the core. Seeing Cody laugh and joke with a man other than my brother was a rarity, and I was loving every second.

I hadn't dated—not even once since Cody was born. I'd been asked out, usually by customers coming to buy flowers for a friend, or a mom, or sick co-worker. All my refusals had been simple, easy. Cody was the primary reason for my resolve to stay single; my *need* for emotional recovery acting as a close runner-up. For years I had been too raw to even consider dating—too fragile. *But what is my excuse now?*

"Need plates?"

I jumped at the sound of Jackson's voice behind me. I must have been staring off into space.

"Did I catch you daydreaming? Was a certain tattooed radio announcer clouding up the brain?" A distinct hint of sarcasm dripped from his words.

I glared at him, taking the plates from his hands and shoveling hot food onto them.

"Are you jealous, Jackson?" I turned just in time to see his face shadow. "Has no one ever called *you* a nice guy—is that it? I simply cannot imagine why not..." My sarcasm trailed off as his eyes roamed over my face, stopping on my lips.

He stepped closer, sending my heart into a reckless spasm.

His arms bracketed me as he grabbed two steaming plates off the counter, brushing my shoulders in the process.

"And what if I am?" he whispered.

"What?"

His stare was the only answer I received before he walked over to Cody and handed him a plate.

****

I snuggled into Jackson's plush leather couch, my stomach satisfied. The banana-nut pancakes were exactly what my post-stomach-flu had needed. I stretched out my legs while Cody lay on the floor with two big throw pillows. That was his favorite way to watch a movie, though there was plenty of room on the couch next to Jackson and me.

Jackson and me.

I sighed. I wasn't sure what had happened in the kitchen, but something definitely had happened. He sat at one end and I on the other, but neither of us watched the movie. I knew this only because every five minutes we were both checking to see if the other was watching or not. All I knew about the movie was that it starred a mangy-looking dog who could talk. Cody kept commenting on how he wished his mom would let him have a dog someday. I rolled my eyes, unwilling to get into yet another debate about how expensive pets are.

The tension that brewed in Jackson's living room was thick—almost tangible. And definitely uncomfortable. I crossed my feet as I saw Jackson pull on the back of his neck. What was he was thinking? He turned his head toward me, and I looked away quickly.

As soon as the theme song of the movie came on and the credits rolled, I jumped up. I needed to get out of this pressure-cooker before I said or did something I'd regret. I had only known Jackson a few weeks, but the "moments of regret" between us had been piling up since day one. I didn't need to add another one. I stretched and fake yawned.

"Code…we have a busy day tomorrow. We need to get back to the apartment and get you to bed. Please thank Mr. Ross for such a nice day."

Jackson stood up. "I'll drive you."

There was something different about his voice, a strain. Cody must have heard it too, because we both turned toward him.

"We're fine to take a cab. It's not that far. You've been driving us around all day. Really, Jackson, we're fine."

"And it's even *more fine* for me to drive you."

I didn't argue. It was pointless. Jackson was probably the most stubborn man I knew, and that included my brother.

After collecting the plates and putting them into the dishwasher, Cody grabbed his backpack. We were out the door a minute later.

Cody filled the awkward silence in the car, asking Jackson a thousand questions about the city, books, pets (nice try, Cody) and traveling. Jackson obliged him, returning interest with questions of his own.

Something burned in the back of my throat. I swallowed it down.

Jackson left his car with the valet at my building and rode the elevator up with us, despite my protests. Cody stuck the key card inside the lock pad then turned around and threw his arms around Jackson's waist even as the door clicked open. Jackson looked a bit bewildered, but he returned the hug regardless.

"Thanks for today, Mr. Ross. I had fun at the zoo…and riding in your car." Cody said then darted inside.

I stood, speechless. Cody had always been a sweet kid: both sensitive and friendly. But even I couldn't have predicted that kind of warm response from him.

The heavy door fell back against my shoulder, inches from closing as I glanced up at Jackson. His eyes were intense as they searched my face for several seconds.

"Don't settle for nice, Angela Flores. You deserve better."

As his gaze dipped to my lips, my insides swam with unexpected want.

"Jackson—"

He stepped closer, my exhale catching in a shaky vibrato that heated my cheeks. I slumped against the doorjamb, praying the solid surface would keep me upright. He swept my hair off my shoulder.

"Maybe I do act like a jealous teenage boy around you...but it's not because I want to be called nice." His warm breath swept across my lips, a shiver tickling the back of my neck.

"Then why?" I rasped.

Hope soared in my chest as I focused on his mouth, the world around me nonexistent as I silently begged him to continue.

"Because you remind me of something I lost..."

He leaned in and pressed his lips to my cheekbone.

The second he pulled away, I was released back into the hands of my cold, colorless reality once more, the reality I'd always found sanctuary in...until Jackson.

Color had changed everything.

Chapter Fourteen

A LONE JOY

Thai Food, Throw-up and Truth—OH MY!

Well, it's official: I hate throw-up.

The only thing worse than cleaning up throw-up, is *throwing up*. But luckily, the times of flu-like symptoms in my adult life—or in this case bad Thai food—are rare. The experience got me thinking though, about life. How staring into a big porcelain pot while vomiting can be a time of introspection is beyond me, but it happened nonetheless.

Why is it that when we are in our most fragile, helpless state as moms, we don't want help? Does anyone else experience this phenomenon?

Asking for help has almost become a foreign concept for me, even when help is offered with the best of intentions, even if it's offered to me by my son. I realized while lying on the bathroom floor that in my desire not to be a burden…that I'm actively training my child to think it's better to be self-reliant than to admit weakness.

Though I believe independence is a necessity in our world today, self-reliance can be crippling. I cringe at the idea that I have taught him to exhaust every effort BEFORE accepting or asking for help. For a woman who has benefited so much from the concept of community and pushed it like a bad habit on this blog dozens of times, I fear that I have missed the boat in this particular life category. A community of friends and family shouldn't be limited to *invitation-only status*. What purpose does that serve in Cody's life to only have people around when life is on the up and up?

My tendencies will quickly become Cody's tendencies if I don't change them. If I never allow him to see me vulnerable, then he might never think vulnerability is okay. I will have done him a tremendous disservice if that is the case. Life is full of moments that drop us to our knees unexpectedly. I want him to know how to reach out, to pray, and to seek help when help is needed. *That* is a type of strong that I missed out on for too many years.

I want better for him.

****

"Good morning!" Pippy sang as I walked into the reception room of the KDAK 97.9 radio studio, Cody in tow.
Pippy handed me a large plastic cup filled with a thick, green concoction. A straw was poked through the middle—apparently the contents of the cup were edible.

"This green smoothie is like magic for a tummy-upset. I got Cody one, too." Pippy pointed to a small table in the corner of the room. My son looked at me for a rescue plan, but I had nothing.

"That's very thoughtful, Pippy. Thank you." I nudged Cody to say the same. He did so, begrudgingly.

Pippy smiled, completely unaffected by our less than enthusiastic response to her thoughtfulness.

I scanned the room. Everyone was here for our first family group interview—everyone but Jackson. Biting my bottom lip at this discovery, I worried that our time together the night before was the cause for his absence. *Had I said too much? Had we gotten too personal? Were my feelings becoming too obvious?*

"Nothing like spinach in the morning." Jackson's voice spoke softly into my ear. As I spun to face him, relief radiated through me.

"Hmm…you can have mine if you feel a craving coming on," I said, careful to make sure Pippy was out of earshot.

"Not on your life, sweetheart."

I'd never admit what his word choice did to me. *Ever.*

The next twenty minutes were spent getting briefed on the agenda for the interview by the station manager. We also heard how our time would be divided up within the hour-long segment. My part would be relatively small, but exciting nonetheless. The radio host was a man by the name of Kent Brown. He was an older gentleman with a round face, large glasses, and a white, wiry beard.

Jackson seemed unusually pleasant this morning. Was the chipper mood due to the fact that we were not sitting in front of

Brian—the *nice* radio DJ? That thought reminded me, I needed to tell Pippy to use more discretion with giving out my phone number. Brian might be cute, but I wasn't looking to date, or at least, I wasn't looking to date Brian.

The interview began with Mr. Brown speaking to the Zimmermans. I enjoyed hearing the couple speak about marriage. They seemed so down-to-earth, yet their relationship appeared extraordinary. They spoke on the importance of *tone*. "Our tone is far more important than the words we speak…it is the indicator of what's in our heart," Tom Zimmerman said.

I turned my head just in time to see Jackson leaning over Cody, showing him something on his IPAD. The compartmentalization of my heart was slowly melding into one big pile of mush. I took another deep breath and tried to regain focus on the interviewer.

The questions that were asked of me this morning were of a new variation, mostly about how I balanced my time between work, social engagements (ha!), and Cody. All of the questions were on the "approved" list that Dee had gone over with me before I left for New York. I appreciated the way she navigated my request and honored my boundaries.

It was hard to believe that Briggs and Charlie would be here in just shy of a week to take Cody back to Dallas. Each day that passed now was like the silent tick of a bomb. Though I was confident in my brother's ability to care for my son, I'd never been apart from Cody for longer than a day. This time, we would be separated for two entire weeks. My stomach rolled in nervous apprehension. As I peeked back over my shoulder, I made eye contact with Jackson. The uneasiness quickly faded into something else entirely.

My time in New York has felt a bit like my own summer camp.

I could remember with stark clarity the day my dad dropped Briggs and I off at Camp Kingston in Boulder during the summer of my eighth grade year. I'd stood on the steps of the registration building, bags in hand, thinking that my life was over. *Seven days with no friends?* I knew no one except for my brother, but unfortunately *his* friends had also decided to attend that summer, so basically I was on my own if I didn't want to spend the week hanging out with sweaty boys. I'd felt so overwhelmed and alone at first, but in mere hours that feeling had faded. How quickly one could connect to people when eating, sleeping, dressing, playing and endless chatter were involved. In a single week I had made closer friendships than I had during the entire previous school year. The experience was remarkable.

Thinking back over our last three weeks spent with the Pinkerton Press bunch, I'd had a similar revelation. We were no longer strangers, or even business acquaintances. The relationships I'd made so far were ones I hoped to cherish for a long time to come. I would miss each of their faces when I left, especially *one* in particular. He was the same one that was currently laughing with my son and pointing at me through the glass.

My heart squeezed again.

Sooner or later I'd have to face the facts: summer camp *always* came to an end.

****

"I won't be at dinner tonight," Jackson announced as we made our way through the lobby of the radio station in Brooklyn.

"Oh...okay." My surprise was not that he couldn't make it, but that he'd felt the need to tell me of his plans, a fact that did not go unnoticed.

"I have a board meeting. They always go late." He sighed, dropping his phone back into his suit pocket, ruffling Cody's hair as he walked passed us with Pippy.

"We'll be fine finding something on our own." I smiled weakly and shrugged a bit, still stunned that he'd shared his schedule with me so openly. What had he expected me to say in return?

He smiled down at me, narrowing his eyes as if dissecting my words in his mind.

"I'd never doubt your resourcefulness."

My face flushed hot, betraying my feelings like a newspaper headline. I reached for my necklace, weaving the tiny pendant back and forth between my fingers. I stared down at my feet, swallowing before speaking again.

"Jackson…I hope you know Cody and I have been grateful for our time with you in the evenings—going to out to dinners, I mean. But please don't feel obligated to us. I know you must have a lot of other clients and work you need to attend to. I realize we've taken up a lot of your time lately."

Through my peripheral vision I saw him cross his arms over his chest, a movement that caused me to look up. His expression reminded me of my first impression of him: Hollywood renegade on a mission to save the world.

"That sounded *dangerously* close to an apology, Miss Flores." He took a step closer to me, lowering his voice into a deep, husky rasp. "You haven't taken anything I haven't offered. Finding food in this city might be easy for a man like me, but finding good company to share it with…not so much."

I was locked into his gaze when I felt a tug at my arm, pulling me back into reality once again.

"Mom…are you ready? We're supposed to meet Peter at the park to play soccer on his lunch break, remember?"

"Oh…right."

Jackson smiled at me as molten lava bubbled-up in my core.

"Don't let your mom take any headers. She has an important interview on Friday," Jackson told Cody with a broad wink..

Cody laughed. "Okay, I won't."

"And do your best to keep the butterfly attacks away from her, too."

Cody hooted louder as he ran back out the doors where Walt was standing talking to Pippy.

"You're so *not* funny," I said, biting my cheeks.

"Then tell yourself to stop smiling."

My face broke into a grin. "I wasn't—I mean—I'm not."

He shook his head, a glint of amusement in his eye. Turning to open the lobby door for me, he whispered in my ear as I slid into the back seat of the town car. "Don't ever play poker, Angie."

Chapter Fifteen

"So how was your date with Caleb?" I leaned back against the shaded park bench, watching Peter kick the soccer ball to Cody.

Pippy sighed dreamily. "It was wonderful…he's wonderful."

I chuckled at her dramatics. "So you're going out again I take it?"

"Yes, this weekend. He's actually going to my dad's birthday party with me on Saturday night. My mom's been planning the event for a while—it's a pretty big deal." She smiled sweetly as I remembered that her dad had been sick. I wasn't sure what the current status of his health was. Jackson hadn't spoken much more about his brother.

"That's great, Pippy." I bumped her shoulder with mine.

"You deserve to be happy."

I heard Cody laughing as Peter dove on the soccer ball to stop it from rolling into a row of blackberry bushes.

"What about you, Angie?"

"Huh?" I caught Pippy's eyes sparkling in question. "What about me?"

She sighed and shook her head. "You deserve to be happy, too, Ang. To find love."

I squirmed in my seat. *How do I even begin to talk to this innocent young woman about the precarious thread that held my life together?* We were as different as night and day when it came to this topic. She was a clean, starched piece of fabric ready to be stitched; I was a tattered, used remnant.

I watched Cody play, mulling a response. "I *am* happy—truly. My life may be more complicated than other twenty-nine year-old women I know, but I have learned to cherish the happy seasons. Cody is-"

"He's a great kid, Angie," she interrupted. "But even I know that it would be impossible for him to fill every gap in your heart, or in your life. My dad always says that complications should be seen as a chance to simplify one's priorities."

Out of the corner of my eye I could see her beaming. I took a sip of my ice water, warmth growing in the pit of my stomach despite the cool beverage.

"When Dee called to tell us that she'd added a single mom to the tour, you weren't at all what I pictured." She played with the straw of her second green smoothie of the day.

I laughed lightly. "Yes, I'm sure my laid back mom attire was a bit of a shock compared to the trendy atmosphere you're used to around here." I gestured toward the city.

"No, that's not it." She touched my knee, drawing my attention back to her. "And *I* wasn't the only one who seemed surprised by you when you arrived."

Even without hearing his name my heart hammered against my chest like a mallet inside a courtroom. Her smiled grew wide when she saw the shock in my eyes. I shook my head; I couldn't talk about Jackson with Pippy. Not only was she his niece, she was his assistant as well.

"Pippy, I don't think—"

"It's true. I know my uncle very well, and he is not easily stunned…but he was that night, the night he met you outside of your building."

"You mean the night I overheard you two arguing about my lack of appropriate wardrobe pieces?"

Pippy laughed. " Uh, yes. I'm sorry about that, but I'll never forget the way he looked at you."

"I think your twitterpation over Caleb has twisted the objectivity of your memories, Pippy."

"No," she said, scrunching up her face as if thinking back. "His face was like that of a man who had just woken up from a long slumber. He's different with you."

My heart squeezed in silent torture.

"Maybe it's because I drive him nuts. He seems to get upset with me often," I countered weakly.

Pippy smiled again, her eyes twinkling in the sunshine. "Not all people are happy when they wake up."

I stared at her, open-mouthed, as she giggled.

"Mom—heads up!" Cody yelled, as the soccer ball sailed toward our bench. I reacted quickly, catching it before it hit Pippy squarely in the face.

"Good catch!" Peter called to us.

I threw the ball back out to them, wondering if someday I might be a good catch for someone, too.

****

Despite my best efforts, I couldn't forget Pippy's words.

His face was like that of a man who had just woken up from a long slumber. He's different with you.

I stood, looking out the window from my fourteenth floor apartment and stared into the inky backdrop of a city that seemed to be in a constant adrenaline rush. There were lights, traffic, noise and movement everywhere I looked. Cody had fallen asleep an hour ago with a book on his face, obviously exhausted. I was grateful that Peter had worn him out earlier. Physical exertion was a necessity to a young, growing boy.

I'd spent some time answering voicemails after our quick trip to the grocery store earlier. It was only a block away. The walk, though hot, was nice.

It was good to catch up, especially with Maggie. She filled me in on the recent happenings at *The Refuge* and was elated to hear about my upcoming television interview on The Eastman Morning Show. Rosie had told her about it, naturally. Maggie's voice always seemed to instill in me a sense of peace and comfort whenever I spoke with her. And as the founder of *The Refuge*, I knew many other women felt the same way I did about her. Our connection was the closest thing I had to a mother/daughter relationship, and I cherished her greatly. Her advice was always sound, honest, and wise.

As she told me about last week's meeting, I was reminded of Jenny—the young woman who had called me a couple weeks back. Maggie let out a deep sigh when I mentioned her. I knew that wasn't a good sign.

"Rosie has put in several calls to her this last week…she hasn't responded," Maggie said.

"But Rosie spoke with her right after she moved in with her Aunt in Oklahoma, right?"

"Yes, I hope she's just busy adjusting to her new home," Maggie said, worry lacing her words.

She didn't need to say more. I knew what *more* could be said. I closed my eyes, saying a prayer for her right then. I'd learned a long time ago that prayer was the most valuable asset I had, especially during situations that were beyond my control.

"Well, I love you darlin'...I don't want to keep you, but please know that I sure do miss seeing you around. Give your boy some lovin' from me."

"I will; I miss you too, Maggie. Love you. Bye."

Maggie had been the one to bring me to *The Refuge*. She'd sat with me for hours as my nurse six years ago while I was recovering from multiple injuries and coming out of an induced coma. In the darkest season of my life, she had given me hope—light. Through Maggie I had met Rosie and connected again with my faith in God. Her invitation had forever changed my life—and my son's life. There were no words to express the kind of gratitude and love I held for her. I often told her that she was my guardian angel.

I touched the tiny wings that sat at the base of my neck on my pendant and thought again about Jenny. I hoped she had a guardian angel looking out for her, too.

After I made my way through the living area to my room, I snuggled down into bed, switching on the bedside lamp. I picked up my black journal and started to write. This time, it was not about the days that marked my past, but of the thoughts that filled my present. I had so many questions, so many unknowns swirling around in my head that what flowed onto the paper was a fluid stream of consciousness. As I pulled back my hand to read what I'd written, my body surged with a sort of anxious anticipation.

Maybe Jackson wasn't the only one who had awakened from a deep slumber.

Awakened

A little pull, a tiny push

A fleeting thought, a heart of mush

My pulse is quick, my breath is short

My skin feels hot, my mind distorts

I need to see, I want to hear

I long to know, I hope he's near

The balance tips, the line is crossed

The risk unknown, the hope not lost

****

Just when I thought I'd met every single mom that New York and the surrounding areas could produce, a new sea of faces would emerge. I'd been sitting at my signing table for nearly two hours while Cody sat next to me and read his adventure book and snacked on dried banana chips—a gift from Pippy.

"I've read every post on your blog. You're such an inspiration to me." A petite red-headed woman leaned over the table to shake my hand. "Can I get my picture with you?"

This question never failed to surprise me. "Sure, of course. What's your baby's name?"

She bounced a little girl on her hip who looked to be about one. "Carly."

"Well, she's beautiful." I held out my hand for the little girl to hold.

"Thank you," the woman said, She extended her phone to arms length and snapped a photo with me. "Do you hope to have more children some day?"

My gut twisted, leaving a familiar ache to settle over me. I looked at her daughter and did my best to smile. "Life is full of surprises."

It was a cryptic answer at best, but standing in line at a pre-book release appearance was hardly the time or place for the truth on that particular subject. The woman radiated joy as she walked away, her baby waving at me enthusiastically. I took a deep breath as I felt a warm sensation press onto my back.

"You need a break?"

It was Jackson's voice. I hadn't seen him in almost two days as he'd been working long hours at the office. Heat rushed into my face as I turned my head toward him.

"I can keep going for a while longer," I said, glancing at the line, which currently held about thirty women.

"That's not what I asked." He kept his voice low, but his brows were pressed into a familiar scowl.

I nodded, feeling a sense of relief at the rescue of his presence.

"Okay, folks, I'm afraid Miss Flores needs to take a lunch break now. We'll resume within the hour." Jackson's voice brimmed with charm and authority, a mix I hadn't heard before.

"Thank you," I whispered as Cody stood and stretched.

Jackson took us into a back stock room where Pippy had sandwiches and drinks waiting for us. Cody immediately plopped onto a folding chair and unwrapped his sub. Jackson tugged on my arm, holding me back a few steps.

"Is everything okay?"

"Yes, why?" I asked him, noticing his hand was still on my elbow.

"You seemed...troubled a minute ago."

I hadn't even known he was in the room, much less watching my interactions with the moms in line. I swallowed hard as I thought again about the woman's question. That wasn't the first time I'd been asked, nor would it be the last, but I the inquiry would never cease to be painful.

I opened my mouth to answer, but Pippy burst into the room, forestalling my words. Thankfully. Jackson dropped his hand from my arm with immediate haste.

"Oh…uh, sorry," Pippy said, smiling at me with eyes full of mischievous delight, "but I have a phone message for you, Mr. Ross."

Jackson pulled his phone out of his pocket, checking his own screen with a look of pensive curiosity.

"No, it's not a business call. It's of a personal nature."

"Oh." After taking two steps in her direction, he turned toward me again, his eyes resembling the color of the dark pockets in the ocean. "May I take you and Cody out tonight?"

Every cell in my body flashed cold and hot in a matter of a millisecond.

"Sure."

"I'll pick you up. Pippy can fill you in on the specifics later."

Pippy trailed behind him as they left the storage room, but not before giving me an over-enthusiastic wink. I bit my lip.

What had just occurred?

Was this a date?

My heart skipped. A dozen times in a row.

Chapter Sixteen

Once when I was around fourteen, my friend Eva invited me to go to the Nutcracker with her family. I remember being completely overwhelmed by the magnitude and luxuriousness of the theater. I'd been mesmerized by the entire production, hanging on every movement and word said by the cast. It was a memory I'd never forget.

Tonight though, would put that reminiscent event to shame.

"You should definitely wear the champagne-colored one," Pippy said on the phone.

I'd been saving that gown, but for what I wasn't sure.

"You think so?" I bit my lip as I ran my hand over the options hanging in the tiny closest in my room.

"Definitely. It's Broadway. That dress is perfect!"

I shifted the phone against my shoulder and ear while I pulled it out of the closet. "Okay…"

"Why do you sound so nervous? You're gonna look gorgeous, and Jackson will think so, too."

"Pippy! Stop…" I sighed. "I can't think that way."

Even though I think about him all the time.

"What? Why not?"

"A lot of reasons—it's comp-"

"Yeah, I know, it's *complicated*. So you've said."

"No matter how I look at it, Pippy, the facts are what they are. And what they are *is* complicated." I ran my hand over the silk of the dress as I laid it on the bed.

"Well, I hope you have a great time tonight. Walt and Jackson will be there at six-thirty to pick you up, and you and Cody might want to eat something beforehand."

"Bye, Pippy," I said, grinning as I hung up the phone.

I couldn't imagine anyone ever being upset at that girl. Talking to Pippy was like talking with Glinda the Good Witch, everything was coated in a layer of sugary happiness.

After a very quick shower, I fixed my makeup and blew-dry my hair, pulling it back into a low twist at the nape of my neck. A tiny gold pin held the twist in place. The simple ornament matched the dress almost exactly. Cody wore his nice dress khaki pants and a red polo shirt.

The phone in our room rang as I applied my lip-gloss. Cody answered it. "Mr. Ross is waiting for us downstairs, Mom."

I exhaled as I looked in the mirror one last time.

"Just. Keep. Breathing," I mumbled to myself as I turned off the bathroom light.

****

Walking into the foyer was like a scene from an old black-and-white movie. Jackson stood near the front desk, his back to us as we approached. The long, silky fabric of my dress danced around my legs as I paced my steps carefully, as if to calm my overly excited heart rate. Cody's eagerness was far from quiet, however, causing Jackson to turn toward the sound of his pounding footsteps.

He laughed as he engaged in Cody's new handshake; the one Peter had shown him a few days earlier. Then his eyes found me. I was still several feet away, but it didn't matter. The gap between us could have been miles, and I still would have felt the effect of his gaze. There was something about his eyes, something so uniquely guarded, yet completely exposed at the same time. The look captured me like a single flame in a dark room. Any attempt at breaking the spell was utterly hopeless.

Cody said something to Jackson before skipping excitedly out the door, but my mind couldn't translate his words. Jackson's eyes were still on me.

He cleared his throat and then extended his arm out to me. I smiled, silently noting that even in my heels he was still several inches taller than me. I was grateful for that small blessing.

As he held the door open, he whispered in my ear. "I was right."

I turned my head toward him, our faces inches apart. "About?"

"That dress."

My insides heated instantly as we stepped outside. "Is that your idea of a compliment, Jackson?"

"No," he said, grinning from ear to ear. "I don't believe in compliments."

I was about to question that statement when Cody called my name. My son was bouncing from seat to seat…inside a limo. I stood momentarily frozen, shocked by the sight. Walt winked as I approached, giving a low whistle as he held open the back passenger door for me.

"You look stunning tonight, Miss Flores."

"Well, thank you for the compliment, Walt." I smirked at Jackson, who laughed heartily while I ducked into the limo.

As I watched my son open and close each compartment, drawer, and cabinet—twice, I realized how many *firsts* we had experienced since coming to New York. And at the root of them all was Jackson. He laughed as Cody talked a mile a minute about each feature he had discovered in his precious few moments alone inside the over-sized vehicle. He hardly came up for air once during our drive to Minskoff Theater.

"Lion King! Awesome!" Cody said, as Jackson handed him the playbill.

Cody walked several paces ahead of us as we made our way to our seats—which were of course only ten rows from the front of the stage. My stomach turned as I thought about the cost of this evening.

"Jackson, I can't believe these seats…this was beyond generous," I said quietly as we sat. Cody was already chomping away on his eight dollar box of candy.

His eyes glistened in the low lights. "What can I say? It pays to have connections sometimes."

I looked around at the beautiful surroundings. "I guess so."

The lights in the auditorium dimmed moments later, as a well-known song sliced through the room. Cody sat up straight, his attention laser-focused on the brightly lit stage. As I turned my head back to face front, I felt a familiar, unapologetic gaze roam my face.

"Thank you," I mouthed to him, sure that my voice would have been swallowed- by the mix of African instruments that were now resonating in the room.

He leaned in, his breath on my neck. "The pleasure is all mine."

And just like that, my resolve to keep breathing failed. Again.

****

Lion King was amazing.

I was touched on so many levels and by so many different emotions. Though I had done my best to stop the tears, a few had slipped out without warning. Jackson, of course, saw my futile attempts to swat them away unnoticed. He smiled at me, squeezing my hand gently, only to let it go seconds later.

The show ran two-and-a-half hours, so it was just after eleven when we got back to my apartment building. We had snacked during intermission, and though Cody had filled up on mostly sugary treats, he was like the walking-dead as we approached our door. Jackson insisted he make the trek up with us. I didn't argue.

Cody gave us both a hug goodnight and thanked Jackson again for the Lion King paraphernalia he'd purchased for him, and then headed inside. Jackson leaned against the wall by the front door, staring at me unabashed.

"What?" I asked, when his mouth turned up into a crooked smile.

"You're nothing like I thought you'd be."

I couldn't help but roll my eyes. *Why was that everyone's favorite line?*

"I keep hearing that, Jackson, yet no one seems to want to elaborate on such a particular statement."

He tilted his head. "I didn't read your blog before you came. I was asked to read it, and I probably should have read it, but I'm not one to buy into hype."

"And… that's what you thought I was…*hype?*" I worked to keep the hurt out of my voice.

"I didn't believe that you could be all the things that you were rumored to be. I thought you'd be a fleeting blip on the radar of this tour. Writing a blog doesn't make someone an author. I thought Dee got it wrong when she signed you. Personal blogs are usually nothing more than a glorified inventory of embellished half-truths."

I sucked in a sharp breath, every suppressed insecurity surfacing again.

"You didn't want me to come," I said, letting his words sink in.

"No, but-"

"Because you thought I was *just a mom.*" My words came out in a broken whisper as I actively told myself *not* to cry.

He pushed away from the wall, his face stripped of all amusement now. "I was nothing short of ignorant to say such a thing."

My eyes welled with tears that seemed desperate to defy me. "I'm not ashamed of being a single mom. Cody is the best thing that's ever happened to me. No fame or fortune could ever compete with that."

He took a step toward me. "I know."

"And you should know that motherhood is the most important job there is-"

Another step closer. "I know."

"And...and-" I couldn't concentrate, his face a breath away.

He put his finger to my lips. "I'm sorry, Angie."

"What?" My eyes widened as he dropped his hand.

Did Jackson Ross just apologize to me?

"I'm sorry. You're far from a *just* anything. I was wrong. There is no hype when it comes to you. In fact, I think your blog is about the most humble piece of literature I've ever read."

"But you said-"

"I've read every word of it." His breath tingled on my lips. "You have something, a beautiful kind of innocence, a goodness. And it's impossible to remain unaffected by it." His jaw tensed twice before adding, "*Impossible.*"

My stomach was a twist of knots and spasms as I saw his eyes drift to my mouth.

His hands came up to my face, his fingers sliding to the back of my neck. And in one smooth, gentle motion his lips were on mine. How he'd managed to both lose and find me within those few perfect seconds I'd never know, but he had. The kiss was a map that led straight to every secret passageway of my heart.

When the kiss broke, he didn't back away. Instead, he rested his hands on my shoulders and held my gaze.

"When I saw you tonight in the lobby…" He closed his eyes briefly and shook his head, as if re-directing. "Walt was right. You *are* stunning."

My brow furrowed slightly. "But you said you don't believe in compliments."

"I don't. Compliments are a wasted effort. But I do believe in truth. And that, Angie, is the truth."

He took a step back, dropping his hands from my bare shoulders. My body must have switched itself onto autopilot. That had to be the only reason why I didn't fall flat on my face.

"I'll see you bright and early tomorrow," Jackson said, backpedalling down the hallway.

As I watched him go, every thought escaped me. I hadn't a clue what he was referring to. I nodded anyway.

He raised his eyebrows. "The interview—The Eastman Morning Show?" He chuckled. "Goodnight, Angela Flores."

Oh, right. Heat flooded my cheeks.

"Goodnight, Jackson Ross."

Chapter Seventeen

Cody had fallen back to sleep on the sofa in the green room, which was adjacent to the brightly-lit room where I sat in a high-back chair in a room full of mirrors. Currently, Esmeralda was "helping me" cover the dark circles under my eyes. I'd suffered insomnia most of the night, replaying a certain moment, with a certain man, in a certain doorway, until sunrise. The only reason I knew it hadn't all been just a good dream, was by the dramatic circles that were now being doused with make-up. I grimaced as I thought about the cameras that were going to make my face their target, and wished I had fought a little harder for a good night's sleep.

Esmeralda did, too.

"Your eyes look tired," she said, painting my face with a thick brush dipped in a beige-colored liquid.

Ya think? I shrugged. "Sorry."

She grunted, yet continued to paint.

I was rescued only seconds later by Pippy's morning salutations. She held a soy latte in one hand and a piece of paper in the other, reading a list of questions which I had already looked over twice. Pippy was anything if not thorough.

"You're going to do great." She rubbed my shoulder for added effect.

"I hope so…"

My gut filled with unease.

The questions would be easy enough to answer. They mostly pertained to what had inspired me to write my blog, and what message I wanted to express to other single mothers regarding aspirations and dreams, yet I couldn't shake the icky feeling. It clawed at my insides like a caged animal trying to escape. I took a deep breath and said a silent prayer.

Walking into the chilly studio, I immediately spotted Jackson. My eyes were always drawn to him, no matter how many people were present. Even at the early morning hour, he was breathtaking. Instantly, the weight of my jittery nerves was lifted from me.

"Back in three," a loud voice boomed through a speaker overhead.

I started at the sound, taking in my surroundings for the first time as I walked toward Jackson who was currently typing on his phone. There were two sets in place within the confines of the studio: a wide desk with a blown-up picture of the New York skyline behind it, and a living room set.

Then I saw Divina.

Before I could even blink she was up from the desk, sauntering over to Jackson. I stopped in my tracks, sickened at the sight of her touching his arm and whispering in his ear as if they were secret lovers.

Jackson continued to stare down at his phone as if unaffected by her obvious schemes.

I propelled my legs forward, unwilling to let her presence alter my destination. I wasn't sure what I was to Jackson, but Divina wasn't going to define it for me, nor would my insecurities about seeing her pressed up against him. As I neared, he turned from her completely, a smile disrupting the concentration on his face.

"Good morning," he said, his eyes full of something unidentifiable.

Heat rushed my face. "Good morning."

"Sleep well?" A fluttering sensation took flight inside me at his question.

"It was a pretty short night." I bit my bottom lip.

"Indeed," he said, his gaze locked onto mine.

Until Divina broke it.

"Jackson, as I was saying…I'm off in an hour. Why don't we go get coffee at Maxwell's? We should catch up," she cooed.

Jackson glanced at her, as if noticing her presence for the first time before finding my eyes once more.

"My day is planned."

She stepped in front of me, running her hand up to his shoulder, making him refocus.

"Well, what about tomorrow, then? We could go-"

His brows creased as he lowered his voice. "The answer is no, Divina. It hasn't changed since the last time we talked. I'll let you know if it does."

"Twenty seconds and counting…" A voice in a speaker called.

Divina's face contorted. Her once playfully seductive expression morphed into stone. She stared at him with a look that could chill a pot of boiling water. Jackson, cool as ever, addressed me again, this time placing his hand on my upper back as he spoke.

"Do you need anything? You'll go on after this next segment."

Divina's hardened eyes flicked back and forth from my face to his arm on my back before stalking away in her red stilettos.

I gawked at him.

"What?" he asked.

"Um…that wasn't awkward or anything," I said, keeping my voice low.

"Not for me it wasn't. She's knows better."

"Oh," was all I could think to say in response.

"So?" He raised his eyebrows at me, reminding me he had asked a question.

"I think I'm okay. Pippy prepped me already on the questions. She's back with Cody now."

He leaned down, his breath ruffling my hair. "I have every confidence you'll do great. Just relax and remember to breathe."

It's not just the interview I need coaching for...

****

I sat across from Divina, an expensive-looking coffee table between us. She crossed her long legs and leaned back confidently as the countdown began. A giant orb of light surrounded me, blinding me to everything and everyone but her.

"Ready?" she asked me, her voice low and sharp.

I took a deep breath, repeating Jackson's words in my head. "I think so."

She looked into the camera a second later while plastering the most convincing smile I'd ever seen onto her face.

"So as promised, we have Angela Flores, writer of the blog, *A Lone Joy,* and future published author with Pinkerton Press. Welcome and good morning," she said toward me, her eyes focused and alert.

"Good morning. Thank you for having me, it's a pleasure." I nodded.

"So it appears you are a virus, Angela," she laughed at her joke, "or I suppose the expression is *viral* in the case of your blog. Your followers increased over three thousand percent within a week's time. Was it hard to adjust—going from a single mother working as a florist to signing a publishing contract and joining a campaign tour practically overnight?"

She rolled the ankle of her crossed-leg in slow, dramatic circles, as if indicating she had all the time in the world. I smiled. I would not let her push me down—this wasn't a playground.

This was national television.

"My first priority will always be to my son, no matter what the future holds. To be honest, other than having this opportunity to visit New York, our lives look relatively the same. I never planned for my blog to go viral, but God has shown me time and time again that my plans are often superseded with a purpose greater than my own. Cody and I feel blessed to be a part of this effort to bring awareness to the resources and tools available for single mothers everywhere."

Her eyes narrowed.

"So you would say that your faith has played a big part in your parenting, then?"

"Absolutely. I'm a big believer in the power of community, and I think church and faith are a prime example of that—at least in my own life."

"And what would you say to single mothers who have no system of belief?"

She was baiting me. I could see it in her eyes, though her lips dripped the sweet poison of everything superficial.

"I'd say that motherhood is the hardest job there is. I may only have one child, but still, raising him has stretched me many times beyond what I felt capable of handling on my own. Whether or not a person has a faith doesn't exempt any of us from needing to seek out support. Parenting is too important to be trapped in the overwhelming feelings of isolation. We need others to root us on and challenge us when struggles arise. The fellowship of others has been my biggest tool."

"You speak a lot about support," she said, a smile spreading across her face.

"Yes, I do." I nodded.

"And what kind of support do you receive from Cody's father?"

What?

The question was a stinging slap to the face.

My breathing went shallow, forcing the words to be released from somewhere in the back corner of my mind. Words not rehearsed; words not prepared.

"None," I said. "He's…"

"Not dead like some of your fans might believe…correct?"

This was the lie I had allowed Cody to believe for years. The sin that ate at my heart and twisted my consciousness with every year he aged. I knew the truth would come out, but not like this. Never like this. Briggs and Charlie knew the truth and a handful of trusted women at *The Refuge*, but they were the only ones. Everyone else believed he'd died when Cody was a baby.

She smirked. "I'm sure you're not the first woman to face this parenting predicament, Angie. Would you care to share how you handled telling Cody that his father is a convicted felon? You're blog is full of such insightful honesty. In fact, that is what your readers say most often about you—how open you are about your life. But weird thing is, I didn't see anything about this detail of your life on your blog. Nothing."

No…

Cody can't find out like this…he can't!

She glanced down at the note cards that lay in her lap as if they were silently coaxing her on.

My ears roared with the sound of pulsing blood. "I'd actually rather not talk about-"

"I'm sure that had to be a very difficult conversation. No child wants to hear that his father's in prison for attempting to murder his mother," she said. "But of course, you had support from your church, right? I'm sure they helped you, or were they led to believe that Cody's father was dead too?"

I stared at her as thick darkness started to cloud my vision, coming from somewhere behind me and tunneling ahead of me with rapid speed.

Divina sat silent now—her ankle still swinging side to side like a hypnotic pendulum.

Murmuring came from somewhere in the distance, and everything felt like it was happening in slow motion. If time was moving ahead, I was stuck somewhere in the past, somewhere paralyzed by fear.

I opened my mouth, but no sound came out.

"I'm sure your fans have a lot more questions for you on that particular topic. I wasn't able to find that particular story anywhere in your blog posts from the past. But really, isn't that the biggest part of who you are? You're not only a single mom who was widowed after all, but a victim of domestic violence whose ex-husband is serving a maximum sentence without parole. That statistic is far more interesting

I believe. Fame doesn't keep secrets," she turned now to the camera. "I'm so glad you were with us today, Angela. For more information on *A Lone Joy*, please visit our website. We'll be back in a moment."

And then…the lights went out.

Chapter Nineteen

A loud, angry voice snapped me out of my stupor.

Jackson.

I watched him break free from the hold of two large security guards. He shot toward the set with long strides of determination and pulled my stiff body to him. He was speaking—no, he was shouting—but the words were a jumbled mix of sounds that bounced off my ears. Nothing could penetrate the defensive wall in my mind once it was up...except...

Cody.

Where is Cody?

And then my feet were moving at lightning speed, Jackson's close behind me. We stopped in front of the green room. Pippy stepped out, her face the shade of ash. As I saw the TV in the back corner featuring a program I'd rather forget, I felt ill. My eyes scanned the room to find Cody.

"Mom?" Cody asked, his bottom lip trembling. "What was that lady talking about?"

Pippy placed her hand on my arm, her eyes telling me everything I needed to know. Cody had heard—what? I wasn't sure, but enough to cause her concern.

Enough to make my stomach twist with nausea.

"Sweetheart." My voice sounded lost, far away, as I dropped in front of him. "I'll answer all of your questions soon, okay?" I hugged him to me, my throat burning painfully as I swallowed.

Cody nodded, but I felt no relief in his compliance. Telling him the truth about his father was the last thing I wanted to do—ever.

****

Cody sat with Walt in the front as Jackson slid into the car next to me in the back. He put his hand on mine, but I yanked it from his grasp. Fury boiled hot inside me.

How did this happen?

I glanced at Jackson, the look on his face frighteningly unfamiliar: Worry.

Jackson never worried.

"I'll take care of this," his voice was urgent, yet hushed.

I shook my head. "You can't, Jackson. It's done."

"No-"

I shook my head again, pointing to Cody as if to silence the discussion. For once, Jackson didn't argue.

We rode the rest of the way to my apartment in silence.

"Do you mind if I have a minute alone with your mom, Cody?" Jackson asked as he followed us into the living room.

"Are you okay, Mom?" he asked, softly.

"I'm okay, baby. I just need to sort some things out right now, okay? We will talk soon, I promise."

He nodded and went into his room, shutting the door behind him.

It was then my tears came—hot, angry, tears.

Jackson took a deep breath, walked to my bedroom and opened the door for me to follow him inside. I hesitated, but I had too many thoughts in my head, too many words that needed to be said. He shut the door behind me.

I turned toward him. "*How?* How did she know those things about me?"

His eyebrows shot up. "You don't think—Angie I would never! *I* didn't even know all of that!"

I slumped against the wall. I knew in my heart he wasn't responsible. But I needed someone to blame and Divina wasn't here, unfortunately.

Tears rolled down my cheeks as my anger morphed into heartbreak.

He stood before me, fire in his eyes as he struggled to keep his voice low. "So it's true, then? He's not dead? He's in prison for assault and attempted murder?"

"Yes."

I could read the torment in his face, his hand twitching with a desire to damage and comfort at the same time. I understood the emotion. That torment lived inside me, too.

I met his gaze. "Exposing me is exactly what she wanted to do, isn't it? She wanted to discredit me?" I swallowed against the burn in the back of my throat. "It's what everyone will believe, Jackson. Any credibility I've built in this tour as a strong, independent, single mom has just been replaced with the image of me as a helpless victim." I shook my head and pushed away from the wall. "But none of that matters in the end; not as much as what she's just done to my family."

Jackson gripped the back of his head like he was holding it in a vice. He stepped toward me, his body so close that I could smell the distinct scent of his cologne: a mix of ocean and cedar wood.

"Listen to me, Angie, she is the one who will pay for this stunt. *Not you.* I just need time to think about how we can combat this—"

"No." I took a step to the side and sat down on the edge of my bed. I needed space to think. "The only thing I need to do is figure out how to tell my son. You can worry about how this will affect the family tour, but now I have to explain to my son how his father tried to murder me...."

I dropped my face into my hands.

"Angie." The hoarse rasp of his voice made my stomach hurt. His tone was full of heat and passion, yet layered with grief. He knelt before me. "You're right...Cody is the priority here, nothing else."

My hands fell away from my face; I stared at Jackson.

"I have to leave town, Angie... but I want you and Cody to come with me."

"Where?" I asked, lifting my face to his.

"My brother's lake house. It's his birthday this weekend, but it would be a good place for you to talk to Cody. I just...I just don't want to leave you like this."

I closed my eyes, head throbbing from stress. "Okay," I whispered.

"Okay." Jackson covered my hand with his and heat surged in my veins. "We'll figure this out."

"You keep saying that..."

"I keep meaning it, too." His eyes pierced mine. "I'll go tell Cody about our trip. It will be good for him....lots of fun things for a kid to do out there. You just worry about packing what you need—no formal wear needed."

That was the best news I'd heard all day.

****

Three hours later we were driving through the luscious countryside of Connecticut. The trip was literally like driving into a fantasy world. Hills, trees, and lakes covered the landscape. Everything was rich and green, nature's beautiful kiss. It was hard to believe we were only a couple hours away from the hustle and bustle of New York City.

Cody filled the hours in the car with his travel quiz games, Jackson playing along while I stared out the window, trying to piece together a plan. Briggs and Charlie would be in New York Monday night, and I needed to talk with Cody before then.

The thought was crippling.

I wanted to go back in time and push Divina off her chair, make her beg for forgiveness for outing such personal information, but even I knew it wouldn't have stopped her. She'd had an agenda. Maybe it'd been her agenda from the first time I met her at the publishing house. Who knew? I wasn't sure how anyone could be so heartless, but the truth was out now. Just like a train that had left the station. There was no reversing it.

I wouldn't let my mind wander much beyond the immediate steps ahead of me. Figuring out what to say to Cody was the priority. Apart from that, I had no control. Perhaps I'd been kidding myself to think I'd ever been in control at all.

Cody knew about my work at *The Refuge* of course. He knew I was helping women out of hardship and hurts, but the details of abuse—especially *my* abuse—I'd kept guarded from him. He was an innocent party to his father's sins. I'd only wanted to protect him for as long as I could.

Now protecting him meant telling him the truth.

I felt a squeeze on my hand, "We're only a few minutes out. Maybe you should take a nap when we get there…my sister-in-law already has a room made up for you and Cody. You'll like Jessie."

"Thanks, but I have a lot of calls to return." I lifted my phone. A list of voice mails and texts filled the screen. I'd have to deal with them sooner or later.

He scowled. "I think you need to lay low for the day. Reception is spotty out here at best. Cody and I can go out on the paddleboat. I think you should rest."

I pulled my hand out from his. "No, I shouldn't. There are things I *have* to do, things I've been forced to do, Jackson. They can't wait."

He remained quiet for the next few minutes. "I wasn't trying to-," he glanced into the rear-view mirror, looking at Cody in the back seat. He flexed his jaw several times, before speaking again. "I just want to help you, Angie. Let me...*please*."

Something warm swam through my veins as my eyes pooled again with tears.

We pulled up to a house that looked like it could be on the set of Anne of Green Gables. The place was gorgeous, easily the most beautiful home I'd ever seen, surrounded by God's most glorious displays of creation. A large, white, Cape Cod-style home encircled by lush green grass overlooked a placid lake. It was truly breathtaking.

Cody burst out of the car, exclaiming how right Jackson had been about our destination. Jackson put his hand on my knee, speaking nothing, but reassuring me nonetheless before I opened my car door. The hot summer air filled my lungs as I followed Cody to the front door. Jackson was at my side.

****

"It is such a privilege to meet you, Angela," Jessica Ross said. "My daughter has told me so much about you. I'm glad you and Cody could join us for the weekend."

"I really appreciate your hospitality, especially at such short notice." I shook her hand and noticed immediately that her smile was the same as Pippy's. That fact warmed my heart. She also had the same dark hair as her daughter, but instead of a short, stylish pixie-cut, Jessica's hair was layered, hanging past her shoulders. There was nothing showy about her appearance; in fact, just the opposite was true. Her beauty was striking.

"We have several people coming to stay with us tomorrow night after the party, so I have you and Cody sharing one of the larger guest rooms at the end of the hall."

We walked through the house, ceilings as high as a mini-skyscraper, dark hardwoods throughout. Everything was in true cape-cod fashion, but above all, the house was inviting and homey.

"Yes, this is perfect," I said, staring into the room. "I hope our stay won't interfere with the party-"

"Oh, no, not at all. It will just be some good friends and some great food. We have a lot to celebrate. Glad you can be apart of it." She squeezed my arm as Jackson walked past me to set our duffle bags on the edge of one of the beds.

"I'm afraid I only packed casual clothing," I said to Jessica, staring at Jackson.

"That's perfect. We are very casual around here," she laughed.

I sighed as Jackson chuckled near my ear. "Told ya so."

While Jackson and Cody changed into their swim trunks to go paddle boating, I found a private spot on the back porch that overlooked Candlewood Lake—which was also their backyard. I punched in the voicemail number on my phone and held it away from my ear. The connection was awful, but I heard Rosie loud and clear. A stream of high-pitched Spanish sentiments flowed from the speaker.

Though I could only catch every third or fourth word, I agreed with Rosie.

Wholeheartedly.

Chapter Twenty

I sat, staring out at the sun setting over the lake while Cody prepared dinner with Jessie. The scene in front of me looked like postcard art.

"Want to talk about it?"

I turned my head toward Jackson, but didn't respond. He tugged gently on my arm, pulling me to sit next to him on the patio sofa. Sitting beside him, I was painfully aware of the six-inch gap between us. Everything about this man was a mystery; I hardly knew him, yet my heart was already more invested than what was safe. *Safe* had gone out the window the first time Jackson had smiled at me.

"I'm scared, Jackson…"

He tensed briefly as he leaned forward to rest his elbows on his knees, his triceps cording as he clasped his hands together. His voice was thick and husky when he spoke, "I can't even imagine all you've been through."

Somewhere deep inside me, a boldness I had neglected for years forced its way to the surface. "To be honest, right now my past doesn't scare me nearly as much as my present. I don't do *this*, Jackson," I paused. "I don't get close to men, but you…" I let my eyes drift over his profile as he continued to stare ahead. "I don't know."

He closed his eyes and exhaled. "You're my weakness, Angie. I don't know how else to explain it."

But before I could question him, he continued. "I'm just not sure you should let me be yours…"

Too late.

"Dinnertime," Jessica said from the doorway.

Jackson and I walked into the house together, the cliffhanger of the century weighing heavy on my heart.

****

Jacob Ross was a tall, thin man who had a smile that stretched from ear to ear. His fingers were bony as they gripped mine, but the handshake was meaningful.

"Can't tell you how thrilled we are to have you and Cody here for a visit. Our kids talk about the two of you every time they call from the city," Jacob said as we sat down to eat. Lasagna, salad, bread and a fruit dish were spread out on the family-sized table.

"Pippy has been a great friend to me, and Cody has loved hanging out with Peter," I said.

Jacob took his wife's hand and then reached for Cody as he bowed his head to say the blessing. Jackson's hand covered mine a second later when he lowered his head in the same manner. My heart thudded hard within my chest.

After the prayer Jacob picked at his food, seemingly more eager to ask us questions than eat. I wondered absently if his interest in people and lack of interest in food was the reason he was so thin.

"We have enjoyed your blog, Angela," Jacob said, smiling. Do you see yourself writing other types of books in the future? You definitely have a gift."

"Thank you. I'm not really sure. I haven't thought too much about what could be next..." My words trailed off as a feeling of dread took over.

"Well, I'm sure Jackson will help you explore the possibilities. He's a very talented-"

"I will, Jacob." Jackson's voice wasn't harsh, but his words were rushed, curt. The tone took me by surprise and seemed to take Jacob by surprise as well. But instead of questioning him, Jacob simply laughed.

"Good."

I helped Jackson with the dishes as Cody cleared the plates off the table. Jessica was mortified that I had requested to help, but Jacob pulled her into the other room with him, ignoring her protests.

As the last plate was rinsed and put into the dishwasher I placed my hand on Jackson's arm. "I need to talk with Cody—tonight."

He stared at me. "Can I do something to help?"

I swallowed. As much as his presence calmed and comforted me, I needed this moment to be about Cody.

"I don't think so."

He nodded. "I'll make sure you have some privacy then. The dock might be a good place to go. It's nice out there this time of night."

"Thank you, Jackson…for everything."

****

I called for Cody to join me outside. His sweet smile sent a pang through my chest as he reached the door where I stood. I didn't want to rob him of blissful innocence. I didn't want to alter his childhood. But my hand had been forced.

As we walked down to the dock, tiny solar lights on the ground lit our path. Cody reached for a small handful of pebbles before sitting down beside me. We took off our shoes and submerged our feet in the water. He threw one pebble at a time into the lake, making tiny splashes.

I took a deep breath, praying silently for the right words to say.

"Cody—we need to talk. I'm not sure what you heard during my interview, but I need you to hear it from me," I started.

"Okay, Mom."

"Do you remember when we lived with Uncle Briggs, before we moved for my job at the florist shop a couple years ago?"

"Yeah. I miss watching cartoons with him and kicking his punching bag in the garage."

I giggled at the memory. "Yes, I know you loved participating in his workouts, but I'm quite happy not to have a gym in our garage anymore." My face sobered as I watched him throw a few rocks into the lake.

"Cody, there was a reason why we lived with your Uncle Briggs—one I never told you about." I took a deep breath. "Before you were born, I'd been scared for a very long time."

He stopped throwing rocks and stared at me in the moonlight. "What were you scared of, Mom?"

I picked up his hand, and traced an invisible pattern onto his palm the way I had done since he was a baby. "Your father."

He scrunched his face, concern crinkling around the edges of his eyes. My gut twisted.

"He had a lot of problems, made a lot of bad choices…and because of those decisions, he became a very hateful man. He hurt me Cody…"

"What do you mean, mom?" Cody's voice quivered.

"When you were two, after I left with your Uncle to make a safer life for you and me...he found us. He tried to take you, and I wouldn't let him. Uncle Briggs showed up just in time...and I had to stay in the hospital for several weeks."

His mouth hung open slightly as his teary-eyes searched mine. "Like...you could have died?"

The salt from my tears remained on my lips as I spoke. "Yes, baby. I didn't want to leave you...I fought so hard to stay, to be your mom."

"But...you told me my dad died when you were pregnant with me. That he was in a car accident. Was...was that lady right mom? Is my dad in prison?"

I swallowed down the guilt that threatened to choke-out my next words, and closed my eyes. *Don't let him hate me, God.* I opened my eyes and gazed into my son's upturned face.

"Yes, Cody. Your father is in prison."

For a second he didn't move, didn't even blink, and then before I knew it...he was on his feet and running away.

"*Cody!*" I cried and he halted, standing stiff with his hands fisted.

His body was turned away from me, facing the house as I approached him from behind. Sobs broke from his throat as he tucked his chin to his chest. "You lied."

Two words.

The two words I'd done everything in my power to avoid.

"Yes. I lied."

I moved in front of him, my heart ripping in half at the sight of his hurt. Lifting his chin with my fingers, I stared into his beautiful blue eyes. "I love you, Cody. It's my job to protect you. I thought I could protect you from my past if you didn't know that truth. I never wanted to hurt you."

"But you…you always tell me lying is wrong."

"It is, Cody. And I spent a lot of time lying for your father, covering up the truth that I should have exposed…"

"So why did you lie for him again?"

The question exploded in my chest like a bomb—the shrapnel cutting off my air supply.

"Mom?"

I knelt in front of him and wrapped my arms around his waist.

"I never saw it like that, Code. I'm so sorry. Please, *please*, forgive me."

Cody sobbed and knelt down beside me, pressing his head to my chest. I rubbed small, comforting circles onto his back.

"I forgive you." He lifted his head and wiped his eyes with the back of his hand. "Is that why you help the women at *The Refuge?* Because they've been hurt, too?"

"Yes, baby. Because for some women it's very hard to leave a man like that. They need help, support, comfort, advice."

Cody clung to me, quiet for several seconds more as the cicadas sang in the distance.

Finally he nodded. "I know who kept you safe, Mom."

He lifted his head and touched my necklace, the one I never took off, the one that had seen me through every hurt and every hope.

"Your guardian angel."

I kissed his forehead. "That's right, baby. My guardian angel from God."

Chapter Twenty-One

Though my nap had recharged me a little, by the time Cody headed to bed at nine, I was right in tow with him. I don't even remember falling asleep, my body and mind were obviously calling out for a reprieve from the day.

I reached for my phone, confirming it was just before sunrise. I grabbed my black journal and slipped on my sweatshirt and shoes. After making pit stop in the restroom and brushing my teeth, I headed out onto the deck and down the steps toward the dock.

There was no better depiction of hope than a sunrise.

The darkness around me lay thick, yet there was a dim light in the distance, blanketing the earth with a dusky gray. I brought my legs to my chin, and wrapped my arms around them as I sat on the grass several feet back from the plants of the dock itself. I stared out into the horizon—thinking.

"You're my weakness, Angie...I'm just not sure you should let me be yours."

So much had gone on yesterday—so much drama and frustration, yet his words ran deep. My mind refused to let go of them without further investigation. I shook my head.

Two weeks.

That's what time I had left here, and now even that much might be challenged. I didn't know what the fallout would be from Divina's interview, but somehow the dream of a future with Pinkerton Press paled miserably in comparison to my dream of Jackson Ross. I reminded myself again that I hardly knew him.

Yet there were times I felt more in tune with him than anyone else.

How was that possible?

As the first brilliant bolt of orange peaked out behind the trees in the distance, I heard footsteps behind me. I jumped.

"Believe it or not, I was trying *not* to startle you. I just didn't want to miss the show," Jackson said, his voice deep and sleepy.

I smiled up at him—hair disheveled, wearing track pants and a t-shirt. I'd never seen him like that. I loved the look.

"Glad you could join me."

He sat down next to me, and for a few minutes we said nothing to each other as we watched the most brilliant colors paint the sky, bringing light to everything around us. The moment was magical, beautiful.

"I love to watch the sunrise when I come here," Jackson said, eyes straight ahead.

"I would, too. It's amazing to see it like this, over the water."

He nodded, smoothing out his hair with one of his hands. I felt disappointed at the return to decorum.

"What?" he said, looking at my face. "Why are you frowning at me?"

I laughed, caught red-handed. "Oh...I uh, was just thinking that your bed-head isn't so bad."

"You were thinking about me in bed?" He grinned so wide his eyes seemed lost inside it.

I pushed him—hard. "No! It's just rare to see you so casual."

"It's rare I get to have a reason to be casual." His face lost all traces of humor as he said the words, like that fact alone was cause for heartache. I wanted to touch his hair then, to feel the strands run through my fingers as I pulled his face to mine. But I didn't move. Instead I sat frozen in place, too afraid of the strength of the emotions raging inside me.

"How did your talk go last night with Cody?"

I stretched my legs out, letting the cool, dampness of the grass seep into my yoga pants. The breeze was warm enough to ward off chill.

"As good as it could go I guess...although, I'm sure our conversation on the subject isn't over." I shook my head at the irony of my words. "He will have a lot more questions as he processes what I told him. The hardest part is knowing I can't control what the future holds."

I felt his eyes on me then. "No…we never can."

A beat of silence passed between us, and I waited for him to say more. I begged silently for him to say more, but he did not. Instead, I decided I would go first. Most of my "stuff" was already out there at this point anyway. Why not tell him everything? I could only hope he would reciprocate in kind.

"I was married at eighteen, right out of high school. We eloped, although my parents were so detached from my life they hardly noticed."

He watched me as he lay back, propping his torso up with his elbows. I scooted around to face him and crossed my legs as I plucked pieces of grass from the earth.

"I thought he was everything I wasn't: charismatic, funny, and charming. He was popular in school, invited to every party and social event. I felt like *somebody* when I was with him, not just Angie-the-forgotten-daughter, or Angie-the-sister-of-Briggs. I felt important, wanted."

"The first year wasn't so bad. He worked for his parent's furniture company. They gave him a lot of flexibility with his schedule. He came and went as he pleased. They spoiled him with freedoms, knowing someday he'd have to step it up and take over for them. It's ironic though; his freedom meant the end of mine.

"What was once a party every few weekends quickly turned into him staying out every weekend. And soon enough there was no distinction between his weekend partying and his normal mid-week life. Dirk grew distant with me, hiding things, lying to me. I knew he was on something in addition to his heavy drinking, but he would tell me I was crazy, laugh me off. But one day he stopped thinking my accusations were funny. He changed into an angry, violent monster almost overnight. I'd seen his anger before, but I never thought...I never believed he would hurt me like he did. I lived in such denial, unwilling to tell anyone the truth about what was really happening. I felt like a failure. I'd banked everything on my future with Dirk—I didn't go to college, I didn't pursue writing, and I didn't think I needed friends.

"There are so many nights I don't remember, so many rages, but somehow those weren't as bad as the in-between times. There was so much uncertainty, so much fear. I didn't know when or what or how he would be set off...only that he would be. That became inevitable. Sometimes he would go for days or weeks without a rage, and I would see a glimpse of who I thought I loved in high school, but the calm never lasted. I did everything I could to make him happy. I thought if I could just *be better*, do more, love more, give more...then he would wake up and realize that he wanted me—more than his addiction. But he never did wake up.

"I left him when I found out I was pregnant. I planned it for weeks, saving up money to start over with Briggs somewhere new—somewhere untouched by Dirk. I never told him about the pregnancy."

I stopped, realizing my heart was racing a thousand beats per minute. I had told this part of the story many times at *The Refuge*, but never like this. Jackson watched me intently as I focused on a single blade of grass between my fingers.

"But he found you," he said.

"Yes."

I heard Dirk's words in my head then, as loud and clear as the night he first spoke them. *"Found you, Angela."*

I shuddered. "He broke into our home in Dallas. Cody was only two. I don't know how Dirk found out about him, but he did. He came to take him, and I...I wouldn't let him."

Jackson sat up, his knee touching mine, his hand balling into a fist at his side.

"He threw Cody into his truck, and I lunged at him, begging him to stop. That's when he stabbed me." My hand instinctively went to my abdomen. "It's a miracle that Briggs came back that night. He was able to take Dirk down and call the cops. I'd lost so much blood by then though. The doctors didn't think I would make it. They were worried about trauma to my head from when Dirk threw me against a wall before grabbing Cody. The doctors induced a coma as a last resort—to give my body a chance to heal."

"And you proved them wrong."

I smiled sadly. "I guess I did."

"Will you show me?" he asked, staring at my hand on my abdomen. His eyes were so sincere, so full of selfless concern. I leaned back slightly and lifted my sweatshirt to expose the scar that resided an inch below my belly button.

I heard a hiss escape between his teeth as his brows furrowed. Then, he reached out, as if crossing a great divide. As his finger traced the length of the scar, a fire trailed across the sensitive flesh.

Eyes still focused intently, he said, "It wasn't enough for you to rob me of my yesterdays...you had to steal my hope of tomorrow, too."

I gasped. Those words were not his—but mine. They were only written in one place, a part of a poem I'd started years ago in my black journal.

He looked up from my scar, his crystal eyes piercing me through. "Photographic memory. I couldn't forget those words."

He took his hand away, searching my eyes for the truth they held, for the hurt that was the heaviest for me to carry.

A single tear slipped down my cheek. "I'll never have another baby."

The words came out like they were separate from me, passing over my lips without caution or restraint. I hadn't spoken them aloud in years. There hadn't been a reason to say them. Jackson went rigid beside me.

A twinge sparked inside me, in the deep hollow of my lower abdomen, within the void that lived under my scar. I closed my eyes briefly, wishing I had the ability to resurrect the feeling of life, the feeling of wholeness. But I did not. The only feeling that resided there now was emptiness. The vacuum had staked its claim; it couldn't be undone.

Though his body was tense, his voice was low. "How are you not hateful or bitter?"

I didn't need to look at him to know it was a sincere question. Not some perfectly constructed string of sympathies like I'd received in the past. This was Jackson, and he didn't shy away from awkward. He embraced it, was comfortable in it even.

"When you have to fight so hard to live—to keep on breathing—you don't relinquish that gift back into the hands of something that will destroy it. I didn't have time to hate, not when I still had someone to love."

"You sound like my brother."

I exhaled at the change in topic, equal parts relieved and surprised.

"Do I?"

It was his turn to pluck a blade of grass and roll it between his fingers; he did not look at me. I held my breath, feeling my heart beat erratically with anticipation.

"Yes, he's very forgiving."

This was new information, a new piece of the puzzle that made him. I didn't dare interrupt. He stared at the lake, as if watching a memory dance upon the water.

"My father and Jacob were cut from the same cloth, even though they never shared the same blood. No one could say a negative word about either of their characters, or how they led Pinkerton. But I never wanted their life of corporate ideals and business meetings. I didn't want to be trapped like them. I wanted to live my *dreams...*" He said the last word as if it were venomous.

I waited, watching how his hair moved in the breeze.

"But that was all before...before I knew what dreaming would cost me," he said, shaking his head.

A cold tingle went up my spine. "What did dreaming cost you, Jackson?"

"Everything. It cost me everything."

He stood then and reached his hand down to pull me up. "Let's go in, and get some breakfast."

With that he was done sharing.

Jackson was the expert at speaking without ever really saying anything.

Chapter Twenty-Two

While Jackson showered, and Cody slept, I wandered down the hall toward the library Jessie had told me about the night before. I had imagined a few crowded bookshelves, but not this. *This* was an actual library. I'd never seen anything like it. The floors were a perfectly polished hardwood. Though every wall was covered with shelving, the room was not dark like I would have assumed. Instead, the ceilings were littered with skylights—admitting a naturally filtered light to illuminate every square inch of it. I stood in one place, turning in a circle to take it all in.

One shelf in particular caught my eye. Though there was order to every linear space, the books on this shelf seemed to be set apart—almost like a shrine. They were red hardbacks, gold lettering down the spines—five in total. I walked toward them.

"The Quinton Chronicles…by Everett Jr.," I said, moving my hand over the spine of each volume. That title jogged a memory. I'd seen these books before at Rosie's house. She had raved about them, but there was something else she had said. I narrowed my eyes, trying to remember what it was. It was something about-

"Best crime novels ever written in my opinion."

I jumped a foot in the air, gripping my chest.

Jacob lifted his hands, simultaneously apologizing and calming me. "I'm sorry; I didn't mean to sneak up on you."

"No...that's quite alright. Jessie told me I should visit the library, maybe borrow a book?" I shrugged, feeling my face heat from the surprise.

"Of course, this is about the best reading property you'll find. This room is what sold us on the house. Jess and I are avid readers."

I smiled. "I would imagine so—with the family publishing house and all."

"Yes, my grandparents and parents passed on their love of books and reading to us at a young age. I think Jackson was barely four when he learned to read."

The image of Jackson as a toddler squeezed my chest. "Bright kid."

Jacob nodded, walking toward the shelf I was standing beside. "Turned out to be a pretty bright man, too."

There was sincerity in his tone and in his words. Everything about Jacob was gentle and genuine. In many ways he was opposite of Jackson, yet they were both strong—both natural born leaders.

"Have you read them?" He pointed to the red books.

"No. I was just remembering my best friend talking about them, though—I haven't read much in that particular genre. I usually stick to light fiction—happily ever afters."

My life looked too much like a crime novel...

"Well, I'd be willing to bet that you'll be hooked after the first chapter of book one. Sometimes we need to get outside the box…shake it up a little. I think you'd be surprised. The plot is impressive. Hit number one on the New York Times Bestsellers with every release."

I could tell this guy had been in publishing—naturally selling story lines with every conversation.

"Romance?" I challenged.

"Yep—although pretty unconventional," he said, lifting one corner of his mouth, just like Jackson did.

"Okay. You sold me."

He laughed. "Take them, they're yours."

"Oh, no… I didn't mean—"

He leaned over and cupped his mouth as if telling a secret. "I can get more. I'm close with the publisher."

I laughed just as Jackson strolled in, hair still a bit damp from his shower. His eyes roamed over the two of us, landing on Jacob. There was a silent exchange between them, thoughts expressed only through their eyes, like a brotherly code.

Jacob's smile never wavered; Jackson's smile never appeared.

"Cody's awake," Jackson announced.

The statement was obviously meant for me, but he stared at Jacob.

"Oh…okay," I said calmly, turning back toward Jacob as he handed me book one of The Quinton Chronicles. "Thank you, Jacob. It was nice talking with you."

"Anytime. I'm looking forward to getting to know you better, Angie."

Two steps into the hallway, I heard an exasperated sigh from Jackson. "Really, Jacob?"

The questioning exclamation was cause for me to stop, curious as to what would be said next, but the only sound to follow was Jacob's laughter. The genuine glee was absolutely contagious. Jackson followed suit a few seconds later with a low chuckle, and my heart knocked hard inside my chest.

I'd never grow tired of that sound.

****

After helping Jessie with party preparations for the last several hours, she'd kicked me out of the kitchen and told me to go relax. Now heavily engrossed in the world of Detective Maverick Quinton and his new partner Reagan Harper, I was grateful for the excuse to read.

She spun around, her hair whipping violently in the wind as she shoved a finger into his chest. "You may think trust is a luxury, Quinton, but in my book it's a requirement! You can't build a house on a wet foundation. Stop looking for reasons to nullify my existence in this case...I'm not going anywhere. Get used to it!"

He stared at her, eyes sharp and narrowed. It wasn't that he didn't notice her—he noticed, too much. He didn't want to need her, he didn't even want to like her, yet there she was, refusing to be ignored. He grabbed her wrist, pulling her bony finger away from his chest. No woman was going to tell him how it was—not even his new partner. He didn't care what abbreviations followed her name; she didn't know him.

She didn't know anything.

"The only thing I'm required to do is make sure that at the end of the day we are both still breathing."

Her eyes grew round, as her hand twisted away from his grasp. For a moment he thought she would sprout tears, proving once and for all that he was owed a different partner—of the male variety.

But she didn't cry.

"You're the worst kind of arrogant there is," Reagan challenged.

He laughed humorlessly. "And what kind is that, sweetheart?"

"The kind that's born out of necessity—like a custom-fit suit of armor. You think its protection, but it's not. A lot of materials are made to look like iron, Quinton. But I can see through your armor, and it ain't made of iron."

"How can you stand this heat?"

My head snapped to attention. Covering my eyes against the rays of the sun, I held my finger into book one of the *Quinton Chronicles* to save my place.

"I live in Texas, remember? It's hot there," I answered, closing the book while holding my place with my finger.

"Want to go out on the paddleboat? I promised Cody another ride."

"Sure," I said, using a blade of grass to keep my spot in the book before setting it down.

Glancing at the book, Jackson asked, "Is it any good?"

"Yeah...I'm surprised I'm so hooked, actually. I don't usually care for this genre. Your brother has good taste."

I knew he heard me, but instead of replying, he jogged ahead, calling out for Cody to untie the boat from the dock.

****

I was definitely sweating now.

My shorts were stuck to my backside like sticky plastic wrap. Twisting my hair atop my head, I hoped a sudden rush of wind would dry my neck. No such luck.

Jackson and I occupied the two main seats on the paddleboat, while Cody sat in the back, facing out toward the water. He had a life jacket on, even though I was confident in his ability to swim. I glanced at my co-captain. The heat had to be overwhelming him like it was me, but somehow, instead of looking like the sweaty pig I was...he looked cool.

That was annoying.

Without warning, Jackson stopped paddling. In one swift motion, he stood, ripped his shirt off, and dove into the water. The boat rocked violently at the sudden movement. I clung onto the side for dear life while Cody laughed hysterically and joined him in the water a second later.

They splashed and swam, leaving me to cook like a grape in the sunshine. I was sure by the end of our time on the lake I would be a raisin. The water was so tempting, but I was not in swimwear.

I slipped my sandal off and tried to stretch my foot gracefully into the water—desperate for some relief, but it proved an awkward task. Even with legs as long as mine, I could barely touch the water with my toes.

Jackson swam over to me, a devious grin on his face. "What are you trying to do there?"

"I'm hot, Jackson. What does it look like I'm doing?"

Sure, I was a little testy. But honestly, my skin felt like melted wax.

"So get in, then." He floated on his back with ease, revealing abs that shouldn't exist on a real, live man. I diverted my eyes.

"I'm not dressed for it."

Guys had it so much easier. If they wanted to swim, they just did it. A simple strip down was all they needed. Not so for a woman though. Nope. There were all kinds of wardrobe malfunctions we had to think through. My tank top was light pink—soaked, it would be nearly transparent, not to mention I was wearing jean shorts. That was likely the worst swimming cloth imaginable. There was just no getting around that.

"Oh, come on, who cares. This is the lake, not a populated beach front."

"No." I shook my head.

I looked toward Cody, floating on his back in his life jacket, making motor sounds. I smiled at him, despite the sweat dripping off my face. In that unguarded moment, Jackson grabbed my dangling leg.

I gasped.

"You have two choices: Jump or-"

SPLASH!

I swam up to the surface, sputtering, as I heard Jackson and Cody laughing.

"Urgh! You said I had *two* choices!" I yelled, shoving a wall of water at Jackson, who was quite amused at the turn of events.

"Yeah, but when I realized you'd never jump, I decided I had better seize the opportunity before you pulled your foot back."

"You are so mean!" I bit the insides of my cheeks, trying desperately not to smile.

Jackson swam to me as I backed up underneath the lip of the paddleboat.

"Say it again," he challenged, his voice low and smooth.

"You're mean," I said with half the conviction as the time before it.

"Say it again."

I shivered, the cool lake water soaking into my bones, stealing my breath from my lungs—or maybe that was Jackson. I couldn't be sure.

"You're mean." I whispered the words this time, their meaning completely lost now.

We treaded water, staring at each other, unsure of what should happen next.

I reached up and grabbed hold of the ledge, steadying myself. He did the same, trapping me between his chest and the boat. My eyes skittered past him, searching for Cody who was still on his back, humming.

My chest ached when I saw the intensity of Jackson's stare. "What do you want from me, Jackson?"

I took in a shaky breath as his hand grazed the top of my head, freeing my hair to fall down my shoulders and back. His fingers combed the length of it while an army of goose bumps marched up my neck.

I stopped breathing entirely.

His voice was so low it was hardly audible. "I don't know."

Yet as soft as the words were, their weight was crushing.

He doesn't know?

Turning to pull myself back into the boat, Jackson gripped my hips and pulled me to him once again.

"Don't, Angie."

"Don't *what?* What is this, Jackson?" I swallowed, reminding myself to keep my voice low. "I don't need any more complications in my life, and that's what *this* is starting to feel like—like one big, messy complication. I appreciate all your help the past few weeks, but I think…"

His eyes grew dark as the arm around my waist loosened.

"You think what?"

I exhaled. "I'm going back in two weeks."

Thoughts and feelings could change, they were fluid—but leaving wasn't. That was concrete.

"Don't you think I know that?" He practically growled.

Another shiver went through me.

"Hey! Guys—look there's Pippy! And Peter!" Cody yelled, pointing to the yard where Pippy, Peter, and the man I assumed was Caleb, all stood waving at us.

Jackson hoisted himself back into the boat then reached for my hand to pull me inside. He did the same for Cody.

Neither of us spoke on the paddle ride back.

Jackson tied us up to the dock and Cody jumped out and ran over to Peter, asking him when they could play pool in the game room. As I started to stand inside the boat, Jackson put his hand out to stop me.

"Here, you'll want this." He tossed me his shirt.

"What? Why?" I asked.

He looked down at me and immediately I remembered. Crossing my arms over my chest, my cheeks flamed.

"I will bring you a towel." He was halfway across the deck when he said it.

"Oh, uh, thanks," I muttered in reply before slipping his shirt over my head.

****

A relationship with Jackson was like playing a game of connect-the-dots, while blindfolded. There was no numeric system that led the way; no big picture set as a guide. There were just dots—haphazardly placed at will. *His* will.

I kept busy by arranging several vases of flowers.

When Cody was in kindergarten, I took a job as a florist part-time, and even now, working with flowers remained one of the most soothing hobbies in my life. My love of flowers was also behind my name change from Angela Luterra to Angel Flores years ago.

As I clipped the few stems, I breathed in a sigh of relief. All I had to do was keep this up, and I could get through this night. I didn't know what Jackson wanted from me, but I knew without a doubt, that my feelings for him were stronger than his for me. That had been made abundantly clear earlier today at the lake.

Hiding in a house the size of this one, was easy. When the caterers arrived, I became one of them. When the bakery deliveryman came with the birthday cake, I led the way the table. I simply never stopped moving.

Pippy introduced me to several groups of people when the guest started to arrive—mainly relatives and good friends. It was quite a gathering for a forty-second birthday celebration, but maybe that was normal around these parts.

As someone made a toast in the next room over, the doorbell rang. Since no one else was close, I decided to add *doorman* to my list of titles for the evening.

Opening the door, my jaw fell slack.

Dee Bradford?

She seemed quite surprised to see me here as well.

"What a great surprise. I didn't know you would be here tonight, Angie." Her perfectly manicured hand clutched her heart as she smiled. "This is my husband, Marcus Bradford."

"It's a nice to meet you, Marcus, and it's nice to see you again, Dee," I said, opening the door for them to enter.

"You're here for the birthday party?" I asked her, puzzled, as we stood in the entryway.

She opened her mouth to answer me, but then looked up and beamed at something behind me. Before I could turn to investigate, I heard a familiar voice at my back.

"Hi, mom."

Dot. Line. Dot.

Chapter Twenty-Three

Again, my mouth fell open. "She's your—you're his mother?" I swiveled from Jackson to Dee.

Confused was an understatement.

"Yes," she said. "We don't usually advertise all the family connections within the company. Nepotism is frowned upon I hear." She laughed as she threw her arms out to hug Jackson.

I watched him, his face calm and composed as ever. I couldn't get past my astonishment. *How did I not know they were related?* Marcus shook his hand.

"Good to see you again, Marcus," Jackson said.

I remembered then that this man was not Jackson's father. His dad had died years ago from a heart attack, leaving his mom as a widower—Dee Ross as it turned out. She had apparently remarried.

But still, there were so many missing dot connections in my brain.

And then I remembered something else—something from earlier that morning at sunrise. I'd heard Jackson say it, but it didn't make sense then, and I wasn't even sure it made sense now, but I recalled it nonetheless.

"My father and Jacob were cut from the same cloth, even though they never shared the same blood."

What did that mean? Dee said she'd been a single mom...she had told me that at our meeting in Dallas...but did that mean—

"You're gonna hurt yourself, thinking that hard," Jackson said, staring down at me. I looked around, Dee and Marcus had already walked past us into the party. I was standing in the same spot, hand still frozen to the door handle.

"I'm just confused. You're mom told me she was a single mom at one time." I kept my voice low.

His eyes swept over my face in a way that made my insides swim.

"Jacob is my half-brother. My father adopted him once he and my mom had married. Jacob was about ten at the time. I came along two years later."

I bit my bottom lip, soaking in this new revelation.

"Come on, let's go to the party." He reached for my elbow. "That is, if you're done hiding from me."

I flushed hot, nodding.

****

There was no shortage of food; it was everywhere. But even still, Jacob didn't hold a plate in his hands. Instead, he held a very familiar thick, green smoothie. I shuddered at the sight of it.

"So you've met our mom?" Jacob asked, bumping his way through the crowded living space to get to me.

"Yes, although that connection was lost on me until tonight." I chuckled.

"I figured she wouldn't have said anything to you about that at your meeting in Dallas. She's all for real first impressions," he said, leaning in so that his voice was muted.

Prickles of anxiety crept up my neck. "What do you mean?"

He grinned and glanced over at Jackson who was getting us something to drink.

My stomach dropped.

Jackson and I?

"And you most certainly have impressed her," Jacob said, drumming his finger on his tumbler glass of green goo, "which is one of the highest complements a woman can be paid. Her approval is worth its weight in gold."

For what felt like the tenth time that evening, I was at a loss for words.

I was overcome with a need to breathe *fresh* air. "Will you excuse me, Jacob? I need to—please, excuse me."

I shuffled through the crowd to the back patio, careful to slide the door shut behind me. The air was stuffy, humid, but I could breathe easier out here than inside. My mind swam with snippets of conversations and jumbled memories. So many things were starting to make sense now. I had been so stupid to assume that a CEO like Jackson would be working with a runt like me out of the goodness of his heart. He'd been requested to—by his mother.

Dots and lines were connecting left and right, but all I wanted to do now was erase them—all of them.

"Jacob said you were out here."

It was Dee, in her designer summer dress and heels. She had not received the *casual* memo apparently.

She leaned against the patio rail near me, studying my profile as I looked out at the dark lake, my manners struggling to surface.

"I'm sorry about what happened—at the interview. Jackson told me how upset you were. He was furious when he called me yesterday, wanting to make sure that nothing had leaked from the inside. And I'll assure you, as I assured him, nothing did. We have done everything in our power to protect you, Angie, but Divina is a ruthless and resourceful woman. Though I understand your reasoning for keeping the whereabouts of your ex-husband a secret, we need to come up with a plan-"

I turned quickly, facing her for the first time. "Who—you and Jackson?"

She was startled by my tone; I was startled by my tone. But I meant it. Playing nice had gotten me nowhere. I was still back rolling the dice moving inch by inch, while these socialites had swooped in and purchased every high-dollar property that Monopoly sold.

I was so out of my league.

"Well, yes…along with our public relations department," she began. "We feel we need—"

"I don't know if I can hear this right now, Dee."

Her eyes narrowed. "You can't let someone like Divina stop you from your future," she said, placing her hand on her hip.

"I don't care about Divina!" I blurted.

This was a showdown. It was like the wild, wild, west—only instead of a dusty dirt road in front of a saloon, it was an outdoor patio, on a summer night in rural Connecticut.

"What's this about then?" she asked.

"Tell me why you invited me on this tour Dee, *really*?"

She squared her shoulders. "Because you're talented."

I raised my eyebrows. "Is that the only reason?"

Dee glanced out toward the water and then back to me. "You're a mother, Angie. So you should believe me when I say that there is no greater pain than watching your child go through life unhappy. I would do anything for my son."

Though my heart contracted at her words, I felt every last morsel of strength leak from my bones. "You told Jackson to work with me, then? With that hope that something might happen with us—romantically?"

"Angie, you likely know as well as I do that *telling* Jackson to do anything is a waste of breath. He rejected my motherly push to get to know you on a personal level prior to you coming out, but..." Her eyes twinkled at me. "But it looks like that's changed."

I leaned onto the railing, my stomach hollowing as I forced the words out, the truth that simultaneously burned my throat and broke my heart. "There's nothing between Jackson and I, Dee."

"You're wrong about that."

My head jerked up, the low voice jarring me back into reality.

Jackson walked toward me.

"You're wrong about that," he repeated.

I spun around, face to face with Jackson, my insides a mess of spams and knots. I watched Dee leave, winking at me as she slid the door closed behind her.

"You…you heard all that?"

He nodded.

Of course he'd heard. My life was anything if not a long list of badly timed events. I fought to swallow the ball of thick molasses that was working its way up into my throat. The anger I felt floated on the surface of my tears, carried by the current of my hurt.

As I blinked my tears away, my back was pushed up against the banister, Jackson's hands in my hair, on the side of my face, his mouth dangerously close to mine.

"She may have asked me to be open to meeting you—but I have my own mind, my own eyes, my own…heart. Everything I've done regarding you has been because I *wanted* to do it, maybe even *needed* to do it. You're not the only one who's scared about what this is between us, Angie." His breath was quick and shallow, skittering across my lips. "I'm scared, too."

A whimper caught in my throat as I lifted my chin a fraction of an inch. It was the only invitation he needed. His lips met mine with such desperate fervency that I was grateful for the post at my back. His hands were in my hair and on my neck, killing any sense of self-control

I had. It was the kind of kiss that made oxygen a second-rate commodity.

A quiet moan escaped me as he pulled back, chest heaving.

"I lied to you." His voice broke my trance. "When I said I didn't know what I wanted from you—I *do* know. I want to be with you, Angie. Every day. All the time."

"Jackson-"

He pulled me into his chest, wrapping his arms around me. "But I need you to know some things before you say anything—I need you to know me."

"Okay," I rasped into his shirt.

"Can we go to the dock?"

I glanced inside the house and nodded. "Yes."

Chapter Twenty-Four

As I walked onto the patio and down the steps after checking on Cody, Jackson grabbed my hand, lacing my fingers through his. In that moment I felt like a teenager, one that needed to text every friend I had to make sure that this was actually happening, that it was for real.

We rolled up our jeans and stuck our feet into the water. The air was still sticky with heat. He laid back, keeping my hand in his. I did the same.

The stars and moon were bright above us, illuminating his face perfectly as he stared up into the vast beyond. No matter what the future held for us, this moment was beautiful. He was beautiful. I wanted to memorize his face, to etch it into the confines of my heart.

"I met her in grad school—Livie. She was my polar opposite in so many ways, yet it was those very qualities that made me feel whole when I was with her. We were part of a study abroad group in Europe. It was an amazing time—traveling where we wanted, whenever we wanted. My major was in literature, hers was in art history.

"One night, while our group was asleep on the train, I had my first itch to write—to *really* write. My father had died earlier that year, and somehow when I wrote, I felt more connected to him than ever before. I started writing my first novel while aboard a train to Rome.

"Livie was my muse and my first reader. Within four month's time I'd finished it. I was happy just to brush it under the rug uncelebrated and unpublished, but Livie wouldn't allow it. She badgered me constantly until finally we came up with a plan—a pen name. I didn't want the Ross name to publish me. If it was publishable, I wanted it to be published because of talent, nothing else. I sent it to the toughest publishing house I knew—Pinkerton Press—under my pen name. Amazingly it wasn't rejected.

"Livie was ecstatic; I was in shock. I kept my identity a secret, handling everything through secured communication while I stayed overseas and continued writing. I wrote three books while I was in Rome, in just over a year's time. I was on fire...on top of the world. By that time, my first book had been published, and the secret identity of my pen name seemed to boost sales and publicity. Right before Livie had to go back to New York to start her own career, I asked her to marry me, promising her that we would set a date once we were both back stateside.

"But once I arrived back in New York, things got even crazier. As year two hit, my fourth book was leaked onto the Internet, and I was forced to reveal my true identity to my publishers—who were also my family members. We took legal action and stopped the leak, and amazingly, we also managed to keep my name concealed. But all the while, I was too busy for anything or anyone. I was focused only on getting my last book out. Livie was patient, God knows she was so patient, but I just wasn't ready to settle down, not even for her. I spent days in my office, typing. She would ask to go places, do things, and I would always arrange for her to go with someone else. That was how I eased my guilt.

"I was in the middle of writing the last book when a big group of family and friends took a winter vacation to Stowe, Vermont. We all stayed in separate cabins, using snowmobiles to travel between the lodge and ski areas. Livie was so excited; she was turning twenty-five during that trip and wanted to learn how to ski."

He stopped then and scrubbed a hand over his face. I didn't move, afraid he would shut down if I did. He took a deep breath and continued, as if fighting an inner battle.

"It was two days after Livie's birthday when she came into my cabin and asked me to go with her to her lesson. But I was under so much pressure to get my first draft to my editor that I told her she needed to find someone else to go with her. We fought—probably the worst fight we'd ever had. I told her she was needy and high-maintenance, that she had to stop relying on me so much…and she told me that I was the most selfish man she knew." He paused. "That was the last time I saw her alive."

I gasped, "No. Jackson…"

"She took the snowmobile out to the mountain, but never made it to her lesson. She was with Jacob and his friend when she fell through a shallow spot in the ice on the lake."

I sat up, staring down at him. Looking at his face caused me physical pain.

"And you blame yourself?"

He turned his eyes to me then and blinked.

"At first I blamed Jacob and his friend, thinking they could have done more for her...I pulled away from everyone. Jacob called, emailed, texted...but I refused to answer him. Though he didn't give up on me for that entire year I avoided him, I had convinced myself I didn't care about any of them. It was my mom who finally told me Jacob had been diagnosed with cancer. That was two weeks before I took the company over to relieve him—to start being the brother I should have been the year prior when he was dealing with all of that on his own. Once again, I proved Livie's words true. I am a very selfish man."

"Oh, Jackson."

I had no other statement. I felt his pain, his hurt, his sorrow...but most of all I felt his guilt.

He sat up, kicking his foot hard in the water, creating a splash.

"I'm so sorry-"

"Stop. Stop being sorry. I don't want you to be sorry, Angie. I want you to hear what I did—*who I really am.*"

I shook my head, processing what he wasn't saying. "So you working for the company, giving up your future as a writer, is what? Paying some sort of penance for fighting with Livie before she died and staying angry with Jacob even though you didn't realize he was sick?"

He stared into the lake, silent. My heart ached for him, for the guilt he carried and the shame he refused to release. I picked up his palm and traced an invisible message onto it, the same way I did with Cody.

I pulled on his arm, forcing him to see me. "Do you know what we say at *The Refuge*? That the only way to let go of our shame is to stop *acting* ashamed."

"I'm only trying to protect you, Angie. I don't have a good track record when it comes to relationships. I was a horrible fiancé and an even worse brother."

I leaned closer to him so that my forehead rested against his.

"I'm not afraid of getting close to you," I whispered.

"That might be the stupidest thing you've ever said."

"Then I'm far past stupid."

He shifted his face and cupped my cheeks with his hands. "Me too."

And then he kissed me in the moonlight.

There was no hope for undoing what he'd begun inside me. I could no sooner undo the reflection of the moon on the lake, or the way the dew weighted the grass in the morning. My heart knew only this: it was made to love Jackson Ross.

We heard a loud whistle from the porch, followed by an announcement for cake and more rounds of toasting. Jackson chuckled lightly.

"You want to go back inside?" I asked softly.

"Sure." He pulled me up and laced my fingers through his again as we made our way across the yard.

Just outside the patio door I pulled him to a stop. "Wait...what's your pen name, Jackson?" My heart started beating a thousand miles a minute as I waited for his answer. He smiled mischievously, his eyes revealing the secret his mouth wouldn't speak.

"Oh, my gosh!"

"Shhh..." Jackson laughed.

I stood, jaw open wide. "Rosie will seriously die...she will *die*! Oh. My. Gosh!"

"Well, I don't want to be liable for that. I have enough legal trouble as it is."

I punched Jackson in the arm. "You're famous—like really, really famous."

"No, Everett Jr. is famous," he said, kissing my temple before he opened the door. "I'm just Jackson."

I smiled wide. "There's no such thing as *just* Jackson."

With that, we slipped quietly into the back of the party crowd, watching Jacob as he made his way to the front of the living room near the cake. Jessie, Peter and Pippy stood by his side.

They were a beautiful family…one I would never forget.

Chapter Twenty-Five

The party went well into the evening—toasting, pictures, hugs and laughter. The Ross family knew how to celebrate, and I suspected Jacob's zest for socializing had more to do with his remission from cancer than his need for a party. Several guests stayed over in the rooms upstairs, including Dee and Marcus. I was glad I'd have an opportunity to speak with her at breakfast in the morning.

Jackson had walked me to my room around midnight, shortly after Cody had fallen asleep. We agreed to keep our interactions under the radar since Cody was leaving in two days. There was still so much left to discuss—our honest conversations this weekend were only the beginning. In addition, I hadn't the foggiest idea of how to talk to Cody about dating Jackson, but at least there was time for that. I had two weeks to figure that part out.

****

I padded down the hallway to use the restroom around seven in the morning when I was immediately put on alert. Something was wrong. Loud voices, raised in anger came from the library—one of which I knew very well.

I had done more eavesdropping in this house than I had in my entire existence on earth, yet I couldn't stop myself. Standing several feet away from the closed door, I listened intently. I could identify three of the voices: Dee, Jacob and Jackson.

"...never expected you to sign your life over, Jackson. We at least need to discuss it."

"No. The company is not your problem to worry about anymore, Jacob. That was the whole point of you moving out here to the country. Let it be," Jackson said.

"Let it be? You stepping in was only supposed to be temporary. You and I both know that Stew is more than capable of taking over. He may not be a Ross, but he worked with Dad and me for ten years. He knows the company better than anyone else. Please just think about it. I only want you to enjoy your life again...to write, to dream, to fall in love. Dad wouldn't want this for you, and either do I."

"You're one to talk," Jackson said.

"Jackson!" Dee's voice was high, angry.

"It's true! Where was *our* vote when you decided to stop treatments?"

There was silence for several seconds, and then I heard Jacob again, his voice soft, tender.

"That is not how I want to finish out my life. All of our days are numbered, mine are just shorter than most. I want to be *me* for as long I'm able to be, to know my kids' voices and faces, to see sunsets and rainstorms, to kiss my wife and take her dancing...those are the things I want to fight for—not extra days pumped full of drugs, too sick to get out of bed. I've accepted it, brother. I hope you will, too."

I didn't hear Jackson's response; I couldn't. I put my hand over my mouth and ran to the bathroom, my throat tight as tears pricked my eyes. This weekend had been filled with emotional roller coasters, but this was biggest one of them all. Jackson's gathering last night hadn't been a birthday bash or a remission celebration. I understood the purpose clearly now.

He was making memories with the people he loved.

He wasn't going to get better.

He was dying.

****

Breakfast was difficult.

I could hardly look at Jacob without wanting to cry. Everyone else seemed to function normally. I didn't understand that. Pippy had never let on that her dad was...that he was still sick. I pushed my plate away, no appetite present.

"Good morning," Dee said, sipping on coffee.

"Good morning," I said, trying to clear the thoughts of cancer and death from my mind.

"I hope you slept well last night," she said. "It looked like your evening improved after I left the patio?"

I flushed. "Yeah, about last night, Dee—"

She waved her hand in the air, "No need, darlin'. I'm just glad you two had a chance to…talk." She smiled.

I wondered what she saw—or what she knew. I couldn't imagine Jackson being open with his mom about the current status of our relationship, but she was a smart woman. Dee wouldn't need the full scoop to know something had changed.

I smiled, touching the pendant at my neck.

"I arranged with Pippy to meet with you and Jackson on Tuesday afternoon."

My eyes snapped back to hers, panic fueling my veins.

"To talk about our next steps of actions, regarding your book and fans."

I exhaled. "Yes, we need to talk about that."

"She told me your son was about to go back to Texas, so I figured we could wait another day. I'll be in town all week. I have some meetings at the company I need to attend."

"Well, thank you. My brother and his wife should be in New York tomorrow afternoon. They are going to stay for a couple nights and then fly back with Cody so he can go to soccer camp. It will be the longest I've ever been without him—almost two weeks."

Dee looked at me with compassion, "I remember those days well. I'm glad you have family you can trust."

Yes, so am I.

We chatted for a while longer, drinking coffee as several others joined us. Two aunts, a few cousins, and a couple from Chicago were present by the time Jackson sat down at the table beside me. He looked like he always did—capable and in control, but still my heart ached for him. I hated knowing what I knew. I hated that I had heard it the way I did.

It was not information I could forget, no matter how hard I tried.

I replayed my conversation with Jackson on the dock last night many times, trying to get a handle on his fierce loyalty to the company—one he has no passion to work for. I knew he felt indebted to it for reasons beyond my limited understanding, but this morning had shed new light on the topic.

Jackson wasn't only trying to right his past wrongs, to relieve his guilty conscious…he was trying to barter with God. His life for Jacob's.

The only problem was: God doesn't barter.

254

"What's the problem?"

I jumped a little at his voice in my ear.

"Just tired," I said. "Spacing-out, I guess."

"You've been staring at that same spot on the wall for several minutes."

I laughed, weakly. "What time do we need to leave?"

"I need to finish up some things here with Jacob. Is two or three okay with you? I know you need to get back to pack for Cody."

"Yeah, that will be fine." I smiled at him, wishing I could take his hand...or kiss his face...but we were in a house full of eyes. "I was thinking I might try and read some more. I'm dying to know what Detective Quinton is up to."

Jackson shook his head, turning so his face was pointed in the opposite direction as the group seated at the table. "I knew I should have kept that a secret from you for a while longer."

"No way, I'm going to soak up every word." I smirked as he turned toward me and groaned as if in pain.

"Maybe I can boot out the president of your current fan-club. I'm on the PTA, ya know. I've got skills."

His eyes dipped to my lips.

"Hmm...I think I'll go out and read right now, actually, since Cody and Peter are headed out to the lake."

As I started to scoot my chair back, Jackson put his hand on my leg under the table, stopping me. The sensation sent my body into a tailspin.

"If you become one of those swooning, young moms who wear t-shirts with *Team Quinton* written on the front, I will be forced to retaliate."

I quirked an eyebrow. "How so?"

"I'm thinking butterflies—lots and lots of butterflies."

I gasped. "You wouldn't dare."

"Try me."

****

Several hours later, I finished book one. Reading was a good distraction while still at Jacob's house. And the cliffhanger? Horrible! How did people read these types of books before the series was completed? I'd go insane. I was already planning out my next pocket of time to read. These books were a peephole into Jackson's soul.

Every girlfriend should be so lucky.

Girlfriend? Is that what I was?

We hadn't discussed titles. We had hardly discussed anything. I for one wasn't going to bring it up. If Jackson wanted to label us as an item, he would have to be the first one to say it. I was old fashioned that way I guessed. At twenty-nine, I was hardly naive, but I certainly wasn't forceful or pushy. I could be patient.

Love was worth patience.

My stomach rolled at the thought. *How had four week's time changed me so much?*

"Hey, I think Caleb and I are going to head out. I feel like I've hardly seen you since I got here," Pippy said, pulling up a chair beside me.

I immediately felt guilty. I'd been avoiding her since this morning. Seeing her pretty, happy face was a reminder of my morning's undercover work outside the library door.

"I know, sorry. I've been sucked into these novels. Your dad recommended them," I said.

Pippy laughed, her eyes lighting up, baiting me to tell her that I *knew*.

"Yes, I know. He told me," I said.

She threw her arms around me, "I knew he would! I just knew it! That means something you know—he never talks about his past, or his books, or-" she stopped, her face flushing pink.

"I know. We had some good conversations this weekend."

She squealed. "What if we're related someday! Oh, my gosh!"

My eyes grew huge. "Pippy! Please—shhh!"

"I've never had a sister, but of course, you really wouldn't be my sister...you'd be like...what? My aunt? Hmm...that's kind of weird, but still we could act like sisters-"

If only she had an inside voice. I was dying—my armpits sweating at her family tree quandaries.

"Pippy, I promise you—*if* and when that day comes, you will be first in line. Until then, please do not talk like that. I don't even know what's going on with us yet," I said, quietly.

She nodded, her grin stretching wider by the second.

She hugged me again, and my heart went to mush, my mind again to Jacob. She pulled back from my arms, about to leave.

"Pippy?"

"Yeah?" Her face was full of vibrant wonder.

"Are...are you okay?"

"Yes," she laughed. "Why?"

"I just...I wanted to make sure. If you ever want to talk...about anything, I'm here for you. I hope you know that."

She nodded. "See? You'll be a great big sister-type. That's exactly what one would say."

I chuckled and shook my head. "Okay. Well, I mean it."

"Thanks. It was a great weekend, I was so glad Caleb was able to meet my folks. I think they both really liked him."

I nodded, my words caught somewhere inside.

Would Jacob be alive to see his daughter get married one day?

"It was a great weekend," I said. "And yes, he is a very nice guy, Pippy."

After she walked away, I felt my body relax slightly.

I had so many questions.

Too bad eavesdroppers didn't get rewarded with answers. I slumped back hard in my chair. I would suck at being a detective.

Chapter Twenty-Six

Land Of Certain

In the Land of Certain, options are slim, outcomes are planned, and pathways are marked

Nothing is original

In the Land of Certain, everything is placed, everything is timed, and everything is controlled

Nothing is impulsive

In the Land of Certain, faith is needless, courage is useless, and trust is expected

Nothing is absent

In the Land of Certain, emotions are balanced, expressions are stoic, and thoughts are passive

Nothing is passionate

In the Land of Certain, you are nameless, you are unknown, and you are pretend

Nothing is real

For the only truth that lives in Certain, is the façade of its own deception

****

I walked out onto the front porch, as Jacob, Jessie, Peter and Dee stood around Jackson's car. The sight of such togetherness immediately overwhelmed me. My experience with a family this size was nonexistent, but my desire to be near it was powerful nonetheless. My chest ached as I watched them, smiling and talking as if their world wasn't breaking.

As if their loved one wasn't dying.

I glanced at Jacob, a wave a shame sloshing inside my belly. Helpless as I was in this situation, there was no excuse for my avoidance of him. He was a good man, one that had so obviously enriched and influenced many of the people I'd come to care about. I was a coward to hide from him—no matter how uncomfortable I was.

The truth was like an itchy blanket, trapping me beneath its rough fibers. My skin screamed at me, desiring nothing more than its removal. Yet the blanket stayed, indignant at my protests for relief.

Jackson opened my door and walked around to his side of the car where his mother pulled him into an embrace that caused something inside me to shift—to yearn. A warm surge of envious-want coursed through me. I'd never known a mother's love or affection. There were years that I'd gone without a well-meaning, well-intentioned touch. Years that were lost to the shadows of my past, but standing here, watching this, was a reminder that touch had a distinct purpose: *love*.

"You're good for him, Angie. Don't give up." The whisper was low, yet the tender voice that spoke was unmistakable.

Jacob was at my side, smiling. His eyes held the same child-like wonder I'd seen countless times in Pippy, the same hope and life. He nodded at Jackson and winked at me. A rush of heat stung my cheeks as he pulled me into an embrace. My throat swelled as I racked my brain for words to follow such a statement. In the end though, I simply said goodbye, forcing a smile on my lips as he closed my car door.

I fought the tears that threatened to pool in my eyes and refused to blink as I looked out the window at Jackson's family.

I hated *time* in that moment. The certainty of what it brought, the injustice of *who* and *how* it robbed from us.

A rebellious tear slid down my face as Jackson started the engine.

Life was so uncertain.

****

By the time we pulled up to my apartment building, my mind was like an overstuffed suitcase. No matter what tactic I tried, I couldn't get the darn thing to close.

There was virtually no line of thinking I could venture down without an overwhelming feeling of anxiousness taking over. Between the fallout from the interview with Divina, my upcoming meeting with Dee, Jacob's failing health, Cody's approaching trip home, and the new developments with Jackson and I...the list of unknowns was growing by the second.

Twice, Jackson had brushed my hand with his while we drove, asking more with his eyes than he did with his mouth. Twice, I had simply smiled in reply.

"I'll walk you up," Jackson said, grabbing our bags from the trunk.

"Thanks," I said, following him inside the elevator. Cody already had our key in his hand, anxious to get inside our room. He'd had to use the restroom for the last half-hour. As soon as the doors opened, he was off, running down the hallway to our door. Jackson laughed.

"If I knew he had to go that bad, I would have stopped."

"Oh, he's fine."

"But are you?" Jackson asked, dropping the bags at the doorway, a concerned look on his face.

My guilty conscious tugged at me. Who was I to be the cause of his concern, not when his only brother was home facing incurable cancer? The fact that Jackson didn't know I *knew* that information was the cherry on top of my guilt-sundae.

"It's gonna work out, Angie."

I swallowed hard. I didn't know which of the many things he was referencing, but I knew his statement couldn't pertain to that one.

Jackson touched my chin and lifted my eyes to his. "Hey, what is it? Are you not feeling well?" He touched the back of his hand to my cheek, as if to check my temperature, a gesture that caused me to feel feverish in and of itself.

"No, I'm not sick. I'm just worried. I heard something this morning and I probably should have told you sooner, but-"

Jackson blew out a hard breath and pulled on his neck, causing me to stop short.

"I told Pippy not to tell you. We're going to deal with it, Angie. I promise. I just need you to be open when we meet on Tuesday morning with my mother."

A cold chill seemed to settle inside every cell of my body.

"What exactly was Pippy not supposed to tell me?"

Now it was his turn to look surprised, although not for long. His features shadowed over again, leaving his standard unruffled expression behind a second later.

"You weren't talking about your blog?" he asked.

"No, what are you talking about Jackson?"

He reached for my hands then, holding them together as he wrapped his fingers around them.

"I need you to promise me something, right here, right now."

I raised my eyes to his, his stare as intense as his words.

"What?" I asked.

"Do not go on your blog site, or anything having to do with your publication—not until we set our next course of action."

The chill was back, trying to win over the warmth of Jackson's hands on mine.

"You're scaring me...why not?"

He took a deep breath. "I'm not trying to scare you, Angie. I'm trying to protect you. Trust me, please. Just stay off your computer for now—whatever damage Divina has caused, it's not an accurate representation of who you are. Reading reviews and commentaries based off fallacies will only work against you. Promise me, okay?"

I closed my eyes and took a deep breath. It was true then. Divina's hard punches had brought destruction—to my name and reputation no less. Her crushing blow wasn't just outing me to the world as a domestic violence victim, but framing me as a deceiver.

I nodded at him reluctantly.

Jackson pulled me into his arms as I let my body melt into him. "So, it's bad then, isn't it? People believe her over me—that I'm a coward?"

He crushed me to him even tighter. "If I ever hear anyone call you a coward, they will live to regret their words."

I heard the elevator ding and a rustling in the hallway as I lifted my head up slowly from Jackson's shoulder. Staring into his eyes I knew he meant it. He didn't see me as weak—and in my book that was about the best compliment I could ever receive. As he lowered his mouth to mine, I heard a gasp followed by two loud thumps.

Everything moved in slow motion when I turned my head in the direction of the sound behind me.

I began to blink rapidly as if that action alone could help my eyes explain to my brain what they were seeing. They couldn't.

"What's going on here, Angie?"

My brother stared at me like I'd just morphed into a bright blue alien right before his eyes.

Charlie smacked him hard in the chest, hissing, "Don't be rude."

"*Rude?* Are we not seeing the same thing here, babe? Because it looks to me like some guy my sister couldn't have known for more than two minutes was about to-"

"Briggs! Stop—I'm sorry. I wasn't expecting you guys until tomorrow," I said, my heart racing a thousand beats per second.

Charlie smiled then, walked over to me, and threw her arms around my neck. In that moment I realized Jackson's arm was still tight around my waist. Apparently, he wasn't nearly as bothered by the interruption as I was.

Charlie beamed. "Introduce us to your friend, Ang."

Jackson took a step toward her, hand outstretched like a gentleman.

"This is Jackson Ross. He's my—he's the CEO of Pinkerton Press."

Jackson raised his eyebrows at me slightly, nodded politely. I was so overly aware of each eye on me in that moment that I suddenly wished the hallway was made of quicksand.

Charlie reached back and grabbed Briggs' hand and pulled him closer toward us.

"Jackson this is Briggs, my brother," I said. "Briggs this is-"

Jackson reached his hand out to him then, lip curled in a smirk.

"Just call me *some guy*."

Chapter Twenty-Seven

The fact that Briggs and Charlie had caught an early flight to surprise Cody and I should have been the focal point of the evening. Ironically though, the surprise had been a little bigger than they had anticipated. *SURPRISE!*

When I spoke to Briggs a couple of days ago after the interview crisis, I'd left Jackson out of our conversation—now I realized why I had. Briggs was a great brother, no doubt, but he would always see me—no matter how old I was—as his sister.

Standing now between two alpha males was enough to make me sweat through my clothing. Thankfully, Charlie broke the ice yet again and asked where Cody was.

"He's inside…he'll be so excited to see you guys," I said.

Briggs grunted.

Jackson stared.

Shoot me now.

Charlie put her hand on the doorknob and looked back at us. "Why don't we all do breakfast together in the morning—Jackson, can you join us?"

His eyes danced in delight at the request. For the life of me I would never understand how he could thrive in the midst of awkwardness—yet he did.

"That sounds great." He looked at me again. "Just let me know where and when. Thanks for the weekend, Angie." He leaned in and hugged me, kissing me on the cheek before adding, "And don't forget your promise."

Jackson nodded at Briggs and then turned and walked away. For a split second I contemplated running after him. If not for Cody, I would have. Any escape would have been better than the upcoming conversation with Mr. Perma-scowl himself.

Briggs crossed his arms over his chest. "I hope you aren't too tired after your weekend getaway, 'cause suddenly I'm in the mood for conversation."

"Lighten up, Briggs. I'll tell you everything, okay?" I pushed him a little to knock a smile back onto his face.

"You bet you will."

With that, my evening had officially begun.

****

After Briggs and Charlie settled into their room, we went to dinner at one of the local pizzerias two blocks over. Cody filled them in on our adventures at the lake house—specifically his paddleboat rides. Though Charlie had looked interested, Briggs had looked irritated. I held out on Cody's bedtime for as long as I could, but one could only put off the inevitable for so long.

We sat now in the small living quarters of my apartment, staring at each other.

"Spill it. What's going on with you and Romeo," Briggs said, leaning his elbows on his knees.

"Briggs—give the girl a chance," Charlie scolded, turning to me and smiling. "He seems very nice, Ang…and he's not hard on the eyes either."

I laughed as Briggs shook his head.

"Well, to be really honest, I'm not totally sure what to call it yet. Nothing is official, but…there is definitely something there. I wasn't looking for this—and he wasn't either." I laughed, thinking about the first night we met. "But I feel something very real for him."

Charlie swooned, cupping her hand to her heart and leaning back against the couch. Briggs was silent—never a good sign.

"Angie, I am so excited for you! When did all this start? What's he like? What have you guys talked about for the future?" Charlie asked, her voice getting higher and higher with each new question.

"Charlie—we don't even know this guy! How can you so blindly encourage a romance you know nothing about?" Briggs threw his arms in the air as I shushed him, pointing to Cody's door.

"I haven't said anything to Cody yet," I said, quietly.

"Apparently, you haven't said anything to anyone, Angie." Briggs whisper-yelled, which caused Charlie to giggle.

I rolled my eyes at him. "Listen, I appreciate your concern, Briggs. I know you want to protect me, but Jackson is *not* Dirk, and I am no longer a stupid eighteen-year-old girl. You aren't the only one who has learned the hard way in life. I have too. I would never jeopardize Cody, or myself—you know that, right?"

He held my gaze and nodded. "Angie, I know you aren't the same girl who chose Dirk, but I won't pretend that the idea of you in a relationship doesn't scare the crap out of me—because it does. I don't even know him!" He stood up and started to pace, running his hands over his face.

"Then get to know him."

He stopped walking and looked at me.

"I don't know what the future holds, Briggs, but these last four weeks have changed me—in here," I said, pointing to my heart. "I used to think that I was too tainted by my past to ever *feel* for someone what I feel for Jackson. I used to think I was too broken—too damaged—to ever be seen as more than just a victim, but I don't believe that anymore. If God is as good as I say He is to all my girls at *The Refuge*, than I choose to believe that He can redeem anything and anyone. Even me. My story is still being written Briggs, and for the first time in eight years, I want someone to share it with."

Charlie reached for my hand, tears streaming down her cheeks. "I believe in redemption too, Angie, and I believe that love can heal pieces of our hearts that we never even knew were broken."

Briggs looked at his wife and smiled lovingly, pulling at his neck the same way Jackson did when he needed to relieve tension. He looked at me and sighed.

"I'll give him a chance, Ang."

I knew that statement was difficult for him to say, and I wasn't about to push him further on the subject. Not being in control was scary—it scared me, too—but I knew his fear ran deeper than that. Not only had he seen my ex-husband try to murder me, he was also the one who saved my life. I would never deny Briggs a voice; he had more than earned it.

I could only hope that his faith would outweigh his fear.

****

As we took a cab to see meet Jackson by a pancake house he'd suggested, I felt my nerves grow with anticipation. After my passionate speech last night, I woke up with a head swirling with doubt. Everything that had happened with Jackson over the weekend still seemed so surreal. I questioned now if my feelings for him could possibly be reciprocated. *Had I been so desperate for him to like me that I had imagined more on his part than what was actually there?*

I hated how much of a girl I really was sometimes.

But when I saw him, my worries quieted. I smiled as he gave Cody a high five, ruffling his hair as he walked past him to our table. Jackson caught my eye and held it as if I were the only person in the room. The warmth in my chest radiated to my cheeks as he met me. Though Briggs and Charlie stood close, Jackson was undeterred as he lifted my hand to his lips.

"Good morning, Angie," he said.

"Good morning."

He turned to each of my family members and offered the same greeting, while keeping my hand tucked in his. As we walked together to the table, Jackson whispered in my hair, "I missed you."

And then...my doubt was gone. I hadn't imagined him.

"So, Jackson, tell us everything you know about the publishing business..." Charlie started.

I laughed as Jackson squeezed my hand underneath the table. He humored her all through breakfast, answering her questions and asking several in return. Briggs played along, too, winking at me when Jackson turned his head to speak to Cody. I knew it wasn't a full-approval, but it was close. It was progress.

Progress was a great place to start.

Jackson ever so slyly paid the bill before it was ever brought to the table. This, in turn, earned several more points in Charlie's book—as if there was ever a doubt where her loyalties were when it came to my love life.

"I'd like to offer my driver tomorrow when you head back to the airport. The town car will be more comfortable than a cab," Jackson said.

I smiled as he spoke to my brother, shaking his hand as we stood to leave.

"Thanks—that'd be great," Briggs said.

When I turned around to speak to Charlie, she was no longer behind me.

"Where's Charlie?"

"Uh—she had to use the restroom," Briggs said, his eyes roaming everywhere other than my face.

"Okay…why are you acting so weird?" I asked.

"I'm not," he said, suddenly taking an interest in his shoes.

Charlie came back a moment later and met us in the lobby of the restaurant, her face pale.

"Hey…are you sick?" I asked, touching her shoulder.

She shook her head, looking up at Briggs who seemed to be asking her a silent question through his eyes.

"What? What's going on?"

Charlie bit her lip and leaned against Briggs who smiled like a kid on Christmas morning.

"She's had a bit of an issue with breakfast lately."

I gawked at Charlie for confirmation.

"I'm eight weeks pregnant."

Chapter Twenty-Eight

As I hugged my sister-in-law, I could feel Jackson's laser-focused gaze on my face. I ignored his stare the best I could; I didn't want to feel what I knew his look would provoke in me. Instead, I launched into a list of questions for her: When's your due date? Who's your OB? How's your morning sickness?

Each and every question was a deflection from the painful reminder that lingered somewhere in the back of my mind: *I'll never have another baby.*

"Want to hear something even crazier? Tori—Kai's wife—is also pregnant. We're due four weeks apart! It'll be so fun to have a prego-pal," Charlie said, grinning wide.

The pit in my stomach grew larger by the second, but I pushed it down, refusing to acknowledge its presence.

"I'm so happy for you, Charlie."

"Our first ultrasound is next week. I'll have to text you a pic since you'll still be here." Charlie linked arms with me as we walked to the curb to hail a cab. Jackson, Briggs and Cody were right behind us.

"Please do."

As the cab approached, Jackson pulled me back as my family piled into the back seat. His eyes were intense, so I focused instead on the open button at his collar. He never wore ties.

"Angie."

"Hmm?"

He hooked a finger under my chin, forcing our gaze to meet.

"I see you," he said softly.

I could only blink, too afraid my voice would give me away. I'd spent years redirecting the pain, and I wasn't about to show it now and ruin a moment of happiness for someone I held so dear to my heart. That wouldn't be fair to her.

"I'm in meetings all day today, but I wanted to make sure you got Pippy's text about this evening?"

I nodded, giving him a weak-smile.

"Okay, I'll see you tonight then."

He touched my arm and gave it a squeeze, aware of the audience around us, one small set of eyes in particular.

"Sounds good." I spun around, slid inside the backseat of the cab, and shut the door quickly. I couldn't stare into Jackson's eyes for a second more. I needed to push through.

"Feeling up for some sight-seeing and art museums?"

"Oooh, yes, good call!" Charlie said at the same time as Briggs groaned.

We laughed in unison, driving toward Times Square to catch the tour bus.

Pippy had texted early this morning to let me know my day was wide-open. She had taken the liberty of canceling my bookstore signings—as I'm sure she'd been instructed to do, along with arranging a special night for Cody, as a send-off back to Texas. I was glad she would get to meet my brother and Charlie. For now, that is what I would fill my mind with: busyness. Tomorrow's meeting, surprise pregnancies, and Cody's goodbye party, would all need to take a back seat.

I could only process so much information at one time.

****

Oh. Sweet. Mercy.

Pippy's idea for tonight might have been perfect for Cody, but coming off a long weekend, and then a day spent sight-seeing around the city, all I wanted to do was sit in a hot bath and close my eyes—for about a year. Instead, I was at an arcade the size of Texas with a thousand and one people running about. When I sat down at the table she reserved for us, I was fairly certain I wasn't going to be able to get up again. I was beat tired.

"Mom, mom! Uncle B and Peter are gonna take me to play Fast and Furious, okay?"

"Sure, sweetie," I said, putting my head down on the table and giving him a thumbs up. I just needed a second to regroup, recharge. I gave Pippy and Charlie my debit card and told them to order whatever they wanted food-wise for the group—I knew if Jackson were here I'd never get my way. I hadn't been allowed to pay for anything in weeks. It was well past my turn.

I tried to drown out the noise around me by closing my eyes and taking several deep breaths.

"A little noisy for a nap, don't ya think?"

I smiled at the sound of Jackson's voice and scooted over. While keeping my head propped on my arm like a pillow, I peeked out from my cozy hideaway to see the gorgeous face.

"How was your day of meetings?" I asked.

He smiled. "You're horrible at deflection."

I shrugged. "I wasn't trying to deflect, Jackson. I was simply interested in your day."

"Meetings are meetings, nothing of interest there," he said, slouching down in the booth a tad to kick his feet up. I noticed then that he'd changed his clothes. He was no longer Corporate Jackson but Casual Jackson. And I'd grown to love that version quite a bit.

"You nervous about Cody leaving tomorrow?"

The question hit my gut so hard I felt nauseous. "That's an understatement. I'm trying not to think about it."

"And how's that working out?"

I lifted my head then. "What are you, Dr. Phil?"

He laughed, the right corner of his mouth lifting into a half grin.

"You look worn out."

"Wow, thanks Jackson. Why don't you just tell me I suck as a human being too? You're on quite a roll tonight."

He laughed heartily, as I pinched my lips together to keep from joining in.

"Five nice things."

"What?" he asked, trying to get his breathing under control.

"Don't you know that for every mean comment you make, you're supposed to offer five nice ones?" I asked, crossing my arms over my chest.

"I don't do empty compliments, remember?"

"Well *I* don't do rude."

"Seems we're at an impasse."

I pushed his shoulder as he snatched my hand playfully. "Seems so."

If we weren't in the middle of an arcade, I'd kiss him right there. The fire that burned through my skin and into my bones from his touch was more than just a little intense. He must have felt the same, because he let go a second later.

"Hey, Jackson!" Charlie said, walking up to the table with Pippy, who was balancing several drink cups on a tray.

"Hey—how did you enjoy your time in the city today?" Jackson asked her, leaving me to regain composure.

"Oh we had the best day—I've actually been here several times on tour with the University, but it was Briggs' first time," she said, sitting down and taking a sip of her iced tea.

"I'm glad. It's not for everyone," Jackson said, taking a glass of Coke off the tray and handing it to me.

"Oh I just love big cities—I don't think my husband would go for it, but I have always loved the city life," Charlie crooned. Her hands animated each word she spoke.

Jackson smiled in response as Pippy handed me my debit card. I took it quickly and placed it back in my purse as he swiveled his head to stare at me.

"Tell me you didn't do what I think you did."

"Okay. I didn't do what you think I did."

He shook his head. "After dinner. You and me. Air hockey. Winner pays."

"It's already done Jackson."

"Nothing is done that can't be undone."

The video-game crew: Briggs, Peter and Cody must have smelled the food because they arrived back at our table about a minute before the food did.

"Tell me about Soccer Camp, Champ...you excited?" Jackson asked Cody just as he was stuffing his face with a cheeseburger.

Cody looked at me and finished chewing before he responded. Good boy.

"It's way awesome. Our coach—Mr. Denny—is really funny. He wears a different hat every day of practice, and if everyone shows up on time and doesn't forget anything he brings us a Slurpee the next day."

"Wow, he does sound pretty awesome," Jackson said.

"Yeah, he is." Cody nodded enthusiastically.

"What's been your favorite part about visiting New York, Cody?" Pippy asked.

Cody tapped his chin like an old man, thinking. "Making new friends."

The collective *"aww"* that made its way around the table in response to his answer melted my heart. It was moments like this that I wouldn't trade for anything in the world. Though he'd never known the love of a father, there was no end to the people who loved and cared for him. My heart ached with pride as I watched him finish his dinner.

As the first one to finish his meal, Cody stood up and smiled. "Who wants to challenge me to a game of Space Invaders?"

"I'll take that challenge, short stack," Jackson said, faster than I could blink.

"Cool!"

A second later, he was out of his seat and walking into the masses with Cody. Briggs smiled at me and shook his head before taking another bite out of his Philly-cheese steak.

"What?" I mouthed while kicking him under the table.

"Ouch…really, Ang? You had to kick me? We're not twelve anymore."

"Some of us still are, apparently."

He rolled his eyes and then lowering his voice. "He cares about you."

My stomach knotted at his words. I was afraid to acknowledge just how much I wanted them to be true. I looked around the table. Thankfully Pippy and Charlie were engaged in *baby talk,* and Peter had just stood up from the table to go join our troop in the battle against aliens.

"I care about him, too."

"I can see that." He shook his head again, putting his hamburger down on his plate. "You were right—what you said last night. Your story isn't finished yet. I never meant to imply that what you've been through wasn't redeemable. I just can't...I don't want to see you hurt."

"I know, Briggs."

"You're different though—Charlie and I have both noticed it."

"How so?"

He took a deep breath and put his elbows on the table. "It's like the difference between watching a game and playing in it. You've been sitting on the sidelines for years, watching everyone else have a turn...and now, it's like you've finally stepped out onto the field."

My brother wasn't the wise guru-type, but every once in a while he struck gold. I knew *exactly* what he was saying. Unexpectedly, my eyes filled with tears.

For two hours we played every game that the giant arcade had to offer—and then some. I watched as Jackson and Briggs hooted and hollered over Cody as he made his way through each new challenge. I was hoping Jackson had forgotten about his little air hockey bet, but of course, that was only wishful thinking.

"It's your turn." He hooked my arm in his and practically dragged me to the air hockey table.

"Jackson, I am totally capable of splurging every once and a while. I want to pay for tonight—honestly."

"And you can—if you win."

"You are insufferable."

"Thanks," he said, plunking the flat disk on top of the table. "You know how to play, right?"

I scrunched up my nose, scrutinizing him. "Of course I do."

He flashed a wicked grin, and I nearly had to brace myself against its affect on my knees.

In the first two rounds I saw the competitive nature that lurked not-so-far beneath the surface in one, Mr. Jackson Ross. I quickly learned that defense was my only strategy. Scoring proved very difficult, but blocking? I could block. By the fourth game, I was growing tired. My sad little bicep was screaming at me to surrender, but I would never do it—not over this particular wager.

"How's your arm doing, Flores?"

"Didn't your mother ever tell you that bullying isn't the way to win a lady's heart?"

He laughed as he pitched his paddle forward, scoring before I could react.

"The stakes have already been set, sweetheart. I'm not playing for your heart—I'm playing for your dinner."

"Ha—funny. Stop talking; you're breaking my concentration on purpose."

He laughed again.

Amazingly, I blocked his next two shots and scored one of my own! I twirled around in a circle, suddenly feeling very good about my concentration improvement.

Jackson laughed again. I scored again.

"Now *you* need to stop it," he said.

"Stop what?"

"If I don't get to bully you, you don't get to dance around."

I smiled, scoring another point.

"And the tides have turned," I said, belting out my best version of an evil-villain laugh.

Jackson was not amused. He crouched down as if he were playing in the air-hockey Olympics. I quickly lost all confidence, and it turned out that I had a reason to be scared. When Jackson was motivated, there was virtually nothing that could stop him. He won. Fair and square.

Because I had agreed to it…I wouldn't be a poor sport. In my opinion, there was nothing uglier than that. If I didn't allow Cody to throw tantrums over losing a soccer game, then I certainly couldn't allow myself to throw one either—no matter how much I wanted to pout.

"Well-played, Mr. Ross," I said, sticking out my hand to shake his as he laughed.

"You're a well-mannered loser, Miss Flores."

I put my hand on my hip. "You really need help in the compliment department, Jackson—regardless of what you believe about them. It's really quite sad."

I laughed as I met up with Cody at the ticket counter. Combined, he had enough to get a rubber snake and a book of temporary tattoos.

"Cool, huh, mom? I got all this for free."

"Yep, way cool." I neglected to mention all the money that was spent to play the games that got him the *free* stuff.

I scratched his head as we rounded up the troops to head out. Walking out to the curb, the summer air closed around us, sticky and hot. Peter and Pippy left together after hugging Cody goodbye and promising to stay in touch. A lump formed in my throat. Jackson was last.

As the cab pulled up, Jackson bent down to see eye to eye with my son.

Briggs pulled Charlie to the car, giving us a moment alone.

"You're a good kid, short stack."

"Thanks," Cody said, his mouth pinched in a half-smile.

"I don't want you to worry about your mom while you're away. I promise I'll watch out for her until you're together again, alright?"

Cody nodded, glancing at me and then back at Jackson.

"Just make sure she keeps her necklace on."

Jackson looked at me before responding. "The one with the angel wings?"

"Yep. It's her guardian angel. She needs to keep it on," Cody said.

My breath caught, the lump in my throat growing larger as I watched Jackson regard him.

"Okay, I will. I promise. Have a great time at soccer camp."

"Okay." Cody rushed Jackson, embracing him in a way that nearly pushed him off-balance. "Do you think you'll visit us sometime—in Texas? Maybe come to one of my games?"

Jackson swallowed. "You'll be my first stop if I do."

Cody smiled. "Bye, Jackson."

"Bye, kiddo."

I looked at Jackson as Cody climbed into the back seat. His usual unreadable expression was replaced by something new—yet unidentifiable.

"Walt will be there at six to take them to the airport."

"Okay."

He took a deep breath. "I'll see you in the morning. Goodnight, Angie."

He kissed my cheek before stepping into a cab of his own.

I realized what I'd seen in his eyes as we drove back to the T. Ross building. In just two week's time we'd be doing this again—only we'd be saying goodbye to each other.

Jackson's face had reflected the answer.

He didn't know what would happen after that.

And neither did I.

****

As Cody got dressed for bed, I noticed a picture on his iPad…something he'd drawn recently.

"What's this, Code?"

He glanced at me over this shoulder and shrugged when I picked up the device.

"It's just a picture mom."

My vision blurred immediately as I realized what I was looking at. I slumped onto his bed. It was not *just* a picture.

"Cody," I breathed.

He stood and came toward the bed. "It's a family."

I could clearly identify Cody and myself—he'd been drawing us for half a decade—but the man next to me?

Cody pointed to the far corner, ignoring the question in my head. "And that…that's my first dad."

The man in a prison-like box off to the side had an X over his face. My stomach churned.

"But this over here…" Cody tapped the man next to me now, along with the other two figures. "This is our New York Family. That's Jackson, and Pippy and Caleb."

I pulled him into a tight hug and thanked God for such a beautiful child.

****

It was just after midnight when I finally finished packing Cody's suitcase and carry-on bag. He'd long since been asleep. My nerves had taken on an entity of their own—threatening to consume me with worry over his time without me.

Taking yet another deep, calming breath, I dragged myself into my bedroom and picked up my phone to set an alarm for our early morning wake-up. I put my hand to my mouth as soon as the screen lit. A message was waiting for me.

An email from Jackson.

I couldn't fall asleep in good conscience knowing that I was still in your debt. Since I schooled you in air hockey—to which you so graciously accepted your fate as the loser—it's only fair that I pay you back in kind.

So Angela Flores…here are your "Five Nice Things":

1. **Before I met you, I would have argued that *humble* and *strong* could never be synonymous. I would have been wrong.**

2. **Kindness is part of your genetic code—of this I'm nearly certain.**

3. If the way you love your son was "standard issue" for parents everywhere, therapists around the world would be out of a job.

4. Your words never fail to match the goodness that's in your heart—you're gracious to a fault. (It's quite annoying actually.)

5. Every minute that I'm not with you, I feel as though I'm missing out on one of God's best kept secrets, one I've been privy to for reasons of which I am still unsure.

*Bonus (only because I hate playing by the rules): No matter if you're lying on the bathroom floor recovering from food-poisoning, or drop-dead tired from a weekend full of drama and chaos...you could trump any and all definitions of the word *beautiful*. Any. Time.

And of this one I AM certain.

Sleep tight.

J

Chapter Twenty-Nine

"I promise, Mom. I'll call as soon as we land."

I hugged him for the seventeenth time since walking outside to wait for Walt. "Okay. I'll miss you so much, buddy."

"I know. You keep saying that."

I laughed. "Well, that's because it's true. Give Rosie a big hug for me, okay? And don't forget to give her the gift I bought her. I wrapped it up in one of your t-shirts so it won't break."

"Got it."

Briggs put his arm around me. "We'll be fine, Ang."

"I know. Okay. You're right. It will be fine."

He laughed.

"Just you wait. You'll know what it's like soon enough," I said.

Charlie rubbed my back sweetly. "Yep, he will. And you can give him all the grief you want, okay?"

"Sounds good."

Walt pulled up a second later. Cody introduced him to his uncle and aunt as Briggs loaded their bags in the trunk.

"Well…this is it. I love ya, sis. Don't worry."

Briggs gave me a hug and climbed into the back seat. Charlie was next.

"Enjoy your time as a single lady. This is New York, Ang. Live a little."

"Ha! I don't even know what that means."

"Exactly," Charlie laughed as she pulled me in for a hug.

"Hey," I said, grabbing her arm to pull her back. "I'm really happy you're making me an Auntie."

Her eyes filled with tears. "Me too, Ang. I want to be a mom just like you, ya know. I told Briggs that last night."

I swallowed hard, fighting back tears of my own as she slid in next to Briggs.

"Okay, Code...one last hug," I said.

"Really, Mom?" Cody unbuckled his belt from the front seat and hopped up onto the curb—again.

"Really. Hey—you're not a teenager yet. You don't get to be sassy about hugging your mama."

He squeezed me tight. "I love you, Mom. I'll miss you, too."

I took a deep breath as I watched them pull away and wrapped my arms around myself. I couldn't imagine what more than a night without Cody would feel like. And in that instant I doubted why I had ever agreed to stay. *Why had I let them talk me into this?*

My phone buzzed with a text.

Jackson: How ya doing, champ?

Me: Currently? Not so great.

Jackson: Take a deep breath. He'll be fine. Repeat that. He. Will. Be. Fine.

Me: Thanks for your email last night. You're better at "five nice things" than I thought you'd be.

Jackson: I meant every word.

Before I could respond, another text came through from him.

Jackson: The PR department will be joining us this morning. I thought you'd want to know.

Me: Oh…okay?

Jackson: It'll be okay. I'll make sure of it.

Nerves swirled in my gut as I made my way up to the apartment. It was the first time in a month that Cody wasn't trailing beside me.

I can do this. Couldn't I?

I stepped into the shower, allowing my anxieties about whatever was to come in the next few hours wash away as the hot water poured over me.

****

I took my time getting ready, as if the extra minutes spent on my hair and makeup would bring me loads more confidence. I would pretend for now that it did. I slipped into a pair of black slacks and heels and buttoned up a silky, light-blue blouse. I also threw a change of casual clothing into a bag, unsure of all this day might hold.

I can do this.

I checked my phone on the way to the office, and sure enough Briggs had texted to say that they were fine, about to board, and that Cody was halfway through his second blueberry muffin.

I erased three possible text-replies back to him. All were way too neurotic sounding. I finally settled on: *Sounds good!*

It was just after eight-thirty when I arrived at Pinkerton. Though I always looked forward to seeing Jackson, I couldn't shake the dread that seemed to overpower me with each step I took. I tried to clear my mind while I rode the elevator up, reminding myself to be open—like Jackson had asked me to be.

Pippy trotted toward me in heels that looked like they needed their own license, and hugged me. "Good morning! I was just coming to look for you. You doing okay without Cody? I was going to stop and get you a coffee on my way, but Mr. Ross told me you'd probably already had some since you were up so early, right?"

I smiled and tried to process the stream of information, picking up on the fact that she was back to calling Jackson *Mr. Ross* since we were back at the office. The girl was classy—no doubt.

"Yes, thank you though, Pippy—for thinking of me."

"Of course. May I walk you to the boardroom?" Pippy glanced at me with a look of concern.

"Sure, thank you."

I was nervous; I hated I was so nervous.

Jackson said I'll be fine. I can trust him.

I do trust him.

I reminded myself of that fact over and over again.

I trusted the Jackson who had kissed me at his brother's lake house.

I trusted the Jackson who had played air-hockey with me at Cody's goodbye dinner.

I trusted Jackson who had emailed me "five nice things".

Pippy stopped at large double set of doors. "Mr. Ross said to send you in when you got here."

"Wait." I put my hand out to stop her from opening the doors.

Her eyebrows shot up.

"Do you know…what this meeting is about?"

Her eyes softened. "No, but I'm sure it's not anything that should worry you."

That assurance didn't exactly bring me comfort.

"Thank you, Pippy."

"Absolutely, sis." She whispered the last word and patted my shoulder before opening the door to let me in. Jackson and Dee went silent as they turned toward me. Six other faces stared at me—all sitting at a long, rectangular table—each I vaguely remembered seeing at a dinner a few weeks back.

Oh gosh, I'm gonna be sick.

"Good morning, Miss Flores."

"Good morning, Mrs. Bradford," I said, walking into the office as Pippy waved briefly and closed the door. Whatever this was, she hadn't been invited.

Jackson walked up to me, his hand touching my arm briefly before gesturing for me to sit down in the chair at the far end of the rectangular table. "Good morning."

Apparently this was Jackson-the-CEO—not Lake-Kissing-Jackson. I needed to get that straight. He was all professionalism here. Business-only.

I sat, the cushiness of the office chair barely registering. My heart was in my throat as I wrung my hands in my lap, the gaze of each man and woman creating enough heat to scorch my face.

"Can we get you anything before we begin? Coffee? Water?" Dee asked.

"No, thank you," I croaked.

Jackson leaned back in the leather armchair at the opposite end of the table, watching me like a pot about to boil. Whatever this was, he was just as unsure of how I was going to respond as I was. *Why?*

Just then the door opened, and a face I had seen only once before entered the room.

What was his name again?

"Good morning, Mr. Vargus," Dee said, smiling at him as he took his seat to the right of Jackson.

Stewart Vargus. That's right.

Jackson's posture stiffened as Stewart nodded at me, smiling. I remembered then, his kindness to me at the dinner party a month ago. He had introduced me to several people, keeping my company like a gentleman until Pippy had arrived. But when he'd asked me about setting up a meeting with him, Jackson had made it clear that no such thing would happen. *"You have no business with Stewart Vargus,"* he'd said. With all the other distractions, I hadn't asked Jackson to expound on his statement that night, but I was certainly very curious now.

Dee remained standing—a fact that did not go unnoticed by me. She asked each man to introduce himself. They did so, each taking roughly five seconds to greet me. I wished I could say the formality made me feel better, more comfortable even, after all, each of them were as human as I was. But it didn't.

Though Dee's face looked calm, she walked over to the window where I could almost see the wheels turning behind her eyes. She laced her fingers behind her back and took a deep breath.

"Though we regret what happened last Friday during your interview on The Eastman Morning Show, Miss Flores, it is time to do some damage-control. It is not only your future career that is in jeopardy, but the family tour that we've teamed you with, along with the integrity of our company it seems."

Everything in me felt compressed and tight. I was sickened by the fact that the exposure of my past would be the cause of hurt for anyone. Dee had taken a risk on me—believed in me though I had never dreamed of any of the opportunities she had given me. And then there were those who had graciously accepted me into their circle even though I was the latecomer on the tour. My heart squeezed tight thinking about my new friends. The Zimmermans, who had coauthored their book of marriage tips and Sue Bolan, who had poured her heart out to serve and train adoptive parents.

I always admired Dee's ability to speak eloquently. But although she was very professional in conduct and speech, she was never condescending. Instead, her voice held the unusual balance of compassion and authority. She turned toward the table fully, her tailored pantsuit hugging her curves as she moved. I felt Jackson's gaze on me more than the rest, but trained my eyes to focus on Dee alone.

"After several lengthy discussions, we'd like to propose a change to our current marketing pitch concerning your upcoming book release and the remainder of this tour. In light of recent events we feel there is an opportunity that has presented itself—maybe even a moral responsibility. Miss Flores, what we'd like you to consider, is adding to your current platform as a single mom. We feel there is a way to salvage your fans and followers who might have been led astray by wrongful accusations that you haven't been forthright. We'd like you to share your story of recovery and hope—by sharing about your past…openly. You would do this by making some substantial revisions and additions to your current blog, your future book, and also in your upcoming interviews."

Every hair on my neck rose as she turned to face me.

I blinked, the men around the table waiting for a response from me, but I couldn't find my voice.

Jackson leaned his elbows onto the table, his gaze intense as he stared at me from what felt like a continent away.

"Angie, do you understand what we're asking?" Jackson asked.

I focused on him as my heart pounded hard within my chest. "I...I understand, yes. I'm just not sure if I'm ready to—"

"Well, I think you'd better *get* yourself ready, young lady," said the man with the big nose directly to my right. "We have quite a large investment wrapped up in this family tour and because of your unwillingness to disclose certain pieces of vital information, that investment is now at risk."

"That's enough, Henry," Jackson barked, red-faced.

"Miss Flores and I had an understanding prior to her joining this tour that her privacy would stay protected," Dee said firmly." She is not the one to blame, Henry. Don't forget that."

"You knew she wasn't a widow?" He asked her.

Dee glanced away. "It's what I assumed."

I swallowed hard as Henry piped in again, "No, it's what she *led* us all to believe—and while I have compassion for her history, she should have been honest from the start!"

"Well, that is neither here nor there. What's done is done," said Ernie Smythe, an older man with stark black hair that I was almost certain wore a toupee. "The facts are that it's not just Divina's stunt that have caused an uproar. Though there are some that say publicity is publicity—no matter how ugly it is, we are not believers in that slogan. The online world has been making a mockery out us for not checking our facts...and out of you." He stared at me.

"What are they saying?" I asked, my voice straining for sound.

They all looked at me with surprise on their faces. "Have you not been online, Miss Flores? To your blog site?" The question came from Stewart.

I opened my mouth, but Jackson cut in before I could utter a word in reply.

"I advised her not to until we had a game plan in place—do you have a problem with that, Stew?"

Jackson's voice was a low growl. I held my breath at the tension that hung in the room. It was thick, uncomfortable and prickly all at the same time.

Stewart ignored Jackson and looked at me instead. "Divina's objective was obviously to discredit you and undermine whatever favor you'd found in the public eye. But we feel that once you speak out, we can steer that course in a new direction—one that will profit you, sustain the company, and allow the tour to pick up momentum again."

Every nerve in my body wavered, along with my mind, as I thought about what was being asked of me. The doors I had closed on my past, the lights I had switched on, the safety-net I had put in place…had it all been in vain? Or was this the path I was meant to take all along?

Whatever the case, Angie Flores had no more secrets to conceal.

Divina had been right: Fame didn't keep secrets.

No matter how much time I was given, there was no real choice being offered to me. I was smart enough to understand that fact. The decision of my *new platform* had already been made.

The minute I had signed that contract, I invited the opinions, advice and counsel of everyone in this room. It was no one's fault but my own that I hadn't fully thought through the ramifications of what that signature could mean.

I may have told my story a hundred times over in the past five years at *The Refuge*, but that environment was filled with those who shared my same past, history and hurt—at least to some degree. What kind of feedback would there be from the rest of the world? The ones who couldn't relate?

"We'll need an answer by the end of the day, Angie," Dee said. "One way or another, we need to address the statements made at that interview. You are in contract with Pinkerton Press, so that responsibility is ours as much as it is yours. We'll support you in whatever capacity we can. We have our most senior editor standing by to help you with any revisions and additions you are willing to make."

I nodded, though I was far from being okay.

Okay was a mindset I had never occupied for long.

For the next hour I sat silently while they discussed my next course of action as if the decision had already been made for me. I guess the truth was...it had. They knew it, just as I knew it. Jackson remained quiet, watching me the way a parent watched a child who was playing with a ball too close to the road.

The cross-talk around the table was mild now that Jackson and I were out of the flow of conversation. Dee had given Stewart control over the rest of the agenda as they discussed a new marketing plan.

The emotional turmoil over what had been asked of me had simply been dismissed—minimized, as if they had asked me to share my favorite cake recipe with the world, and not the intimate details of my life—and near murder.

As I sank further inside myself, trying to process the steps ahead, Jackson slapped his hands on the table. I started at the noise, and the room fell silent.

"Everyone out. We're done here!"

"Jackson—we have several other issues to discuss before—" Stewart began, lifting his hands in a diplomatic gesture.

"*Issues?* Do you even understand what we've just asked of Miss Flores? I'm ashamed that not one of you has even bothered to ask her *a single* personal question since this meeting began, much less how you might support her in it! If my father or Jacob were in this meeting today they would be embarrassed! Here you sit, talking about investment plans and shareholder trends and marketing campaigns when there is a woman at the end of this table who deserves more respect for what she has lived through than everyone in this room combined. So, no, I don't care about your issues. We're finished here today!"

My mouth hung open in shock as I stared at Jackson. Each man stood and left without so much as a sigh of disapproval over his outrage. Dee walked over to him and patted him on the shoulder while she flashed me a pride-filled smile. She strolled out the door last, closing it behind her.

And then it was just Jackson and me.

Chapter Thirty

My mind was working overtime trying to process what had just happened. I looked at Jackson who was standing now and leaning over the table, tension rolling off him with every heaved breath. Finally, he lifted his head, and our eyes locked for the first time since his outburst. My emotions battled each other as I saw the distress on his face. My chest pulled tight like an overextended rubber band.

I wanted to make this better, to fix it.

My heart pounded under his gaze. "Jackson, I'm sorry for-"

He put his hand up, cutting me off mid-sentence.

Dropping his head, he sighed heavily. "Why...*why* would you apologize, Angie?" His voice was soft, yet strained.

"I just—I guess I feel responsible in some way for-"

Before I could finish, he took three quick steps toward me and took my upper arms in his hands. He squeezed just hard enough for me to switch gears from my own thoughts and refocus on his intense stare.

"If there was one thing—just *one thing* I could help you see Angie, it would be your constant willingness to accept blame that isn't yours. You are *not* responsible for what went on here today. My anger is *for* you—not *because* of you, don't confuse those motivations." His eyes roamed my face. "When I asked you to come to the meeting with an open mind, this was not what I envisioned. Please believe that I would never try to manipulate you into telling your story…not for the sake of the tour, or even this company. But with that being said, I believe in you Angie."

In a sea filled with unknowns, a wave of relief crashed over me.

It was then I realized that Jackson wasn't in the sea.

Jackson was the wave.

Letting go of my every inhibition, I broke out of his grip and fell against his chest, hugging him tight. In that moment, there were no words to express what his support meant to me.

Seconds passed as he held me, his hand pressed to the back of my head. I could hear the steady beat of his heart as I breathed in that perfect scent of ocean and cedar wood.

I pulled away from him slightly, my eyes misting as his hands slid down my arms. He gripped my fingers and led me to a chair. Once I sat, he pulled another one over and sat across from me. Our knees bumped, creating a flurry of warmth in the base of my belly. My eyes focused on the window in the corner as I processed through the jumble of information in my head.

"The first time I told my story was about two years after the night Dirk was arrested. Even though I could rationalize that he couldn't physically hurt me anymore, my mind was still tied to him—controlled by fear. It took every ounce of energy I had just to survive and take care of Cody. But Maggie, my mentor at *The Refuge*, wouldn't give up on me. She just kept telling me that someday my story could help inspire hope for someone else—someone who needed to see a light beyond their darkness." I shifted my gaze to my hands. "One night...the fear subsided long enough for me to open my mouth."

"And what happened?"

I steered my eyes back to Jackson. "A woman found me after group that night. She told me...she told me that I'd given her the courage to confront her past. That she was going to put in the work so she could stop the cycle from continuing." Tears filled my eyes as I thought of that moment. "That woman is now my best friend—Rosie."

Jackson's smile was tender as he said, "There are a lot more Rosie's out there, Angie—I know I don't need to tell you that—but the statistics of abuse are alarming." He sighed. "Taking this platform could potentially reach tens of thousands of women. Your voice and influence could mean the difference for them, but I need to be sure it's what *you* want to do. This is *your* story to share. Nobody owns the rights to it but you."

I dropped my eyes again. "I do want to help other women, Jackson. I have no greater passion in life, but do you really think I'm ready for that kind of exposure? Telling my story is hard enough when it's told to women who can relate to it."

"But why would you limit its impact?"

"Because I *hate* my story." I pushed my chair back and stood up, suddenly needing to move as my voice broke with emotion.

That was the truth.

No matter how much work I did to change myself, my story would never change.

My past was the shadow no light could outshine.

He leaned forward, hands clasped in his lap as he watched me pace. "Have you ever seen an artist work on a blank canvas?"

I shook my head, fingering my necklace.

"There are hundreds of hours poured into a painting before it even starts to resemble the masterpiece it will become. Your portrait—just like your story—isn't complete yet, Ang. You're only seeing what's there now...not the whole vision of what could be."

I stopped in front of him. "I don't know if I have that vision, Jackson."

"Then I'll have it for you."

****

Cody called just after lunch.

The flight had gone well, and they were headed home to rest and get everything ready for camp. He was excited to play with Dillon, especially since he had a cool new iPad to show him. I was glad to hear his voice, even if it was only a few hours since I'd seen him last.

It was hot outside, but I needed to think—alone. Pippy had told me where the smoothie shop was just a few blocks down, so I walked there. Strawberry/banana blend in hand, I made my way to Central Park. I was incredibly grateful for my wardrobe change into shorts and a tank top. As I found the shade of a large tree, I sat down and crossed my legs underneath me.

I watched the busy world buzzing past as I pulled out my journal and pen. The scenes of dogs playing, kids running, businessmen and women rushing…were completely chaotic, yet oddly familiar. I may not know this city or its inhabitants, but what I saw before me…was life.

I took in a deep breath, warm air filling up my lungs.

Life.

That was what I had been given back.

****

"Sis?"

Briggs knocked on the wall before pulling back the privacy curtain. I wanted to answer verbally, but no sound came out. My throat was so dry, like the inside of it had been rubbed with sandpaper and dust. I coughed for a minute straight until I could swallow a drink of water. I'd been awake for a couple of hours, doctors and nurses running tests, and policemen asking me questions regarding the night of the attack.

Finally though, they had allowed my family to visit: Briggs.

When he stepped into my room I was surprised. He looked awful, like he hadn't slept in days—maybe he hadn't. I was sure I didn't look much better though. How good could one look when they'd been in a coma for seven days?

"You look good, Ang," he said, his smile not quite reaching his eyes as he walked to my bedside. He sat down on the edge.

I smiled at his lie.

"Where's Cody?" I whispered, trying to avoid another coughing fit.

"Cody's perfectly safe and healthy. My Chief's wife is watching him while I visit you. I wasn't sure if I should bring him up yet—I didn't know if you'd be..."

I nodded, knowing what he meant. Though I ached for my baby, I understood that Briggs was only trying to protect him; it's what he did best. The doctors weren't sure of the extent my injuries had on my brain before the coma was induced. There were no guarantees I'd wake up the same person as before. Briggs didn't want to expose Cody to that kind of trauma. He had seen enough already.

I grabbed his hand and my brother squeezed it, tears pooling in his eyes.

They were the first tears I'd seen him cry since he was a young boy.

"Thank you, Briggs," I whispered. "I know what you did for me…and for Cody."

"When I saw you on the ground—I've never felt anything like that before, Angie. I wanted to kill him. I don't know how I didn't do it, to be honest," he said with a shaky exhale. "But he's gone now, and you're safe. He's never coming back."

I nodded, the police had told me that, but they also told me what Briggs had done to save me.

"I'm so sorry, Briggs—for everything. For not listening to you all those years ago, for all the lies and the secrets, for the pain this last week must have caused you." Tears slipped from my eyes in a steady stream.

"The only reason you'd have to be sorry—is if you waste the life you've just been given back."

****

I tapped the journal with my pen.

I'd been staring at it for a while now, waiting for inspiration to jump out and pull me in like Mary Poppins and the sidewalk paintings. So far the page was still blank. There were so many questions swirling in my head: What do I share? How many details do I provide? Do I start at the beginning or work my way back? I laid my head on my hand at the same moment my phone rang.

It was Jackson.

"Hey."

"Hey, where are you?"

"The Park. Trying to write…something…anything."

He laughed. "Been there before. I'm about to leave here…I'd love to help."

"That would be nice. I, uh, I called your mom."

"She told me. And you're sure?"

"Yes. I'm still scared, but I know you're right. This is bigger than me now. If I stay silent and let Divina have her field day, I give away a huge opportunity to help the cause that's closest to my heart. That regret would be far worse than my fear of speaking out."

Several seconds ticked by. I opened my mouth to ask if he was still there when he spoke again. "You're amazing, Angie."

"I wouldn't have made this decision if it weren't for you."

"Okay, well, I'll have Walt come pick you up, and we can head back to my place. We can order out or something."

"Or I can just make us dinner like normal people."

"I'm afraid I'll get too spoiled if I let you start that."

I smiled. "Good, that can be my insurance policy then."

He laughed. "You play dirty, Miss Flores."

"Oh, there's still so much you have to learn, Mr. Ross."

He laughed again. "We'll be there in twenty, sweetheart."

The spasm that knotted my insides went wild.. If this difficult day could be saved...he had just managed to redeem it with that one word. *Sweetheart!*

****

After stopping at the store to grab ingredients for chicken enchiladas, we headed to Jackson's condo. Rosie had taught me her grandmother's recipe, and I'd admit, it was goooood. As the enchiladas baked, Jackson repeatedly asked when they were going to be ready.

"Geesh...you have about as much patience as my nine-year-old."

He smiled proudly. "I refuse to think of that as a negative."

"Suit yourself. They still have thirty-minutes to go."

He grumbled as I wiped my hands on a towel and walked out of the kitchen. Jackson had changed into cargo shorts and a navy t-shirt that stretched across his chest and back in a way that made me flush when I looked at him. He had almost caught me staring, but I was glad I had been at the stovetop. Cooking gave me something to do other than gawk at him.

"So, let's sit. Tell me what you have so far. Are you working on your forward—for both the blog and book?"

"Yes. I thought that would be a nice way to summarize, and then I can go into more specifics throughout. Your mom thought it could also be what I base my interview questions on next week."

He nodded, scrutinizing me.

"What?" I asked.

"You adapted to all this very quickly."

I shrugged. "A learned habit, I suppose. But since I have nothing on my page, I don't think I've exactly come to terms with outing myself quite yet."

He pulled his chair up close, slid my journal out from underneath my hand, and pushed it out of my reach.

"Uh, I might need that, Jackson. I thought you were going to help me write."

"I am."

"Okay?" I looked at him confused.

"Close your eyes."

"What?"

"Trust me, Angie. Close your eyes."

With one more look of uncertainty, I closed my eyes and sighed. It was unnerving to know that Jackson was watching me—my face felt hot under his gaze. I tried to relax.

"Tell me who you are."

"Jackson, I don't see how-"

"You don't take directions very well, do you? Why don't you stop thinking about why my method won't help and instead use that energy to answer my questions, okay?"

I smiled. "Fine."

"Who are you, Angie?"

I took a deep breath. "I'm...I'm a twenty-nine year old single mom."

"And?"

I stretched my neck from side-to-side, drawing the kinks out of tight muscles, but careful to keep my eyes closed so I wouldn't invite another lecture.

"I'm a loyal friend and a good sister."

"And?"

"I'm a fighter—a survivor."

"And?"

I exhaled, searching for something deeper. "I'm a believer in second chances, in redemption. I believe that hardships can be overcome and that strength is often built out of weakness."

I felt his touch on my hand. "And?"

"And though I can't change my past, my future is still unwritten. I'm a work in progress. I want the legacy I leave for Cody to be one of truth, not superficial perfectionism."

"Open your eyes," he said softly. "That's where you start."

I looked up at him, waiting for him to elaborate. But in true Jackson style, he did not. Instead, his challenging gaze held me captive, probing me to think deeper.

Swallowing the thick emotion in my throat, I answered, "My legacy?"

He nodded, and then an invisible blanket of warmth wrapped around my shoulders: Inspiration.

Chapter Thirty-One

My name is Angela Flores.

This was not my given name, nor was it my married name. Instead, it was a name I chose, one I hoped could symbolize the freedom I so desperately desired. I hoped a name change could restore every broken promise, every painful memory and every trace of the woman I once was.

And though there is much to be said for a name, my expectations could never be met by the filing of some simple paperwork. The name changed, but the woman I was did not change with it. She didn't know how many years of hard work, intensive therapy and consistent support it would take before transformation took root.

My story is not pretty. It is, in fact, far from pretty.

The sketches of my life that I hold dear are the ones that are filled with obvious joy, happiness and pleasure. Most of which are shared with my son. However, those sketches are only fragments of a much larger picture, a picture I've been afraid to show until now.

Though I can pinpoint the poor decisions I've made, the ones that led me straight into the mouth of the lion's den, I am no longer a prisoner of shame. My wrong does not negate the wrong done to me and does not excuse it. That was a sentence that took me years to say.

I want to be more than a survivor.

Survival was once my only goal. If I could live to take another breath, if I could keep my son safe from abuse, if I could hide under the radar...then I had met my goal. But I realize now, surviving is not living. Life is more than just a beating heart; that is only where life begins.

To overcome is to live beyond the fundamentals of survival. In my case, overcoming meant finding hope for something more—something outside of my shadow. I do not pretend to know all the answers, or to have walked the path of every victim of abuse, but I do understand what it sounds like to lose your voice.

To liberate those lost to silence is the legacy I want to leave behind.

I know I cannot do it alone. The statistics are far too daunting, but I can share my story. I am but one daughter, one sister, one mother...yet I am the voice of many. My story may not look exactly like yours, but the faces of oppression are all around us.

I am no longer a victim of domestic violence. I am no longer lost to the darkness of isolation, lies and hopelessness. And though the details of my past are grim, my future will not be marked by the same fate.

My name is Angela Flores, and I hope my story will be one that reminds you to fight, to live, and then to dream anew.

Progress is made one brush stroke at a time. May we never stop painting.

Angie

Jackson had spent the majority of the evening on the couch reading after we ate. I wrote and wrote...and then re-wrote. When he finally heard me lay down my pen, he sat up and reached out his hand. I worried my lip at him, unsure.

"Let me read it, Angie, come on," he said. "I'll even say *please.*"

I lay my hand on top of the journal, hesitant to release it to him. "It would be a lot easier if I didn't know you were a best-selling author."

"Well, then pretend you don't."

"A little too late for that," I said.

He beckoned me again with his hand, a glint of mischief in his eye. I'd seen that look on the paddleboat, right before he pulled me into the water. I decided that it would be best to give in now rather than have him kidnap my journal by force. I was way too ticklish to win that contest.

"Fine."

I handed the volume to him and then started to pace as the soft tick of the clock in his dining room reminded me to breathe. I glanced at him only once before the roll of nerves forced me to look away. Posting a blog was so different than writing for an instant critique. It wasn't the first time this evening that I wondered if I was crazy for taking on this task.

After several minutes had passed, Jackson put the journal down on his lap and held out his hand to me again. With a crooked finger he gestured me to come closer. I swallowed. *Is this how he was going to break it to me gently?* As I crept nearer, he took my hand and pulled me down next to him on the arm of his chair.

"This is perfect, Angie," he said, his voice thick.

I bit my lip again, hiding the smile that wanted to break loose.

"Really?"

"Yes…this needs to get sent to Sally, the editor, tonight. Don't change a word."

I turned the smile loose with, a feeling of accomplishment swelling in my chest. Jackson smiled back, but this time when we made eye contact one question surfaced to the forefront of my mind: How could he believe in me without hesitation, yet abandon his own talent so easily?

As I stared at him, my heart ached for the hope he'd given up, for the dreams he had deserted. And in that moment I knew with full clarity why he was so passionate about my future.

Because he had given up on his own.

There were so many should haves and could haves that hovered in the space between us, so many past regrets, hurts and losses—whether due to pride, circumstance or guilt. But in the end none of that mattered. The truth was: we were not so dissimilar.

Beyond the wealthy CEO who sat beside me now, was a young man who had dreamed of influencing the world and sharing a voice of his own. I wanted to know him.

"What about you, Jackson?" My voice was soft, but the passion that surged through my veins was strong.

If Jackson was allowed to want for my future, than I was allowed to want for his.

"We're not talking about me right now, Angie," he said, a shadow crossing over his features.

"But I want to."

He narrowed his eyes. "There's nothing to talk about."

"Why are you so willing to see in me what you won't see in yourself?"

I slipped off the arm of his chair and perched on the edge of the coffee table directly in front of him. We needed to have this conversation—sooner rather than later. Neither of us knew what later held.

"My course has already been set, Angie. This is my life now; my responsibility is to this company. I've accepted it. You should, too." His gaze was penetrating.

I picked up his hand, lacing my fingers through his. I needed him to see me, to hear me, to stop whatever pretense of denial he'd been living under for the last two years. His breathing changed as my pulse echoed loudly in my ears.

"I won't accept that statement. Your life is more than a responsibility—especially one that's formed from a guilty conscience." I took in an unsteady breath, pushing myself to continue. "I overheard you talking with Jacob in the library. I know he's not going to get better, Jackson." I leaned in to touch his face with my free hand as his eyes continued to burn into mine. "I know you're grieving over his decision to stop treatments, and I know you must be hurting...but giving up your dreams won't fix anything."

Jackson's body tensed at my words, his chest rising and falling at a faster rate than seconds before. His eyes were a fusion of torture and beauty. They called to me, squeezing my chest like a vise. His hands gripped my bare knees gently, anchoring me as he leaned in close. "I don't have any dreams, Angie. They expired the day Livie died, and they were buried six feet under the day that Jacob told me he was stopping treatments."

The air was pushed from my lungs as I let his words sink in. There was a part of me that still hoped it was all a misunderstanding, that I had overheard wrong. I wanted to reach for him as he slid his hand over his face, as if trying to clear his mind, but I kept my hands to myself, for the moment.

"Help me understand, Jackson," I whispered. "Does Jacob expect you to—"

"It doesn't matter what he expects me to do. What matters is what I *should* do, what I should have done a long time ago."

"But it didn't sound to me like he wanted you to give up your-"

"Well, it sounds to me like you already know everything." His eyes dared me to challenge him.

So I did. I knew he wanted to argue so that it would deflect from this conversation, but I wouldn't engage him in that. I wanted answers, not a battle.

"Hardly. A three-minute conversation outside the library door is not *everything*, Jackson." I reminded myself stay calm. "Tell me about Jacob."

"He's dying."

And with that, the tender-Jackson I had seen glimpses of was gone. His curt response stung, as did the truth behind his words. It took me more than a second to recover.

I did my best to keep the emotion I was feeling out of my voice, but I doubted my acting abilities were that good. "How long...how long does he have?"

He shrugged. "Could be as little as six months or as long as five years. No one knows for sure."

An icy shudder went through my core as I watched his face, and the lie of his indifference stared back at me. I knew the unnatural calm was a coping mechanism, but still, it broke me to see his resolution. He felt far more than he was letting on. I'd heard his voice when he spoke to his brother that day in the library.

"Do Peter and Pippy know?" I thought of my sweet friend who I'd come to love like a sister and pushed the threat of tears down again.

"Yes. They knew before I did—they made the decision together, as a family."

This stopped my heart mid-beat.

Oh, Jackson.

I closed my eyes, feeling the heaviness of his guilt. His opinion hadn't been heard...possibly because he hadn't been there to say it. The dots were connecting again. *Were those calls he hadn't taken from his brother, the ones he had ignored for months, about that?* I felt sick to my stomach. By the time Jackson had shown up at the company to take on his brother's position, Jacob had already decided. I wanted to be wrong, but deep down I knew I wasn't.

"Jackson-"

"Angie," his voice was soft, but his eyes were not. "I know you're only asking because you care about him and the twins, but rehashing his decision isn't going to change anything for me."

"That's not the only reason I'm asking, Jackson. I *do* care about them, but I care about you even more."

The truth slipped out without thought. His eyes grew wide at my admission. It was the closest I'd come to saying it all—baring my heart completely, my heart that now beat wildly against my chest. It surprised me again how strong my feelings were for him. And I knew in that moment that they weren't going to lessen with time, in fact, the force that pulled at my desire for him only confirmed the laws of gravity.

He pulled me into his lap, and the next instant my hands were in his hair, my hip twisting against him. He kissed me hungrily as if afraid I'd disappear. I was aware of his hands on my back as I pressed into his chest, equally aware of the heat that built between us with each passing second. I wasn't sure who would have more self-control—but I hoped it was him. No part of me wanted this to stop.

I craved his kisses more than I craved my next breath.

My lips felt swollen and hot when Jackson pulled back, his hair a disheveled mess between my fingers.

"Angie—I need to take you home, sweetheart."

I nodded, my breathing heavy and ragged.

With a groan, he gripped my hips and pushed me back onto the coffee table opposite him. He leaned forward, resting his elbows on his knees as he scrubbed his hands over his face again and again. Heat radiated off my body as my gaze remained focused on his lips. He caught my eye and gave a short, breathy laugh in response. My face exploded into flame.

"You can't look at me like that, Ang. Not when I'm trying my best to be a gentleman."

I bit my lip. "Sorry."

He nudged my leg with his playfully. "Thanks by the way."

"For what?" I asked, my scalp tingling under his gaze.

"Caring."

If he hadn't stood up to grab his car keys, I would have kissed him again.

Chapter Thirty-Two

The following morning, my book forward was posted on several online sites, including the front page of Pinkerton Press and my blog, along with a new profile picture. The response was overwhelming. Emails filled my inbox, so much so that Pippy had to manage them for me so I could write.

And write I did.

For the next three days, I did nothing but eat, sleep and write. I was holed up with the Senior Editor, Sally Miller. My days started before eight and ended sometime after the midnight hour. We outlined the inserts and additions that would need to be added to my book. The work was exhausting, but strangely gratifying. Seeing the pages of my blog in book format, each entry with its own chapter heading, caught me by surprise.

On those pages, the stories that made up my life were written.

That thought was absolutely surreal.

The only breaks I had were when Jackson brought me food or when I called Cody—twice a day. His voice made my heart ache to be with him, yet his happiness was obvious. He said he missed me, but I knew he was not counting down the hours, nor did I want him to be. He was having fun at soccer camp and visiting with Briggs and Charlie.

At the end of the three days, I talked to Rosie during the car ride back to my building and then I slipped into my covers just after 2:30 a.m.—barely coherent. She had helped with Cody's pick-up earlier that day since his soccer schedule was tricky to orchestrate with Briggs and Charlie. She'd asked about the latest with Jackson—as if she had some sixth-sense that more had happened between us, but I didn't have the energy for that conversation. Instead, I yawned, and promised her a rain check convo. She, of course, was not satisfied with that answer, but when I fell asleep with the phone still to my ear, I could only hope she understood.

I don't even remember hanging up.

BAM.

BAM.

BAM.

I sat straight up in bed, confused at the sound that seemed to echo through my dark room. I rubbed my eyes and threw the covers off, straightening my tank top and sleep shorts as I walked to the front door. The strong, pounding rattled the chain at the top of the panel.

As my fingers unlocked the last of the bolts, a cold chill ran the length of my body. In my delirious state, I hadn't looked out the peephole. I hesitated as my hand hovered over the doorknob, but it was too late.

The door flew open.

I opened my mouth to scream as his face registered a second too late. His hands were around my throat before any sound could escape my throat. He pressed his thumbs into my trachea. Black spots blinded my vision in a way that was much too familiar.

"You should have kept you mouth shut, you lying wench. Nothing happened to you that you didn't deserve. You're the one who thought you could keep him a secret from me—hide him from me— but that just shows how stupid you are. How stupid you've always been. No one believes you, Angie. You're pathetic." He dug his nails into my skin. "It's your fear that gives you away every time. It's how I found you—it's how I'll always find you."

I pushed at him, twisting under the pressure and pain trapped inside me. Tears squeezed from my eyes as his hands tightened around my neck. My body sagged limply as his strength overtook me.

This was it.

He was killing me—again.

Bam.

Bam.

Bam.

I jumped up, my body shaking so violently I feared my bones might crack as I gasped for breath. I touched my face, wet with tears. Then I heard the sound again.

It was a dream—just a dream.

Yet somehow, it was more than that. I walked dizzily to the front door, hesitant to even look out the peephole. I pressed my palm against it, trying to take in a full breath.

Dirk's in prison. I reminded myself. *He can't be here.*

I peered out—fear still clinging to me like a wet, sticky substance.

I took in a shaky breath in recognition of the face that stood on the other side of the door.

I undid each lock with hands that trembled so hard they missed the chain latch—twice. The knob turned and opened, and a very agitated Jackson stepped inside an instant later. I crossed my arms over my chest, not realizing until that very second that I was still in my camisole and sleep shorts.

"Angie, I've been calling you for over two hours,"—he started gruffly, but stopped mid-sentence. "What's wrong?"

His eyes scanned my face, concern etched onto his every feature.

As his arms reached for me, I took a step back, trying to get my bearings through my sleepy delirium. The image and feeling of Dirk's choking hands around my throat blurred the lines between reality and fiction. Jackson's gaze sharpened as I retreated, but his voice calmed considerably as if he was trying to talk someone down off a ledge.

"Angie, why are you shaking like that sweetheart? Talk to me— *please.*"

I nodded, blinking several times as if to convinced myself it was really Jackson that stood before me now and no one else.

"I...I had a nightmare," I whispered. "It was...so real." I shuddered again..

His arms encircled me, holding me tight for several minutes. Neither of us spoke a word. Finally, he moved me over to the couch then grabbed a thin blanket off my bed and wrapped it around my shoulders as he pulled me close. I covered my face with my hands as I rested against his chest. I breathed deep as the details again invaded my mind like images of a horror movie—one that was much too close for comfort.

"Can you tell me about it?" Jackson asked softly.

I calmed myself, as his hand rubbed my arm in gentle repetition. "Dirk was here—at my apartment. I heard knocking and opened the door without checking to see who was there. He choked me, before I could even scream or cry out. And then he..." I shook my head as another shudder went through me.

"He what?" Jackson said, anger lacing his tone.

"He said I should have kept my mouth shut—that I'm just a weak, pathetic liar that no one will ever believe."

Jackson's arms tightened around me as he kissed the top of my head. "Sweetheart, he's the one who is pathetic, not you." He kissed my head again and smoothed out my hair as it hung loosely down my back and around my face. "He can't hurt you anymore."

If only that were true.

He still lived inside me somewhere—within every fear I owned.

"Do you have these nightmares often?"

I shook my head. "I used to have them almost every night— but they've only just come back recently."

"You've been working too hard, Angie. What time did you get in last night?"

I bit my lip, not wanting to answer him. Jackson had left around ten, only after I assured him that I would be leaving as soon as I finished up my last couple of paragraphs. Sally had gone home hours earlier, yet somehow in the quiet solitude, I'd found my second wind. Jackson had already stayed hours later that normal, waiting around for me, but I knew he was tired. He had kept the same hours I had all week, attending more meetings than I could even keep fathom.

"What time, Angie?"

"Around two."

He exhaled hard. "No wonder you didn't answer your phone! You were still asleep."

I sat up straighter and looked at him—suddenly conscience that I hadn't yet brushed my teeth, a stale taste on my tongue. "Is today Saturday? What time is it?"

His mouth curled on one side, though I knew he wasn't exactly amused. "It's almost noon. You were supposed to meet me at my place at nine—for breakfast, remember? When you didn't answer my calls I assumed you were just running behind, but then…"

My heart flooded with warmth at his unspoken words.

"You were worried about me?"

He lifted my tangled bed-head hair, and let his fingers run through the strands gently, making my belly swim with sensations that felt brand new to me.

"Yes, Angie. I was worried about you."

I swallowed hard, hearing the emotion in each syllable that Jackson so rarely shared. A giddy pleasure built inside me as I watched him. I pursed my lips together, trying to keep the smile off my face— but resistance was impossible.

"That's funny—my distress is funny to you?" he asked, his voice laced now with mischief.

Uh-oh.

"No Jackson—don't, *please*!" I shrieked, scrambling to get off the couch as he pulled me back toward him, poking at my ribs and tickling me so fast my head spun.

He laughed as I squirmed. Unfortunately, he had a hold of my foot before I could re-direct him. He laughed even harder as my hysterical giggles started in. I was helpless when it came to tickling. Cody had learned this long ago.

"Say it, Angie."

"Mercy! Mercy!" I cried out between breaths.

"And?" He baited, trapping my left foot in his hand, half my body on the couch, the other half on the floor.

"I'm sorry—I shouldn't have stayed...that long when I told you I was leaving."

He dropped my foot.

"Okay, and that, sweetheart is an apology I'll accept."

I stood up and punched him in the arm then escaped quickly toward my bedroom.

"I'm taking a shower," I called over my shoulder. "Do not come in."

He kicked back against the couch and put his feet up on the coffee table. "Wouldn't dream of it."

As I closed the door I thought I heard, "Or maybe I will."

****

When I walked out into the living room, fully dressed, Jackson was watching TV—a basketball game. He smiled at me, his eyes sparking to life. My stomach clenched. Being with Jackson in such close quarters was going to be the death of me.

"I have a surprise for you tonight," he said coolly, hands behind his head as he slouched on the couch.

My eyebrows shot up. "Really? What is it?"

"Did you not hear the *surprise* part of that sentence?" He laughed.

I mock-kicked him, only he caught my leg, knocking me off balance. His arms braced me as I fell into his lap in one swift movement—almost as if he'd planned it. I laughed as he grinned like the Cheshire cat.

"I hate surprises, Jackson," I said, warning him.

"You'll like this one." He stared at my lips and the floor of my stomach bottomed-out.

I pushed myself up to a sitting position, ignoring his protest when I scooted off his lap. "You seem pretty confident about that."

"I am." He winked. "Quite."

I studied him, trying to guess what he had in store. Knowing Jackson though, the possibilities were limitless.

"Should we make a wager?" he asked. "If there is even the tiniest hesitation that you might not love it—I'll gladly succumb to any fate you choose for me."

I bit my lip, toying with my necklace. "Fine, but I'm warning you—I'm the girl who reads the endings of books after the first chapter. I don't like surprises."

He gaped, but swatted my hand away as I reached up to close his mouth, "That should be a crime. You're the worst kind of book reader there is—spoiler!"

"It's not a spoiler…I just want to make sure everyone ends up happy! Then I'll enjoy the journey so much more."

"That's messed up," he said, shaking his head.

I laughed. "Hey, I've never claimed otherwise."

He silenced me then with his lips on mine, and suddenly my concerns of a surprise evening were no more. Jackson didn't need a wager—his kiss was enough.

****

After lazing around all afternoon, telling story after story about our childhoods and family life growing up, Jackson stood up abruptly at 4:00.

"What are you doing?" I asked, shocked as his hand was on the knob before I could even stand.

"I need to get ready for our surprise date tonight," he said, smiling.

"Oh, so it's a date?"

He lowered his brows as if questioning my sanity. "Of course it's a date—what did you think it was going to be—a new type of green smoothie combination? No wonder you hate surprises."

I laughed hard as he watched me, grinning in amusement. He walked over to me then and pulled me into an embrace that made me instantly weak. "There's just one requirement."

I eyed him suspiciously. "What?"

"You have to wear your gold dress."

I shook my head and laughed. "I just wore it to Broadway two weeks ago, Jackson."

His facial hair scratched across my face lightly as his lips found my ear. "Sweetheart, you could wear that dress every day, and I'd never complain."

He pulled away before I could respond and opened the door, "I hired my on-call driver, Russell, to pick you up in an hour and a half. I'll be waiting for you."

I opened my mouth, but like usual, Jackson made it impossible to refute. He always had the last word because there was usually nothing left to be said after it.

Chapter Thirty-Three

On the way to my mystery date, I called Cody to check in. He had played his first scrimmage and was full of stories—all of which made me laugh. Apparently, Charlie got sick during the game and had thrown up in the bushes, but as Cody put it, "I told everyone it was not gross—she is just pregnant." I smiled at his sensitivity as a twinge of remembrance ran along my lower abdomen.

"I love you, buddy, and I miss you to infinity."

"I miss you to infinity, too, Mom," he said. "Are you with Mr. Ross right now?"

"No, why?" I asked, surprised.

He paused for a second.

"Cody? Why did you ask that?"

"You just sound really happy…like you are when you're with him," he said, his voice slightly hesitant.

"Well…I'm actually going out on a date with him in a little while…how do you feel about that?" I asked, unsure if telling him now was the right thing to do or not.

"I like him, Mom. He's cool," he said, cheerfully. "Uncle Briggs and I talked about him last night."

My heart rate suddenly increased as I thought about what their conversation must have entailed. Surely Briggs would not have shared more than I would have agreed to, he wasn't that stupid. "What did you talk about, exactly?"

"Well—I don't want you to get mad," he said.

"Cody, I'm not going to get mad. You can tell me anything. You know that."

He sighed. "I asked him about my dad—my dad that hurt you."

I closed my eyes, taking a deep breath before I could respond. "Okay. What were you curious about, bud?"

"I just—I wanted to know if he was the reason you haven't married anyone else."

"Oh, buddy, we've talked about this before. You are my first priority."

"Yeah, but mom?"

"Yes?" My heart was in my throat as I croaked out my reply.

"It's just...I really liked my New York family," he said matter-of-factly. "I miss them."

I sighed.

"I told Uncle B that maybe you could marry Mr. Ross and maybe he could be my new dad—like the real kind of dad?"

I held my necklace pendant and fought back tears. "I don't know what the future holds, buddy, but you are a very loved young man whether our family grows or not."

"I know, Mom. Um—Uncle Briggs has dinner ready. I love you."

"Okay—Cody?"

"Yeah?"

"I love you more."

As I hung up the phone and slipped it into the clutch purse that Pippy had picked out to match this very dress, the town car rolled to a stop. Instantly, I was filled with a nervous energy as I looked out the window at my surroundings.

The Manhattan Harbor.

My door opened, and as I stepped out, careful to hold my dress up, I saw him. Jackson smiled regally, waiting at the edge of a long dock wearing khaki dress pants and a light blue polo.

"Here you are, Miss," Russell said, as he closed my door behind me.

"Thank you." My breath caught at the sight just beyond where Jackson stood.

No...way. Was he serious?

Jackson must have figured out my shock was completely immobilizing as a second later he was at my side, smile undeterred.

"You surprised?" Jackson asked arrogantly.

I nodded, speechless.

"And you're not unhappy?"

I shook my head.

He laughed.

"Great, now that we have that settled, let's board."

I turned to him, my eyes growing wide with awe, "We're—we're going on that boat?"

He chuckled. "Yes, though technically it's called a yacht. The captain is fairly particular about that fact."

My mouth gaped as Jackson dragged me forward toward the dock. "I can't believe this is your idea of a date night."

"Believe it, sweetheart," he whispered against my hair as tiny prickles ran up my spine and neck. "That dress deserves its own yacht."

I laughed then, stepping onto the beautiful plank floor of *The Cecilia*. The captain and three young men dressed in white coats—two with chef hats stood steps away from where we entered the yacht.

"Good evening, Miss Flores," the older man in the captain's hat said as he kissed the back of my hand. "I'm Captain John

Cogswell—but people know me as Captain Cogs around here. I hope you enjoy your evening tonight. We will be taking a romantic tour around the harbor, and I'm sure Jackson will point out all the essential highlights as you eat our spectacular four-course meal prepared by Ivan here."

I noted the casual way in which Captain Cogs referred to Jackson, deciding that they must know each other quite well outside of this date night. Ivan introduced his two staff members and then left immediately to return to their preparations in the galley. I was still in shock as Captain Cogs smiled and pointed out the various amenities on the 75-foot-vessel.

Jackson led me to the small table inside the saloon, surrounded by gigantic windows that seemed to span from floor-to-ceiling. It was still fairly warm outside, so I guessed that he wanted to eat in the air-conditioning. I didn't blame him for that. It would be much more enjoyable than sweating in this silk dress.

Jackson pulled out my chair as I took in the beautiful décor around me.

I glanced up at him as I settled onto the offered chair. "I am still in such shock Jackson—this is absolutely incredible."

"Cogs was a good friend of my dad's. He was happy to oblige my request—especially since it involved a gorgeous young woman."

"Jackson—that might be a new record for you. Two compliments in less than twenty minutes," I teased.

"I told you, I only speak the truth," Jackson said.

My face warmed as I unfolded the napkin and placed it on my lap. The waiter bustled in with the wine and a plate of shrimp appetizers.

"Before I wine and dine you, I wanted to tell you something."

"What is it ?"

He slid his hand on top of mine. "I had a friend of mine do some checking for me...on your ex. He's still in prison, Ang. No chance of parole for him anytime soon. You're safe. I hope that can put your mind somewhat at ease so you can sleep without the nightmares."

My eyes filled with tears. "Thank you." *You're amazing.*

He said grace and then we dug in. For the next two hours, we ate course after course of the most delicious food I'd ever had in my life. Our dessert was banana foster, and it was to die for. After two glasses of wine my head got a tad fuzzy, and decided I was probably more of a lightweight than I thought. It'd been years since I'd had any alcohol.

Jackson asked a lot of questions about Cody: What was his first word? What had he been like as a toddler? What kind of student was he? With every question my heart became more and more tethered to the man who sat across from me.

Jackson had never talked so much in one setting, it was refreshing. No, it was wonderful.

"So tell me, Miss Angela Flores," he said, pushing his dessert plate aside and leaning onto his elbows. "How might a man such as myself convince you to dance with him?"

I pursed my lips, mirroring his posture as I leaned onto the tabletop , even though the action was against the manners I had worked so hard to teach my son.

"I think he should simply start by asking."

"Hmm...you're big on the asking thing," he said, brow furrowing slightly.

"Yes, it is such a strange request."

He rolled his eyes. "Dance with me?"

I smiled, knowing for Jackson that was probably the best *ask* he could produce and still be himself. I touched my necklace, making him wait a good five seconds for my answer.

"I would love to, Mr. Ross."

"Good answer." He smirked. "Another few seconds and I would have resorted to tickling."

I shot him a dirty look as he grabbed my hand and led me to the aft deck. The sky had darkened considerably, but the lights from the city were breathtaking. From where we were now, the Statue of

Liberty was visible and completely illuminated. But even more beautiful were the stars that had appeared sometime while we were eating.

The night was beyond perfection.

On evenings like this one could not dispute the existence of God.

Jackson tugged my arm as a hard gust of wind blew my hair off my face and shoulders. I regretted not pulling it back—but I also had never expected to be in the middle of the harbor on a yacht either. Not all things could be planned for I guessed.

I laughed as a sweet acoustic melody began to play through the speakers that surrounded the deck. He slid his arm around my back and I scooped my hair to lay over my left shoulder, trying to avoid it whipping either one of us in the face with the constant breeze. Jackson's planted a kiss on the right side of my neck, and my knees weakened beneath me.

"I love it when you wear your hair like this," Jackson said quietly, his cheek pressed to mine.

And just like that—a few hair whippings suddenly seemed so worthwhile.

He held me as we danced under the stars, song after song playing in the background of the most perfect night I had ever experienced. We'd spent hours talking today, but the silence we shared now felt like an even deeper connection.

I let my mind wander back to Cody's words from earlier.

"...I told Uncle B that maybe you could marry Mr. Ross and maybe he could be my new dad—like the real kind of dad."

The truth was: I wanted Cody to have a dad too, but until recently, I didn't have a shred of hope for that. This was a scary path for my mind to travel down, and an even scarier one for my heart. But my feelings for Jackson had intensified since my internal revelation at the lake house last weekend. They had staked a claim, woven their plans into my soul, and had utterly paralyzed me with their power. Yet tonight, another truth gripped me as I swayed to the music.

I was no longer the woman I was six weeks ago, nor was I the same mother, friend, or sister. Love had thawed every frozen emotion. It had exposed every unfounded insecurity, and freed every imprisoned truth.

Love was the strength to my every weakness.

Falling in love with Jackson had changed everything I used to be. And it had allowed me to dream—again.

"What are you thinking about?" he asked, holding my body against his as a cool breeze blew against my back and bare shoulders.

I smiled and shook my head. "You first."

I thought he would refuse my deflection, but as usual, he surprised me.

"I was thinking that I don't want you to leave next week."

My chest ached. I didn't want to leave.

"I know."

"It feels like you just got here—hard to believe that was five weeks ago."

"I know."

He was quiet for a minute more, and then pulled away slightly to search my eyes. "There are so many things I wish I could promise you, Angie," he said, his eyes reflecting the beautiful torment I could sketch in my sleep. "So many things I want for you—and for Cody, but I won't make promises I can't be sure I can keep." He kissed my lips softly, closing his eyes before he continued, "But I-"

"Ahem...Mr. Ross?"

You have got to be kidding me.

We both turned to look the second staff member Ivan had introduced us to, now turning all shades of red as he realized his social faux pas. He looked at the ground as he spoke to us.

"The Captain wanted to me tell you we're in route to be back to port in thirty minutes, and the fire place has been lit in the saloon for your enjoyment."

I felt Jackson's body relax as he nodded his head once. "Thank you."

The young man nodded in response and disappeared.

"So much for perfect timing, eh?" he said.

I laughed, hoping we would finish this conversation inside.

Jackson tugged on my hand to take me in, but first I asked to look over the railing. He smiled in agreement. I leaned over and stared into the dark water below as the wind whipped my face and hair. The moment was powerful. I closed my eyes, committing it to memory.

Jackson leaned on the rail next to me. I could feel the heat of his body before he spoke.

"I never expected this."

I knew exactly what he meant; I hadn't either.

Yet, it was one surprise I wouldn't trade for anything.

Chapter Thirty-Four

Unfortunately, once we got back inside to the saloon to enjoy the remainder of the evening, fate had other plans for us. As I turned toward Jackson on the couch, hoping to continue our conversation from the deck, his eyebrows furrowed slightly as he looked at me.

"What's wrong?" I asked.

"Didn't you have your necklace on tonight—the one with the angel wings?"

My hand went to my neck only to discover that it was bare. Panic fueled every cell in my body as I stood, hoping that a spotlight from heaven would illuminate the frail chain and pendant. No such thing happened.

"It's okay—let's just retrace our steps," Jackson said, taking charge in my frantic state.

I nodded, my hand still at my throat.

But *somewhere* never revealed itself.

As we searched the Aft Deck, I was suddenly struck with a sinking feeling, one that twisted and gnawed at my insides as I remembered.

The wind.

I had leaned into the wind over the railing to look into the dark waters below. *Had it slipped off my neck?* The ocean was the only place we couldn't check.

Though I would have liked to believe that the strength it took to overcome years of physical abuse would keep me from breaking down over some small trinket tonight…it did not.

Losing that pendant was as if a part of me had been severed from my body.

There was no way to describe the kind of value that necklace had held for me, or the hope it had provided over the last eleven years. It was the last gift I'd ever receive from my Granny; the last connection to her unwavering faith. So many times I'd been empowered by its steady presence. Because of it, so many conversations had begun with Cody about the importance of believing in what is unseen, and so many tears and prayers had been absorbed within its delicate design.

In a blink the treasure was gone.

After a full hour of combing the yacht with the help of Captain Cogs and his staff, I had to no other choice but to accept my dreaded theory. Jackson shook the crewmember's hands as we left, and I did my absolute best to hold it together until we got into Jackson's car that he had parked at the marina. The second I sat down in the passenger seat an explosion of grief burst from inside my chest. If only my embarrassment of such a display was more powerful than my feelings of sadness and loss in that moment, but that was not the case.

Though the engine was running, Jackson didn't move, except to pull my head onto his shoulder as I cried. He was quiet as he rubbed my arm softly.

"I'm...sorry," I said between sniffles, "This...is a horrible way...for me to be...after such a great night."

He laughed lightly and brushed his hand over my hair, moving strands away from my face. I was sure I looked like a hot mess of mascara and snot. Again though, my care-factor seemed to be as lost as my necklace for the moment. I took a few deep breaths, calming myself as Jackson finally put the car into reverse and exited the marina. We rode quietly, each lost in our own thoughts. My eyes that felt swollen from crying. Just when I thought I might have pushed him away due to my female inclinations, he said the one thing that could justify my emotional response to such a loss.

"You've had that necklace for a long time, haven't you?"

I smiled weakly. "It had belonged to my Granny—I think I told you about her before?"

He nodded. "Yeah, she collected the angels, right?"

I swallowed the thickness in my throat. "Right. I got the necklace in the mail randomly—about six months after she passed. It'd been given to her on her wedding day by my grandpa whom I never met. She said it was her guardian angel, and that is what she always called him. I've worn it every day since I was eighteen." Several rogue tears escaped down my cheeks. "My necklace and my black journal were all I had from my old life in Colorado. Cody's never seen me without it on."

"He was pretty sure it was your guardian angel, too. I remember him saying that."

I nodded.

Jackson left his car with the valet and walked me up to my door, despite my insistence that the courtesy wasn't necessary. Naturally, he ignored my protest. I took my key out as he placed his hand on top of mine, stopping me from inserting it.

"If there was any way for me to get the necklace back for you—I would."

I turned to him, tears filling my eyes again. "Thank you, Jackson. I know you would. Despite this necklace drama, the night really was perfect. I loved everything you planned." I put my hands on his chest as I looked up at him. "I'll never forget it."

He touched my cheek. "I won't either. Goodnight, Angie."

"Goodnight."

He kissed me on top of my head before I walked inside and shut the door behind me.

Lost

How can one measure the value of invaluable?

How does one quantify the price of priceless?

Worth does not coincide with a cost,

Importance can't be found on a scale.

True treasure may be absent of wealth,

For a fortune is known only by the heart.

I was up early Sunday morning—due in part to my unusual sleeping habits of late. It was too early to chat with Cody, and I was sure my brother wouldn't appreciate his cell ringing at this hour, especially on his weekend off. Instead, I trudged my way to the restroom.

After showering, I decided it was best to avoid the mirror, as my bloodshot eyes were evidence that my necklace was indeed gone. The loss wasn't just an awful dream like I had hoped. Sigh.

Pippy texted last night to remind me of the lunch date at 1:00 this afternoon with the authors on the family tour. It was going to be my first time seeing them since the drama with Divina. Though there was only a week left of signings and interviews, I couldn't help but feel like I had been ostracized from the pack. Jackson had assured me that working on the revisions of my book were my top priority now, but I wondered if they saw it the same way.

I guess I'd find out soon enough.

I decided to take advantage of my unplanned downtime and read Book Two in The Quinton Chronicles. After reading the prologue, I had unknowingly traded my humble setting for a life of criminal investigations. I was completely absorbed. I held my breath numerous times, gasped out loud, and shed more than one tear as the dynamic between Detective Quinton and Reagan had begun to change. He was finally beginning to trust her instincts as she proved herself to him more and more. I bit my lip as I got to the climax of the story; my heart was racing.

Reagan had just walked to her car after leaving the precinct for the night, not knowing that the brother of the drug lord who had recently been murdered, would be waiting for her. I was a ball of nerves as I drew my legs up underneath me.

She pulled the door open and slumped hard into the driver's seat as she rolled her neck from side to side. The long day had stretched into an even longer night, but the grueling hours had been well worth it. A small smile tugged at her lips as she put the key into the ignition. Quinton had finally acknowledged her efforts— finally given her the pat on the back she had been waiting for since their partnership began six months ago.

She turned the key, but nothing happened. She tried again, furrowing her brows in frustration as a light clicking sound was the only indication she had done anything at all. Reagan had just upgraded her car, trading in her old model for newer one, for precisely this reason. She hated falling prey to a world of mechanical issues—one she knew nothing about—so instead, she was meticulous about the demands of proper car maintenance. Always.

What's going on? But the answer found her before her mind had time to fully process her question.

Her seatbelt tightened on her chest, digging in to the side of her neck as a rough hand covered her mouth. She bucked her head forward, trying to loosen the suffocating grasp, but to no avail. She pawed at her door, frantic to find a way to escape. Her attempt was only met with a harder pull as the belt strangled her against her seat.

"Stop squirming, Princess. I have no problem letting you die right here." The dark voice behind her said.

She closed her eyes, trying to calm herself as the raw panic of adrenaline surged through her body. Finally, the belt slacked enough for her to breathe through his thick fingers.

"There you go. Now listen carefully-"

The phone next to me shrilled, and I almost jumped off the couch. I fumbled with the answer button, dropping the cell twice before succeeding in answering.

"Hello?" I said, my voice a higher than-pitch than normal.

"Hey…you okay?" Jackson asked.

I blew out a deep breath. "No I'm not okay…I'm about to have an anxiety attack while reading your book!"

He chuckled. "What part?"

"Oh, uh, well, let's see…the part where you let Reagan walk into a death trap in her car. Jackson, you better have Quinton come out and save her, or I swear I will throw this book at your head the next time I see you."

He laughed harder.

"I'm serious, Jackson."

"I know…that's what's so funny."

"This is why I don't read this genre…I cannot handle the suspense. I hate it."

"Oh, so you just want to read the kissing scenes then? Is that what you're saying?"

I flushed instantly, biting my lip as a smile spread over my face.

"No," I lied.

"Well, I would gladly reenact some of those with you, but I actually need to head out of town for the day—possibly overnight."

"Oh?" I said, trying to keep my disappointment off his radar. *Too late.*

"Yeah. Something's come up that I need to deal with—work related."

Code for: I'm not going to tell you.

"Oh…I hope everything's okay? It not…Jacob, right? You'd tell me if something had happened?" My throat suddenly went tight.

"He's fine, but I'll tell him you said hello."

So Jacob's a part of this spontaneous trip? Interesting.

"Ang?"

"Yeah?" I asked, realizing I had zoned out for a second.

"Yes, I'd tell you something like that."

My heart warmed. "Thanks."

"Hope lunch is good today."

Crap! I jumped up, letting the book fall off my lap onto the floor as I pulled the phone away from my ear to check the time.

12:30 p.m. stared back at me. I pushed the door open to my bedroom.

"Oh my gosh…I have to go. I totally lost track of time while reading *your* dang book!"

He gut-laughed into the phone again, causing me to momentarily forget why I was so panicked.

"I'll let you go…for now. I'll call you tonight. Hope you can get to the kissing scene by then."

"Whatever. Bye, Jackson."

"Bye, sweetheart."

I tossed the phone on my bed and smiled, replaying his voice in my mind. That word would never grow stale. Nor could my feelings for the man who spoke it.

****

Lunch turned out to be a lot of fun, although I was fifteen minutes late.

Pippy, of course, was a ball of energy, buzzing in and out of every conversation as many topics were discussed—most lighthearted in nature. My heart warmed as I looked at each author, appreciating them all for different reasons. They were a wonderful mix of wisdom, humor and friendship.

The drama from my interview with Divina was not talked about—and I was incredibly grateful for that graciousness, although they did address the new forward for my book. My stomach dipped when Mr. Zimmerman brought it up, but he only offered his encouragement and support. His sincerity caused my eyes to water. Sue

Bolan squeezed my shoulder as we parted ways, nodding her head at me in affirmation. My relief was apparently quite obvious, especially to the little spitfire who sat next to me.

"Want to get Ice cream?" Pippy asked as we sat at our now deserted lunch table.

I smiled. "How is it that you're so tiny—when I swear you eat sugar like most people drink water?"

She shrugged. "Maybe it's the green smoothies."

I rolled my eyes. "I highly doubt that, but I'll take your word for it."

She looped her arm in mine as we exited the building and made our way onto the street. Instantly, my body craved the air-conditioning once again. It was hot—probably the hottest day I'd experienced while in New York City. Pippy didn't seem bothered by the temperature, and since I was the one who resided in Texas, I didn't say a word either.

"I noticed your dad drinks these green concoctions too," I said, testing the topic with her.

She nodded enthusiastically. "Yes, he's the one who got us hooked, actually. They've done great things for him since...since his diagnosis." Her smile remained intact, and her expression was still light, but the hesitancy in her words hit home.

"I really enjoyed meeting your parents, Pippy. Cody told me yesterday how much he missed his *New York family*."

"Aww…that is the sweetest thing I've ever heard," she said, squeezing my arm a little tighter as we continued to walk.

The Ice Cream Shop was two blocks away. I had never been more grateful for ice cream in my life as sweat ran down the back of my neck and into my shirt. My long, black shorts stuck to my legs with each step we took.

"How's Caleb?" I asked.

She smiled, goofily. "Wonderful."

I chuckled. "Good."

"How's Jackson?" Her eyes twinkled with mischief as she asked. I rolled my eyes a tad before answering. "He's…a little bit of wonderful as well."

She squealed, scaring an old lady who clutched her chest as she passed out table.

"You loved the yacht, right?" Pippy asked.

The question startled me. "How did-"

"I know all things," she gloated, briefly. "Well, I just know his schedule mostly. I'm the one who arranged for your car service."

"Oh, well…thanks. Yes, it was a great night." I decided to leave out the part where I lost my most valuable earthly possession. I was trying to keep my mind off that depressing fact.

"Awesome."

"Have you…" I hesitated, not sure if I wanted to know the answer to my next question. "Have you set up many dates for Jackson?"

Pippy laughed. She tugged open the door to the Ice Cream Shop and shook her head.

"Ha!—No, he's hasn't really dated since-"

"Since Livie?" I finished.

She nodded, touching each flavor label on the glass that protected the ice cream from the heat. It was as if she was waiting for one to speak to her: "Pick me," or "I'm the one you've been searching for." The unconscious action was quite amusing.

Pippy finally decided after sampling her top five while I stuck with my old faithful: Cookies n' Cream. Who could turn down Oreos crushed into vanilla ice cream?

We sat inside the tiny parlor at a table that barely held our cups and spoons. "So, they were really…in love?" I asked, trying to sound casual about it all…like I was talking about a dog I saw at the park.

Pippy looked at me with compassion. Clearly, she fully comprehended the intent of my question.

"Yes, they were really in love…but that was years ago." She pursed her lips before continuing, "Listen, Angie…you do not need to worry. He's had a few dates, gone out with a couple of women since Livie…but there has been no one like you. Not even close."

"What was he like—before he came to work at the publishing house?"

Pippy smiled as if recalling a found memory. "He was…relaxed. Weird, huh? I mean, he's always been annoyingly brilliant. Even as a young child I knew that much. But since he's been here…I don't know how to describe it, really. He's just always on alert. He doesn't miss anything, and yet, he misses everything at the same time."

My heart seized at her keen judgment of him. I nodded in full agreement.

"The day he showed up at the office, I was working as an assistant to one of the secretaries. I was a senior in high school, so I had my afternoons free." She scraped the inside of her dish, carefully getting every last drop of ice cream onto her spoon. "But it was really crazy to see him there…my dad was totally shocked when he walked into the board meeting and Jackson was there, sitting at the table."

I listened intently. "So your dad didn't ask him to come?"

She shook her head. "No. He knew Jackson's dream was to write—he never wanted him to give that up, not for anything. He was preparing his successor, but Jackson…"

"What? Then why did he do it? If someone else could take over the company...then why did he do?"

Pippy stared into her dish, suddenly quiet.

I realized then how insensitive I must have been to ask these questions of her—when her father, who was the former CEO, was at home, dying.

I reached for her hand. "I'm sorry about your dad, Pippy."

She looked up, and smiled faintly. "Thanks, Angie," she said, spooning her last bite into her mouth. "That topic doesn't make me uncomfortable—just so you know. We're really open about it within our family. We talk about it a lot."

Why was Pippy suddenly so uncomfortable then...if the issue wasn't about her dad? I wasn't sure, but I wasn't about to monopolize the conversation again. I cleared my throat.

"Jackson said you all decided together—about his treatments?"

She nodded, a sweet expression gracing her delicate features.

"Yes," she said, tucking her short dark hair behind her ear. "I cut all my hair off when he did his first round. We matched."

Her eyes sparkled as she pulled her phone out to show me a picture. Her dark hair was practically non-existent in the photo, many inches shorter than the pixie-cut she sported now, but her warm expression of love was the same one she wore now.

My heart broke for her...all over again. "And you're okay with his choice? No more treatments?"

She nodded, her lips turning down slightly as she answered. "The treatments made him so sick, and when he wasn't sick, he was exhausted. I'm not going to pretend that the decision wasn't hard, it was. But watching someone you love be miserable is really unbearable."

I squeezed her hand, feeling my eyes grow damp. "You're an incredible young woman, Pippy. I am so glad to know you."

Her smile spread wide. "I'm so glad to know you too, sis."

Grinning together over melted ice cream, I submitted yet another beautiful moment to memory. There were some people that just couldn't be replaced...Pippy was in a category all by herself.

Chapter Thirty-Five

"So have I been replaced—is that why I never hear from you these days?"

I rolled my eyes at Rosie's dramatics, though I knew she couldn't see me through the phone. Some things never change.

"Yep. As we speak, I'm actually bursting at the seams with itty-bitty Latino women for best buds," I joked, slumping down onto the couch in my temporary apartment.

She huffed. "Very funny, chica. The only acceptable replacement would be in the form of Mr. I'm-a-hot-brooding-CEO."

I laughed—hard. "Well, even he couldn't replace you."

"Good answer. So…I want details. I've waited long enough."

I put my book down on the coffee table in my mini-living room. I filled Rosie in as best I could. She, of course, had a lot to say. It was strange to talk to her about Jackson, stranger still that she had never met him. Up until my trip to New York our lives were very similar. We lived in the same town, knew the same people, were invested in the same things. The only big difference was the fact that I had a son—one she had practically adopted as her own.

"I need to meet this man. Are you sure there are no secret siblings? Another brother you could throw my direction?"

"Oh, Rosie—I wouldn't hold out on you if there were. I promise."

"Alright." She sighed in true Rosie-fashion. "So what's gonna happen after you come back? What has he said? Are you going to try and do the whole long-distance thing until someone gives in and moves?"

I shook my head, wishing I had that answer. I had hoped that we were going to discuss the future last night on the yacht, but the search for my necklace had put quite a damper on such a conversation.

"I wish I knew," I said. "I think he feels for me what I feel for him—though he hasn't said it yet."

"Well, of course he does! Maybe he's just waiting for the right moment. You said he's a writer—they're usually dramatic."

I smiled. I hadn't told her about the whole Everett Jr. scandal. I wasn't quite sure if it was my secret to share. I'd joked with Jackson about what Rosie's reaction would be, but hadn't actually asked him if I could let the cat out of the bag. When I did—she would flip.

"I don't know. He's not super-dramatic—but he is calculating So, maybe it's that. Or maybe he just really doesn't know how it's going to work out between us?" I said, more to myself than to her.

"You love him," she stated.

"Yes. I love him," I confirmed for the first time aloud.

She went quiet. I was beginning to think she had fallen asleep on me—payback for our last phone conversation.

"Rose?"

She sniffled. "It's like a chick-flick. So romantic."

Oh golly. She's crying.

"Well, we don't know the ending yet," I reminded her gently, touched by her love for me.

"Endings are only as great as the journey that made them."

"Where did you hear that?" I asked.

She snorted. "How do you know that I didn't just make that up?" I opened my mouth but she cut me off first. "Fine, I read it in one of the tabloids at the supermarket."

I shook my head. Apparently God had given me several irreplaceable people in my life: those who had wisdom beyond their years, those who wrote brilliant pieces of literature, and those who could quote tabloids.

****

After eating a dinner supplied by the convenience store next to my building, I curled back into bed to finish my book—*finally!* Things had gone from bad to worse for sweet Reagan. Not only had she nearly died in the front seat of her car at the hands of a horrible mongrel named Chaz, she was in a no-win game of blackmail. If she did not destroy some very particular evidence against their main suspect, she would be dead within twenty-four hours.

And so would Quinton.

There was no choice. Her own life she would risk—but not his.

I bit my nails as I turned each page faster than the next. As she went inside the precinct to search Quinton's computer, I was literally sweating.

She leaned over his laptop, and carefully entered his password, which she had memorized a long time ago. Her hands shook as she glanced over her shoulder several times. She scrolled through the pictures they had uploaded earlier that evening. If he submitted them to evidence, Quinton and she were as good as dead. But he'd been as tired as she was, and the submission process was tedious. Reagan prayed he'd left the task for tomorrow.

He had.

Her eyes filled with tears—relief covering her like a thick, warm blanket. She cradled her left arm against her side, fairly certain her shoulder was dislocated. She moved quickly, deleting one picture after the next. She'd lose her job. She'd lose her good reputation. But she wouldn't lose him.

She shook her head, correcting herself. The thugs wouldn't kill him, but she would lose him.

With every click Reagan was breaking his trust, which in turn, was breaking her heart. When her job was finished, her breathing was rapid. Tears streaked her cheeks as she closed his laptop. It was finished, in every sense of the word. She texted the number that Chaz had given her—and prayed she had done enough.

I turned the page and was greeted with the words *The End*. I lifted my phone, checking the time so I could text Jackson, but as I held the cell, Jackson texted me.

Jackson: You still awake?

Me: You are evil.

The phone rang. I answered it immediately.

"What's your problem? Not enough kissing scenes?"

"No! Not even close!" I mock-yelled.

He laughed. "Oh, I'm so glad I texted. I was afraid you went to bed already. I just got in for the night."

"Jackson you wrote a horrible cliffhanger."

"Makes you want to read the next book, huh?"

He had me there. Yes. Marketing-wise he was smart, but he was also a little evil.

"So…where are you?" I tested, changing the subject.

He sighed deeply. "I'm…in D.C."

I don't know what I was expecting, but I was surprised nonetheless.

"You sound tired—how was your day?" I snuggled down into my covers.

"Well, let's see…the last three minutes have been good," he said coolly. "But yes, I am tired."

I heard him yawn and instantly I wished I there with him. Just talking to him sent my heart rate into an erratic rhythm. Would be the first of many late night phone calls to come in our future? Was this what our relationship would look like? Calls and texts at the day's end?

"Do you want me to let you go, so you can rest?" I asked reluctantly.

"Not a chance. You're the only redemption to my entire day."

I smiled. "Glad I can help you salvage the last few minutes of it."

I heard some soft shuffling sounds in the background and figured Jackson was climbing into bed. My cheeks flushed hot at the thought.

"I should be back tomorrow evening. I have another meeting here in the morning, so I'll plan on meeting you at the office tomorrow afternoon if you're still there."

I furrowed my brows in concern. "Jackson, you're okay, right?"

"Yes, sweetheart." He sighed. "I'm okay."

It was nearly two in the morning when we hung up, sleepy delirium finally cutting our conversation off. I had never seen the hours tick away so fast. I could have talked to him till morning…I couldn't wait to see him again.

I fell asleep instantly; grateful that tomorrow evening would be closer when I awoke.

****

It was almost noon when Pippy came into my tiny workspace and announced that I needed a new email server—one solely purposed for my fans and readers. Apparently, logging into my personal email account was no longer kosher. I stared up at her, confirming that I was indeed seeing *stress* on her face, a look I wasn't accustomed to from her in the slightest.

"Hey—what's going on? Can I help you with something?"

"I have a few things I need to get done before Jackson gets back, so I wrote down what you need to do to get it all set up under Pinkerton's domain. Here is the info from the IT department. Can you do it for me?"

"Sure, Pip. Anything else—you seem a bit out of sorts."

"I'm fine—there's just a lot happening today is all," she said, her smile not quite reaching her eyes.

"Oh…okay. Well, let me know if I can help with anything else."

She nodded, gave me a quick hug and exited.

Weird.

I stared down at the note Pippy had given me and logged into my email—something I hadn't done in about week. My mouth hung open as I saw the chaos before me.

So. Many. Emails.

Most of them were a carbon-copy of comments that were left on my latest blog post—The Forward—but many were direct, personal emails written to me. I gulped, scrolling through them, reading each subject line. I understood Jackson's warnings now about reviews…some were wonderful, some less-than-kind, but others were just straight-up nasty.

I felt a slight pull at my conscience, remembering the promise I had made to Jackson about not reading commentaries…but I had promised that prior to our meeting with the PR department. That promise I had kept. There was no such promise on the horizon now.

I scrolled on.

One in specific caught my eye—a name I could almost feel as I read it—like salt to an open wound.

Divina.

I clicked on it, heat filling my body as I read her words.

Angela,

As I'm sure you already know, I have received a bit of flack regarding our interview. Though I will not apologize for my accurate research or for my resourcefulness in gathering it, there are those who feel you may have been a tad blindsided by my eager approach. If you would like a rematch—just say the word.

We will make the necessary adjustments to get you onto our Friday show if you respond by Monday. If not, I hope you enjoy Texas. I'll be sure to comfort Jackson in your absence.

Divina

I clicked out of my email immediately, and pushed back against my chair, crossing my arms over my chest. *Over my dead body would she comfort Jackson.* I furrowed my brow. *Okay, maybe the crime novels were getting to me a bit more than I thought.*

I seethed as I looked at the date. She had written it last Thursday. *Had no one read this? Had Pippy responded and forgot to tell me?* No, the email had been unmarked. It hadn't been read. A lot of these hadn't been read, I noticed. Pippy was simply too busy to keep up with all of these—I could understand why.

I clicked into another unread email, bracing myself after reading the subject line:

Sick Publicity Stunt

Angie,

I am embarrassed to say that prior to the latest information about your domestic violence scam, I was a big fan. In fact, I got many of my single mom friends to follow your blog. We thought you stood for the same things that we did. We thought raising our kids to be moral, upright citizens, even when lacking a fatherly figure, was the ultimate goal—one you shared. We were wrong. I am disgusted by the helplessness you displayed during your interview and by The Forward for your new book which followed only days later.

Is this some sort of sick game you're trying to play to make money? I thought you were better than that. Creating some sort of false reality for fame is both twisted and wrong. You should be ashamed of yourself.

Not a fan,

Felicity Cornwell

The words sank sharp hooks into me. Progressing like a slow-moving train wreck, I was compelled to continue reading email after email.

Though the good emails far outweighed the bad, I just keep clicking onto them, absorbing each word like a dagger to my heart. Divina had done this. She had created this mess and though I knew her offer had to be self-serving, I quickly felt the need for justice—for a chance to speak and not be railroaded by some exotic, long-legged witch of a woman.

Before I fully realized what I was doing, I clicked back into Divina's email...and responded with fury.

Divina,

Friday is perfect. I'll be there. Just tell me when.

Angie

The second I hit send nausea rolled through me and sweat coated my palms. I reached for my necklace—gone. Loss on top of loss. I felt even sicker.

Could I really do it? Did I even have a chance up against her?

Then I had another thought: *What would Jackson say?* Should I have asked permission—I wasn't sure how all that worked. I was unfamiliar to the strength of my anger, and I was grateful for that fact. I did crazy things when I was angry. My last decision was proof of that.

But I wouldn't take the challenge back.

Not now.

She may be my Goliath—a freakishly pretty Goliath—but I wouldn't stand down. Not this time. This time I'd take my slingshot with me.

I *would* have the last word.

Chapter Thirty-Six

Just after six Jackson tapped on the door of Sally Miller's office. We'd been going over my latest revisions for the past couple of hours, and I was beyond relieved to see him—until I remembered what I had agreed to in regard to Divina's show. I swallowed the brick of guilt and smiled. His face reflected his usual stoic demeanor of professionalism as he looked at me. His eyes looked tired, yet I could still see some warmth in them—a tiny sparkle I'd seen up close several times now.

"May I see you in my office when you're done here, Miss Flores?" he asked.

"Sure," I said, nodding.

He shut the door, and I felt my face heat from the inside out. Sally did a double take from me to the door, but then quickly went back to her correction overview. After another painfully slow thirty-minutes I was able to leave. My feet could not move fast enough.

I knocked twice and then entered Jackson's office, turning around fully to close the door. But before I could face the inside of his office again, he was there, walking me backward in quick succession until my back pressed against the wall. I gasped as his hands gripped my hips and then slid up my waist to the back of my ribcage, sending shivers of desire up my spine. As his fingers reached the nape of my neck, his mouth crashed into mine, my hands flat against his chest as my legs fought to remain standing.

Though kissing Jackson was at the top of my most-enjoyable-things-to-do list, this kiss was different. It was rushed, desperate…lost. I tilted my head back in order to catch my breath; he in turn kissed my jaw, then the spot below my ear, then the pulse at my neck.

"Jackson-" I whimpered.

"Hmm?"

"Jackson—stop."

Immediately, he stopped and placed both his hands on the wall on either side of me, breathing intensely. I stared at him, wishing I could take back my soft command, but I knew something wasn't right. *He* wasn't quite right.

I touched his face gently with my hand, careful not to rouse any more desire between us. My suspicion was confirmed when he looked away. He never avoided my eyes.

"Tell me," I said, quietly.

Muscles in his jaw twitched as his breathing normalized, but he didn't respond.

"Jackson—*please*. What's going on?"

He pushed himself off the wall, turning to rake his hands through his hair and then down his face. His suit coat was already off—lying on his office chair. He stood staring out his massive window in a green dress shirt and slacks. As much as I'd like to believe this unfamiliar tension was about my upcoming departure next Sunday, I knew that wasn't the case.

I stayed where I was, back against the wall, until finally he sighed. A heart wrenching sound of defeat.

"You won't understand, Angie. I don't even know if I understand anymore."

I was confused. No, I was more than confused.

"Then help me understand. Maybe it will help you, too."

He turned, eyes roaming my face as if he was contemplating what I had just said.

"Have you ever made a decision, claiming it was for one reason, believing it was the right thing to do when you made it, but all along there was another motivation behind it?" He was looking out the window again as I walked toward him. "A selfish one."

I had no idea what he was talking about—no reference point. But his torment was tangible. I ached for him in this moment. He was raw, worn, and tired. I put my hand on his shoulder.

"Jackson, you are *not* selfish."

He turned sharply, eyes suddenly focused. "I have *always* been selfish. Have you not listened to a thing I've said? I am not like you, Angie. I'm not good-natured. I'm not gentle or tender or consistently kind. I *am* selfish!"

"That's not how I see you," I said, firmly.

He shook his head and exhaled loudly, running his hand down his face and over the scruff on his jawline face. A full minute passed as we stood at an impasse. I could be stubborn too. I was shocked that Jackson was the first to bend.

He relaxed his shoulders, which in turn relaxed the strain in his face.

"I shouldn't be venting here, or to you. Forgive me?"

His tone was sincere, and that fact grieved me more than I cared to accept. That he didn't feel he could vent to me, hurt. But this wasn't about my feelings. It was about him. I tried to pull that perspective into view. Touching his arm again, he wrapped his hand around mine and gave me a faint smile.

"I'm here for you when you need me," I said.

He pulled me in, his arms around me tight, as he planted a kiss on top of my head.

"I know," he said.

Yet somehow, I wasn't really sure he did.

****

The tension in the office on Tuesday was nearly insufferable. At first I thought it was just Pippy and Jackson who were acting off, but unfortunately they seemed to set the atmosphere for the entire building. Jackson made it clear that he didn't want to talk about the company at dinner last night, which for the moment was good considering it probably wasn't the best time for me to bring up my impromptu decision regarding Divina.

I worked tirelessly to get approval on the final drafts of several of my revision chapters, while writing two new ones documenting my escape from Colorado to Texas, and my first nights at *The Refuge*.

Jackson was in yet another meeting. I hadn't seen him but once this morning when we had shared a minty kiss for all of five seconds under the cover of his town car. Other than Walt, we'd been safe from any peeping eyes. Then we'd gone our separate ways. His demeanor changed the instant he walked inside Pinkerton Press, as if the part of him that I got to see—the part of him that I loved the most—had been left outside.

I decided I would corner Pippy, make her tell me what was going on, only I didn't see her either. Most likely she'd been invited to the "secret meetings", which for all I knew could be about a possible alien invasion, or how to keep peace in the Middle East, or the latest recipe for safe play-dough. Urgh. It was driving me a bit insane.

It was late afternoon when I finally listened to the growling in my stomach and made my way down the hallway toward the elevators.

I made sure to pass by Jackson's office, just in case he was suddenly alone. He wasn't, but the door did fling open a second after I passed by. I don't know what shocked me more when I turned around—the fact that Stewart came out, or the fact that Jacob was with him. I felt my eyes widen before I reminded myself to smile. Stewart's eyes softened as they found mine.

"Good afternoon, Miss Flores," he said.

"Good afternoon," I said, trying to recover from my surprise.

Jacob walked over to me and put his thin, lanky arm around my shoulder.

"Walk with me?" he asked, warmly.

I nodded as he quickly spun me back toward the elevators. I didn't see Jackson, and maybe that was Jacob's goal. Maybe I wasn't supposed to see him. Stewart walked in the opposite direction, leaving us alone. I pressed the button to the floor of the café.

"How are you, Jacob?" I asked gently.

"I have no complaints," he said. "How are you?"

I swallowed, pondering his answer. "I'm doing well, thank you."

He looked at his watch. "Were you on your way to get lunch now? It's nearly four."

I smiled, sheepishly. "Got caught up with writing."

He nodded slowly, still smiling. "I knew someone else like that once."

The door opened and Jacob gestured for me to follow him. I did. There weren't many people in the café as four o'clock wasn't a normal lunch hour, but those who were there flocked to Jacob. I'd seen how people reacted to Jackson—with respect and head nods and handshakes. That was not the reaction they had with Jacob, however. He was a hugger.

Jacob was the personification of warmth and love.

I bit the insides of my cheeks as the fifth hugger made their way over to him. After his greeting sessions were through, I grabbed a bowl of fruit and a protein bar and met him at a small booth against the far wall. It was strange the way I felt around Jacob, like I'd known him a lot longer than I actually had. Maybe it was the fact that I was in love with his brother, or how his daughter was now one of the dearest people in my life...I didn't know. But there was an understanding with him—a comfort I felt whenever he spoke to me. I tried not to think about what else I knew about him.

"How's Jackson?" he asked me.

The question startled me. He was just with Jackson, surely he knew how he was. "Um...weren't you just meeting with him?"

He laughed lightly,. "I like you, Angie. I can see why he feels for you what he does." He clasped his hands together on the table in front of us. "What are your thoughts on how he's doing?"

I put my fork down, despite the growling in my stomach. I had my own questions, and Jacob it seemed, was the man most equipped to answer them. "Stressed—but he won't talk to me about it. I don't know what's going on."

His perm-grin drooped slightly. "Yes. I'm working hard to change that—so far though he's not too receptive to my attempts to help him. Stress is the natural by-product in a job like his, but…"

"But what?" I asked.

"I don't want to speak for Jackson. I'm in enough hot water with him right now, but he can be so hard-headed that sometimes it takes some drastic measures to get him to see what he should be seeing."

I leaned in, lowering my voice. "Is he in some kind of…legal trouble?"

Jacob patted my hand gently, like a dad to a daughter. "No—not exactly. He just needs to make a decision that at this point he's still refusing to make."

I huffed out a breath I'd been holding. "Jacob tell me what to do…if I don't know what's going on, then how can I help him?"

He stared at me for several seconds, his wide smile returning.

"Jackson and I are over a decade apart, but it's never felt like that. I swear he thought like an adult when he was ten. It was painfully annoying at times to have a younger brother that was wittier, smarter, and a heck of a lot more talented...but he had this idea that following in the footsteps of his dad and I was what was expected of him. That's not how it was. His father—like me—saw the potential that Jackson lived up to when he was writing," Jacob's eyes were focused elsewhere, as if far away from me. "But then several difficult things happened at once—and he let it all go. Though I appreciated his help and support when he came to relieve me, I never wanted this for him."

I nodded, feeling the emotion behind his words.

"When life feels out of control we often go back to a place where control can be found—even if it's the wrong place," Jacob said.

"He told me about Livie."

He nodded. "I'm glad to hear that."

"But I keep feeling like there's more to the story..."

Jacob sighed. "Guilt is a dangerous thing, both when you've done wrong, and when you've been wronged."

"You mean he can't let go of her?"

He shook his head as if to disagree with my question. "I was with her...when she died. It was a tragedy that I'll never be able to make sense of this side of heaven, but I was there when she said her final words."

I gaped at him. "What did she say?"

I instantly felt guilty for asking such a question, but Jacob continued as if he had expected it.

"She said four words: Tell Jackson I'm sorry."

My eyes pooled with tears. "Their fight. She was apologizing for their fight."

"Yes."

"Oh gosh. No wonder…"

I couldn't even speak the words aloud as every scolding I'd received from Jackson over my misuse of those two little words came flooding back into my mind. He hated those words: *I'm sorry.* And I finally thought I understood why. It wasn't because Livie had spoken them with her dying breath, but because he'd never been able to speak them to her. I closed my eyes briefly and cleared the emotional lump building in my throat.

"So what do you want from him? For him to step down as CEO?" I asked.

"Yes."

Though I'd asked Jackson many times why he was choosing the family business over his writing career, or why he had given up his dreams for the regrets in his past, I couldn't imagine telling him to quit. That was *his* decision to make.

Something in the way Jacob answered though, something in that simple, one-worded response told me he wasn't just being *asked*.

"Jacob, believe me when I say that I want Jackson to pursue his talents as much as anyone, but I don't think that forcing his hand to make that decision is what he needs. If you push him out, do you really think he's just going to run right back to writing again? I don't."

Jacob seemed to consider this. "It's not just up to me—there are others involved, but yes, my hope is that he will not only turn to writing again, but that he'll see a future with the woman who loves him."

I looked away, my face flushing hot. "It's that obvious?" I murmured.

"Both ways—yes."

I smiled, hoping he was right about that as he took out his phone and checked the screen.

"I need to get going, Angie. My bride is waiting for me. She's been out doing some damage to my bank account with my daughter."

Oh, so Pippy wasn't in the meetings today after all. I was relieved to hear that. Being pinned between her boss—who was also her Uncle—and her father, would not be easy.

"Okay, thanks Jacob. It was nice to talk with you."

"No, thank you," he said, picking up my hand and planting a kiss onto the back of it. "You're a treasure, Angie."

And then he was gone.

I opened the seal of my fruit bowl and stabbed at a watermelon chunk, but apparently eating was not in the cards for me today. I jumped as a piece of paper was slammed down next to me at the table where I sat. A large hand was attached to it…one I knew quite well.

"What is this?" Jackson seethed.

Uh-oh.

I smiled up at him, hoping to find a hint of understanding.

"Jackson, I don't know if now is the best time to talk about that." I sighed, picking up my water and taking a swing.

"And when would be the best time, Angie? Friday morning? When I watch you on TV!" He gripped the back of his neck, obviously working hard to stay calm since we were in the very open and public café.

I leaned back, hoping he'd sit down. He remained standing. This fact bothered me—a lot. I crossed my arms over my chest like a child in time-out.

"And you're just an open book about all your life decisions," I said. "If you want to talk with me about this, than you can sit down and stop looming over me like some kind of middle-school bully."

He glowered at me, but sat down in the seat that his brother had filled only moments before.

"Cancel this," he said firmly, pointing to the paper, which appeared to be some kind of confirmation from The Eastman Morning Show. I'd been stupid to think I could hold onto that information without him finding out.

"Jackson, I need to set the record straight-"

He laughed darkly. "You won't even get a word in, Angie. That woman is a viper. It's her life's ambition to hunt her pray and eat them alive. The first time was bad enough—how could you even *consider* this? I thought at first it was some kind of mistake, that is until I saw your email attached to the bottom of it."

I sat up straighter, not willing to be intimidated by him.

"Aren't you the one who's always telling me how strong I am? Telling me that I should share my voice with the world? Well, here's my chance. I'll admit it was a quick decision, but it's done now."

"When did you even make this decision? What brought this about? You never even told me you were thinking about talking with her again."

He was right. I hadn't thought about it—not once.

I stared at him, unwilling to answer with the truth that was sure to get me into even deeper trouble. But a second later he rubbed his hands down his face in frustration, lowering his voice as he leaned across the table.

"You read them—your reviews?"

"Yes. They are *my* reviews to read, Jackson. I can't just live in a Lala-Land bubble for the rest of my life. I have to deal it—the backlash."

He looked up at me sharply, though his voice was still low. "Think about what you're saying, Angie. It's all the backlash that Divina created—the same woman you're wanting to talk with again on live TV."

"I just want a chance to be heard—to state the facts in my own words."

He shook his head, reaching out to take hold of my hands. I was surprised that he did something so personal. We were not in a private setting; we were at his work place. "Angie—*please*. Whatever bad reviews you've read, it isn't worth going back on the show with her. I don't want to see you get hurt again."

I let his words soak in. I cared about what he thought, and deep down I knew he was probably right. I'd most likely fry on that hot seat again, but something tugged at me even deeper. Sure, I had initially made the decision out of anger, but it didn't feel rash to me anymore.

I *needed* to do this, to face my fear.

"I can't explain it, Jackson, but I feel like I need to do it. I can't let my fear control me—not anymore. But...I do want you with me."

He closed his eyes briefly and took in a deep breath.

"Fine," he said eyeing me narrowly. "I'll be there."

Chapter Thirty-Seven

Wednesday came and went quicker than I thought possible. The tension around the office was less, though Jackson was still *off*. He drilled me for over an hour on our way home while stuck in bad traffic, asking me the kinds of things that Divina was likely to throw my way. I winced several times as if proving his point, but I didn't go all comatose like last time—so at least I was making some headway. He laced his fingers through mine, as we walked into my apartment just after seven.

He looked so tired when he walked me to my door. I was supposed to change for a nice dinner out—Jackson had made us a reservation, but I just couldn't do it, not when I knew he wasn't sleeping at night. Not when I knew he had so much more on his plate than what he was sharing with me. We didn't need to go out. We just needed to be together.

"Jackson, why don't you come in, and I'll just go grab us a pizza next door? We don't need to go out anywhere tonight. I just want to be with you."

He stared at me for a moment and eventually nodded. I smiled, reveling in the mini-victory. I left him inside to make the call while I ran to grab the best New York Style pizza I'd ever had. Cody and I had enjoyed several slices there when he was here.

On the one hand, the idea of leaving Jackson in four days made my stomach hurt, but the idea of seeing my Cody again filled me with joy. It was hard to reconcile one feeling over the other.

When I got back, I knocked twice, but there was no answer. I used my keycard then, balancing the large box as I used my foot to prop and hold the door. Before I had even turned around, I knew what had happened. He was asleep.

His suit coat was off, as was his tie and shoes, and he was spread out on my couch. I quietly set the pizza box down and went into my bedroom to change into my yoga pants and t-shirt. If he was going to get comfortable, I would too. He snored softly as I made myself a plate of pizza and grabbed book three in his collection.

I read for over two hours. He never woke up.

I put the book down as I realized that once again I was an anxious ball of worry over the characters that Jackson had created. My gasps were going to be responsible for waking him if I didn't stop soon. I picked up my phone and texted with Cody, him on Charlie's phone, and then finally went into my bedroom to sort through my laundry. One of the nicest perks of living at the T. Ross building— laundry service. I would miss that.

Finally, I heard some movement. I peeked my head out into the living area and Jackson was upright, but still looked half-asleep as he scrubbed his hands over his face. I walked out quietly.

"Hey, feel rested?" I asked.

He looked up at me, a bit startled and then smiled lazily.

"You should have woken me up," he scolded sleepily.

"No. I'm glad you got some sleep. I kept myself busy, although I'm afraid your pizza's cold. Can I warm it up for you."

He just started at me, blinking.

"What?" I looked down at myself self-consciously. Okay, so I did look a little homely—or a lot. I felt my cheeks heat.

He held out his hand to me and pulled me down next to him. "You're too good to me, Angie," he whispered into my hair.

Goosebumps traveled up my arms and neck. "There's no such thing as too good."

He laughed. "That sounds like something I'd say."

I kissed him on the cheek and got up to grab his dinner. Sadly, he left soon after. So to soothe myself in his absence, I picked up his book. Only I didn't start where I left off, I went to my suitcase and pulled out book five and flipped to the back. I needed resolution, something happy, something promising.

But that was not what I got.

I stared at the last page, wishing the words to rearrange themselves. Wanting the ending to say something other than what it did. But there it was. Jackson did not write a happily ever after. He had written quite the opposite. I didn't know what made me sadder: That the characters I loved didn't love each other enough? Or that Jackson's writing was behind that outcome.

Rosie may have been right when she quoted that *endings are only as great as the journey that made them*, but what's the point of a journey if it ends in heartbreak?

My sleep was fitful at best.

****

I stayed in the car, watching for Jackson to walk out of his building Thursday night, the night of the National Publishers Association dinner. I literally stopped breathing when I saw him. Someone with his good looks should come with a warning label. Seriously. I had to work so hard to fit into the "not-so-bad-when-I-try" category, when Jackson rocked the "super-hot-and-didn't-try" category. He ducked into the car and still I couldn't exhale.

His smile spread wide as his eyes found me.

"You know, I used to think I was partial to certain dresses you wear, but I'm starting to think my partiality has nothing to do with the dress, and everything to do with the woman who wears it."

I finally released the breath I'd been holding and smiled back at him, cheeks heating.

"You look really…good, Jackson." I said.

He smiled and reached for my hand, lacing my fingers through his. "You're the only thing that will make this night bearable for me—I hope you realize that. These things are the bane of my existence."

I laughed as he winked at me.

We talked for the next hour and thirty minutes, avoiding mention of my pending departure, his secretive work drama or my interview tomorrow. What was left was a lot of hyperbole. We each asked each other a "what if" question that had to be answered. The game made the time go by quickly and taught me a lot more about the man I had fallen so deeply in love with in just six short weeks.

****

The dinner was held as a massive building that looked like a replica of the Coliseum. It was gigantic. There were fountains, gardens and pathways everywhere I looked. It was gorgeous. We were far enough away from the city that I could see the outlines of the stars in the dimming night sky. The amount of people who were there for the event was overwhelming. Close to a thousand at least.

Jackson linked my arm and walked me into the grand ballroom, where we found our seats. Cocktails and appetizers were served shortly after and the speaker—an elderly gentleman—was quoting out of his favorite books of the year when my phone vibrated over and over.

Jackson looked at me with concern as I quietly took it out of my silver clutch.

Rosie.

She had left a message. I bit my lip and Jackson nodded his head toward the door, as if signaling me to go ahead and call her back. I smiled, relieved at his sensitivity. Cody wasn't with Rosie tonight, but still, she knew I was coming to this dinner. We had texted about it earlier this afternoon.

I excused myself as quietly as could, lifting my dress a tad to walk without stumbling over the hem. As I made my way outside, my phone struggled to find a good signal. Every time I click into her voicemail the call would drop. I walked a little farther around the building, focused on the screen of my phone. Still nothing. I lifted it up and moved several feet back and forth, even though rationally, I'm sure this made no difference at all.

"Ms. Flores?"

I turned, startled.

"Stewart—I mean, Mr. Vargus? Hi, how are you?"

"Doing about the same as you it looks like. I was trying to return a call, but can't seem to find any good coverage out here for some reason. Glad to know it's not just me."

I smiled as he did the same. His face was so kind—the type of face you'd picture your favorite uncle having, or your favorite English teacher. I imagined him to be in his early forties. His eyes were warm, though the sudden awkwardness between us was quite apparent.

"I uh…I heard about your interview tomorrow," he said.

My stomach knotted, unsure where this was going. I didn't need to hear anything negative, especially not the night before I head into the ring with her.

"Yes," I said simply.

"Well, I think you'll do excellent. You're quite well-spoken, and I have every confidence that you can put that miserable woman in her place."

"Thank you—that vote of confidence means a lot. I'm not sure how it will go to be honest, but I feel as ready as I can be."

"That's good, I-"

"What are you doing, Stewart?"

We both turned as Jackson made his way over to us—anger on his face.

I don't know why I felt guilty in that moment, but I did. It was like I'd just been caught fraternizing with the enemy—*but why was Stewart the enemy?* Jackson's hand was on my arm before I could speak. It was a protective gesture, but again, I had no idea why he was trying to protect me from Stewart. My face grew hot with embarrassment as I looked from one man to the other.

"Stay away from her," Jackson growled at him in a tone that made my bones hurt.

Stewart lifted his hands in surrender. "Jackson, we were just having an innocent conversation."

"Innocent? Yeah, I know all about your definition of *innocent*, Stew."

Though Stewart's eyes hardened, his face remained relaxed. I didn't know how that was possible. The tension made me want to cry, but I didn't. Jackson never reacted poorly due to awkwardness…in fact, I'd only seen this reaction from him one other time, at the board meeting. Coincidentally, Stewart was there for that as well.

"Jackson, he's right, it was nothing-"

His brows furrowed in response to me, our faces close. "Don't defend him. He doesn't deserve it," Jackson looked back at Stewart. "Believe me, he has no problem taking care of himself."

This finally seemed to spark a reaction from Stewart. His face had lost the peaceful look of a minute earlier, and now it was hard as granite.

"You have some nerve, Jackson."

I flinched, as Stewart stepped toward us, but Jackson held my arm tight.

"Isn't it about time you move on from your conspiracy theories? You weren't the only one who lost someone that day." Stewart gestured toward me, as if I was some kind of solution to this mounting tension.

My head started to pound as Jackson stepped in front of me, dropping my arm in the process. I didn't know what to do. It was like a bad bar scene, though no one was drinking, and everyone was in formalwear.

Jackson's voice dropped several decibels. "You mean I wasn't the only one who lost someone they *loved* that day...right, Stew?"

When Stewart threw the punch, Jackson must have been anticipating it because he quickly dodged left, yet somehow his bottom lip was dotted with blood when he shoved Stewart back. The fresh distance seemed to alert them both to their surroundings—and to me.

Time was an irritating scab—one I wanted to scratch in order to alleviate the itch underneath. Suddenly, I knew exactly what it felt like to be on one of those trashy talk-shows, the ones where half-way through the curtain was pulled back for one last shocking reveal: This was the big reveal.

Stewart was the friend of Jacob's who'd been with Livie when she died. *Had he been in love with her, too?*

"I apologize for this, Mrs. Flores. Things got out of control. It won't happen again. Goodnight," Stewart said before walking off.

I nodded after him, purposefully keeping my eyes off Jackson.

"Goodnight."

Chapter Thirty-Eight

Jackson bent over a railing nearby, pressing his split lip with his hand as he stared into the pond. My insides quaked with so many emotions at once. I didn't know where to start—but one thing was for sure, I wasn't leaving until I was finished. I wanted every piece of information…and I wanted it now.

I deserved that much.

My heels clicked against the paved pathway, and Jackson turned his head, standing upright as if preparing himself for battle.

"I didn't mean for that to get so out of hand," he said.

I glared at him, hand on hip. "Stewart was the one with Livie when she died? That's why you hate him?"

His face darkened at my tone. I continued, undeterred.

"Were you accusing him of having feelings for her? Tell me what's going on, Jackson."

His eyes found mine again, begging me to understand. I waited impatiently for him to continue.

"Stewart's known my family since I was a boy. He and Jacob were best friends growing up, and he was my father's assistant before Jacob took over the company. He was next in line because I had always told them I didn't want to be involved in the family business." He stuffed his hands into his pockets. "While I was busy writing, Stewart offered to escort Livie to different functions and events. And like the selfish idiot I am, I agreed. I trusted him. My family *still* trusts him."

He practically spit the last words out of his mouth.

"What happened?"

"I found a letter from her—to him, explaining that she needed to put some distance between them…that her feelings were becoming something more than friendship and that she loved me—that she was going to marry me." He looked at me. "She was with him when she died."

"But what did Stewart *do*, Jackson? Do you think he had some plan to steal her away from you?" I asked.

"Does it matter? They had feelings for each other!"

"Seems like you're assuming a lot based on one letter. What if it was one-sided? What if she was taking a precaution by intending to give him that letter—and his feelings for her were only platonic? There are a thousand scenarios Jackson-"

"Yes, and I'll never know the truth, will I? Because I killed her before I could ask any of those questions!"

My mouth hung open as I let his words burrow into my heart. Tears pooled in my eyes as Jackson held his ground—his eyes like steel.

"Your drive to stay at the company has more to motivation behind it than your guilt over Livie and Jacob...doesn't it?"

He didn't answer, which was my answer.

"Why, Jackson—say it!"

"Because I don't want *him* to have it!"

I closed my eyes, letting the truth wash over me like acid rain.

"You would rather stay miserable—give up your life and your dreams for a job you hate, than to let Stewart take your place? Is that seriously what you're saying?"

"Yes."

I blew out a breath I'd been holding for some time—maybe weeks.

"You need to ask him to tell you the truth. There has to be another side to the story than only her letter. Maybe you're right and maybe you're wrong, but you need to ask. If Jacob can still trust him like he does, don't you think you owe it yourself to find out the facts? To stop basing your life decisions on assumption and guilt? Because the only person you're really punishing is *you*." I walked closer to him. "And what about Jacob? Does staying miserable atone for him, too?"

"Leave it alone, Angie," he warned.

"No. Jacob loves you—he wants better for your life than this. He told me so."

He laughed humorlessly. "Did he? Did he also tell you that he's plotting with Stewart to sway the board to vote me out at the next board meeting?"

I closed my eyes at the hurt in his voice.

"I'm sorry, Jackson. No, he didn't. I don't think that's right, but I do think he has your best interests in mind."

Jackson linked both hands behind his neck.

"And that right there is where we differ, Ang."

"What?" I asked.

His arms fell away, his face anguished yet hard.

"We're *too* different."

My stomach dropped as my knees were tempted to do the same.

"Stop saying that…just tell me what you *mean*, Jackson?"

His eyes grew soft as my bottom lip trembled with uncertainty.

He exhaled. "You have a big day tomorrow…we'll finish this later. Come on. Let's get out of here."

By the time we made it to the car I felt like I was dream-walking. Miraculously, I was able to hold my tears in during our silent ride back to my apartment. When Walt pulled up to the curb, I opened my door before he had the chance.

Jackson followed me inside the lobby, and pulled back on my arm slightly as I walked past him. "Get some rest tonight, Angie."

And just like the first night we met, nearly six week ago, I had nothing to say in reply.

****

I laid on the bed, forcing myself to breathe and not to cry. I didn't know anything yet...or maybe I did. Whatever was going on between us would have to wait until after the interview. He was right about that. I needed sleep and I needed to focus. I curled onto my side on the mattress and spotted my phone atop the nightstand. Suddenly, I remembered Rosie's voicemail—the one I didn't get a chance to hear. I placed the phone on the bed with me and called up my voice mail on speaker. My best friend's voice filled the room.

"Ang—sorry to call while you're at the dinner tonight, but I knew you'd want to know this. Jenny, the girl we couldn't find from *The Refuge*, the one who moved to Oklahoma to be safe...well, we found her. She's in ICU...and it's really bad. I guess she went back to her boyfriend a couple weeks ago. Last night he beat her up so bad that the neighbor didn't even recognize her when she got to her house the next morning. You're doing the right thing, Ang…with the book and the interview. There are women that need our help. Okay, I love you. Call me back. Bye."

I closed my eyes and let her words wash over me. Unknowingly, she had just fueled the fire—the fire that needed to burn into the interview tomorrow. There were bigger things amiss in this world than Jackson Ross and Angela Flores.

Chapter Thirty-Nine

Before I even sat in the makeup chair, I wanted to vomit. But every time the nausea rolled in my tummy, I'd replay the voicemail in my head.

I'd been shocked to see Walt at the curb this morning when I was expecting to catch a cab, but Jackson wasn't inside the vehicle. Considering how we parted last night, that wasn't a huge surprise, but his absence stung. A lot. That's when I took out my phone and listened to Rosie's voicemail...five times in a row.

The fire was stoked.

As I followed a young man with a headset toward the studio, I reached for my necklace out of habit. My hand trembled when it came up empty. For a slight second, the fire dimmed as panic crept up inside me. And then I saw him.

Jackson.

His eyes were glued to me as I walked through the studio. They were the piercing eyes that meant business, the ones that demanded respect from his employees, and the ones that showed no favoritism. But they were exactly the ones I needed most in this moment.

I drew from their strength..

In that moment my fear dissolved, vanishing from my body and my mind completely. A fear that had owned me, that had enslaved me, that had subjected even my sub-consciousness to its cruelty. But this man had reminded me over and over again that I was safe. That I was whole. That I was enough.

And I finally believed it, no matter where we stood now.

He stood several feet from me as the current segment came to a close. I could hear his breathing and feel the warmth of his body, but neither of us spoke. His presence beside me was enough. I wouldn't ask for more, not when there were too many unknowns hovering in the space around us.

As I watched Divina walk from one set to the other, my name was called over the deafening speaker overhead. Jackson's hand found mine. It wasn't the intimate touch of intertwined fingers, but a simple hold, a reminder.

He squeezed briefly. "I believe in you, Angie."

I nodded as I walked to the living room set that I knew all too well.

I ignored Divina's glare as I sat, choosing to hear Rosie's message in my mind one last time before the countdown was over.

And then it was just us: her and I.

Under the spotlight.

Again.

Her long legs were crossed at the ankle and curled to the left of her chair. Her eyes were a dark mask of makeup, while her fuchsia lips fought them for attention. But I looked past it all as she spoke.

"We're here again today with Mrs. Angela Flores, a new author and blogger of *A Lone Joy,* where her life as a single mom has been documented in detail. And since our last interview there have been some new additions made to both your pre-published book and your blog—correct? Is that what you're here to talk about today?"

"Yes, thank you, Divina. I have made several major changes to my manuscript, thanks to our last interview," I said through my smile. "Your tough questions that day have actually given me the confidence I needed to speak out about an issue that is very close to my heart: bringing awareness to the crime of Domestic Violence."

"And that is because you yourself were a victim?" Her voice was laced with false sincerity.

"Yes, I was in an abusive marriage for nearly four years."

Her eyebrows shot up as if she was surprised, although I knew she wasn't. "And what were your reasons for staying a victim for that long? Why didn't you just leave the first time he hit you?"

And here we go.

"Though it's nice to believe in the-first-time-will-be-the-last theory, that is rarely how women respond. There are often a lot of emotional, mental, physical and financial ties to a woman's abuser. Leaving can often feel more daunting a task than the abuse itself, but that is the lie I want to speak out against most. No woman or child should be trapped under the hand of abuse. The cost of freedom might be high, but it's worth is far more valuable."

Her eyes shot daggers at me. "What help do *you*—a single-mother, who has limited resources, possibly hope to offer? You are only one person."

I sat up straighter, fire burning in the base of my belly. "That's all it takes: one person. It was one person who reached out to me, just one person who told me there was hope. One person can mean the difference between life and death, Divina. We all have been given a voice—and I'm ready to use mine."

She leaned in, as if to circle her prey. "But I find it interesting how you didn't use your voice before—not until I informed your readers of this secret in your past did you decided to *speak out*. We often keep secrets for one reason: because we are ashamed. Isn't it hypocritical of you to ask these kinds of women to identify themselves when you *didn't* for so long?"

I took a deep breath, pulling myself back out of the hole that wanted to consume me. I wouldn't let it take me. Not today.

"No. Leaving your abuser is only step one, but recovering from abuse is a life-long journey. I have shared my story before, although I never shared it publicly until recently. I believed it was my job to protect certain people in my life from the details of my abuse—but now I believe that even the ugliest and darkest parts of our lives can be redeemed for good. I used to be ashamed of my story, but I know now that the only way to break the hold of shame is to stop acting ashamed. For me, that is a lesson I am still learning, daily."

Her eyes narrowed as she scrutinized me and went in for the kill—luckily, I'd been waiting for this moment. "After our last interview, we were inundated with responses from our viewers. There were many that seemed to question your character and your credibility. For a woman who often chooses to hide behind her faith, what response do you offer those who deem you and your new agenda nothing but a quest for fame?"

I looked from Divina toward the camera. "There will always be people who don't understand. People whose lives have been untouched by the hurt and destruction of abuse, and those people bring me a great sense of hope. In my opinion, a perfect world is one without the oppression of others. So until we can all share in that same sense of freedom, my quest will be for those who still need to be told it exists."

Divina quickly cut to a commercial break, and just like that, the interview was over. She glared at me for a long second as the camera moved away from us. Throwing down her note cards, she rose and walked over to the news desk, saying nothing more.

I smiled. The satisfaction was intoxicating.

I stood. As the bright lights went off in the living room set, I was finally able to see out into the darkness of the studio. Jackson was still there, a look of pride filling his every feature. I walked to him, my smile unbreakable.

"You were...amazing," he said in a voice that caused my heart to knock against my chest.

"It felt good."

"It *was* good," he said.

Together we walked out of the studio and into the parking lot. We faced each other in the sunshine, his hands in his pockets as he looked at me. A gust of wind seemed to bring back the memories of last night, my momentary satisfaction fizzling as it's invisible fingers ruffled our hair..

"We need to talk," he said.

"Here?" I asked, motioning at the parking lot.

"No, are you free tonight?"

The question stung. I'd been with him nearly every night since I'd arrived in New York, why would I have made other plans?

"Of course," I said.

"I'll come over at seven—we can go for a walk, okay?"

"Fine," I said, suddenly feeling a bit like when my dad took the family dog for a "drive to the farm". This scenario felt eerily similar.

"Walt can take you back to your apartment if that's where you want to go. I have a meeting in an hour...so I'll take a cab."

I hadn't been planning to return to my apartment, but now that's exactly where I wanted to go. Something told me that going to the office was not going to be beneficial today.

"Okay."

"Okay, I'll see you tonight," he said, hesitating as his eyes roamed my face.

The urge to vomit was back again, only this time I had no remembered voicemail to soothe my nerves.

It was going to be a long wait until tonight.

A very, very long wait.

Chapter Forty

It wasn't a total waste of a day while I waited for Jackson. I was actually able to video chat with Sally from my apartment on some ideas I had for the new chapters, documenting specific details of my emotional recovery. I'd spent most of the morning looking through my journal and remembering certain lessons while going through the steps outlined in *The Refuge* curriculum.

I had also called Maggie to ask her advice. As usual, she was very encouraging, and I learned that Jenny had made it out of the ICU. Her status had improved greatly in the last twenty-four hours. Her boyfriend was in custody and awaiting trial. I said a silent prayer for her as I ended the call.

In the afternoon, I walked down the street to get a peach smoothie. The day was cooler than usual—especially for July. The sun was out, but it was hidden behind the clouds, and there was little humidity to battle with. My hair was grateful for that fact.

And then…I watched the clock.

As the last couple hours ticked by, I grew increasingly anxious. Did Jackson want to talk about work? About Livie and Stewart? About us…?

We had never had the official *define-this-relationship* talk, but Jackson didn't seem the type to need to make a declaration in order for something to be. Up until the last few days things had felt like they had progressed with us, like we both felt for each other what we hadn't yet said aloud. But the last seventy-two hours had been a game-changer of sorts.

Jackson had been different—distant.

I didn't believe he was still in love with Livie, although it had been quite a shock to learn she was still connected to his life—to the company, through Stewart. Why couldn't he just let go? Was his regret over how he ending things with her—or how he wasn't there for his brother during his treatments, still that strong? It was a complicated mix of layers upon layers of rationale that I probably wouldn't understand, but I needed to try. One of us had to put forth that effort.

Finally, the witching hour was upon me.

Jackson knocked on my door. I opened to find him wearing dark camo shorts and a grey t-shirt. He looked so boyish, hands in his pockets, as he waited for me to lace up my shoes. We walked together down the hall and into the elevator, not saying much. The tension rolled in my stomach like bad Thai.

As we crossed the street and made our way to Central Park, I noticed how he stayed away from me—how his arm never brushed mine, how our hands never touched—not even accidentally. He was guarded. With each step we walked, my sympathy for him waned. In its place was a mounting level of frustration.

When he sighed, I decided I was done with the silence.

"What's going on, Jackson?" I asked, my voice stronger than intended.

He glanced at me. "That's a loaded question."

"Well, then you should probably start talking."

He exhaled loudly, running his hand through his hair.

"They've given me an ultimatum."

I stopped, causing him to stop as well.

"Who has?"

"Jacob and Stewart are calling a board meeting—asking for my resignation."

"They have the votes they need to push you out?" I asked.

"They think so...they want to vote Stewart in."

"Why...I don't understand?" I asked him.

He nodded. "There was a contract signed between my father, Jacob and Stewart before he died. It stated that Stewart would have the same rights to the company as any Ross successor. If something had happened to Jacob, Stew was next in line. But since Jacob was still alive to vote me in when I showed up, Stewart took a back seat to me. Now Jacob wants to reinstate the succession. He claims that Stewart should be in the CEO position…not me." He pulled on his neck with one hand and then start walking again. "The legalities are a bit more complicated than that."

"So what are you going to do?"

"I'm gonna play their game. I've called some secret meetings myself…to win back some votes before next week's board meeting."

I nearly stumbled over my own feet when I heard him say that. "You…you're going to fight them? *Why* would you do that, Jackson? You aren't even happy there!"

"Happiness is an illusion, Angie."

As we walked into a shaded area of trees, I let out a frustrated cry. He turned sharply at the sound—his face startled. I stopped walking, unwilling to pretend that the more steps we took would take us somewhere, but I knew they wouldn't.

I swallowed, feeling like I'd just been slapped in the face. "Is that what you think I am, then? Just an illusion?"

He stared at me, the answer in his eyes loud and clear.

I took a step forward, picking up his hand. "*I am real*, Jackson. This—what we have together—it's real." My voice cracked under the weight of emotion, straining to be heard. "I've lived in an illusion before—my marriage was one."

He blinked, looking at our joined hands silently. I stared up at his face, the pressure building within my chest. I was overcome with the words I had read recently circling inside my head. I could recall them easily…because they were his words.

"I know how your series ends, Jackson," I said.

"What?" His face was both stunned and confused.

"I read it—I skipped ahead," I said defiantly.

His features darkened as I felt his hand slip from mine. "And?"

"It's awful, Jackson—heartbreaking! I couldn't believe you just left them like that—Quinton and Reagan." I folded my arms in front of me, catching his eye momentarily. "But I get it now…I *so* get it."

He laughed, humorlessly. "Is this where you psychoanalyze me, Angie? Why don't you just tell me how you really feel!"

"Fine." I refused to look away from him. "I think you're acting like a coward."

"What did you say?"

"You're. Acting. Like. A. Coward. You tell yourself that you can't be happy, that you can't dream—that you can't love again because of all your regrets." I threw my arms up gesturing in every direction. "But look around you, Jackson. You're the one who hasn't moved on." I lowered my voice. "I don't understand why you keep fighting for a life that makes you miserable…not when your life could be so much more."

For a brief second, his hand reached for me, but he pulled it back before contact was made.

"I tried to tell you," he said quietly, shaking his head. "I shouldn't have let you get so close to me."

My breathing faltered, my body shuddering at his words. I took a step closer and put my hand up to his face, my heart aching as I spoke. "That was never in your control, Jackson. No one gets to tell my heart who it will love." Tears spilled down over my cheeks before I could stop them.

"You can't love me, Angie," he pleaded. "Please don't love me—you deserve a better man."

"I already love a better man. He just can't see that you're one and the same."

He closed his eyes as I held his face between my hands.

"Angie."

"Haven't we both lived with enough regret?" I whispered.

His jaw flexed in the moonlight, as he took my hand away. "I'm saving you from another one."

I shook my head, pain shredding my heart in two. "No, Jackson…denial never saves us, it only delays us."

He watched Reagan, as if in a dream. She'd just loaded up the remaining boxes into her trunk and was walking back to lock her front door.

During the last year, Quinton's life had been flipped upside down by this woman—turned inside out. They'd each sacrificed and risked their lives with the hope of saving the other.

But sometimes, even the best intentions, even the strongest courage, even the deepest love...cannot save us from ourselves.

As she glanced down the street one last time, she confirmed what they both already knew: True love was only a dream.

Heartache was a cold, seeping pain, one that chilled me to the bone.

It had all been so civil: Jackson walking me back, kissing my cheek, driving away. Yet nothing in me *felt* civil. Nothing in me wanted to believe that our last words had just been uttered. But they had. The only promise spoken to our future was a weak, yet dutiful goodbye.

By the time I got inside my apartment, my head was pounding in equal measure with my heart. I wanted to scream, or cry, or hit something, but the throbbing in my skull kept me from all of those. I walked into the room and nearly tripped over the suitcase I had pulled out earlier. It was then that I was jarred back into the present.

The reality that I was leaving in just over twenty-four hours was suffocating. I lay on the bed, curling up as small as I could and touched the spot on my neck that had once brought me comfort, strength, and hope.

But now what lay under my fingertips was the same thing that lay heavy in my chest: Emptiness.

Chapter Forty-One

I was brushing my teeth when I heard a knock at my door. Abandoning my task, I hustled to answer. My stomach leapt to my throat as I reached for the knob. But on the other side was not the most stunning eligible bachelor I'd ever laid eyes on…it was Pippy.

She entered like her usual ray-of-sunshine self, handing me an orange smoothie concoction, which she said she added an energy boost. Tears filled my eyes even as I smiled at her.

"Don't start that yet," she warned. "I'm not ready to say goodbye."

I nodded obediently as one rogue tear slipped out.

"What can I help you pack?" she asked. "Can I put your dresses into garment bags?"

"Sure," I said, humoring her. She had insisted we pick up a few bags the other day; she couldn't stand the idea of my formal wear going inside my suitcase. As we walked into my bedroom. Just the sight of those dresses felt like too much to bear.

Pippy lifted each gown up like it was a piece of lost treasure, and carefully tucked it into the garment bag. She was unusually quiet, which told me she had something to say.

"What is it, Pippy?" I asked, sitting on the bed.

She smiled, sheepishly. "I heard what happened."

My insides dropped as if a giant magnet inside the earth's core was pulling them downward.

Was Jackson just going around announcing the end of our never-to-be-defined romance?

"He told you?" I all but whispered.

She shook her head, slowly. "I overheard them talking about it."

"Them who?" I asked.

"My dad and Stew."

My mind was reeling. "Okay...what *exactly* are you talking about?"

"The Publishers dinner two nights ago. When Stewart punched Jackson. What did you think I was talking about?" She asked, her eyes round with interest.

"Nothing. So...what did Stewart say?" I said, scrambling to change topics.

Pippy continued to eye me like a mental patient as she spoke. "He said that he was sorry for getting out of control and hopes it won't hurt the company. That such a thing would never happen again...and that he wishes Jackson would give him the chance to explain the truth. But he won't listen to anyone."

"What was she like—Livie?"

She exhaled loudly. "She was kind and beautiful and spunky…"

I glanced at her. "But?"

She shrugged. "I don't know. I guess I just never felt the chemistry between them. She was just always there, ya know? Everything was so expected with them. They were each other's safe choice."

"Do you think there was something more going on with her and Stewart?"

She shook her head. "My dad grilled him relentlessly on that subject once her letter surfaced. Whatever attraction they felt for each other was never acted upon. Despite what Jackson thinks, Stewart loves our family…he would never willingly hurt him. He is much too loyal to the company and to my brother to do something like that. It's not his character."

"Jackson won't let it go. He's gonna fight for the company so that it's not passed on to Stewart."

Pippy ignored me. "You have the spark."

"What?"

"What I never saw between him and Livie. There's tension and passion and...joy when you two are around each other. It's like watching the best romance drama unfold. He loves you. I know he does."

I fell back on the bed, covering my eyes with my arm.

Pippy did the same, quietly breathing next to me, as if waiting for some romantic sentiment to come out of my lips.

"It's over, Pippy. Jackson didn't choose me. He chose her—he's still choosing her."

Pippy rolled over and put her arms around me. With or without the ties of a marriage, Pippy was the little sister I had always wished for. I refused to lose her.

****

Hope was a funny thing.

Once you had it, it was hard to kill.

All night I waited for him to call, or text, or even come over. To tell me he'd been wrong, to tell me his past couldn't be fixed by penance. But my waiting, it turned out, was all in vain.

With one last look at the building that had been my home for the last six weeks, I walked out to the empty town car Pippy had reserved for me. Walt took my bags and put them into the trunk while I climbed into the all-too-familiar backseat.

"I took the liberty to provide you with a lock for your each of your suitcases, Ms. Flores. Here's your key."

I thanked him and tucked the key into my purse. He guided the car into traffic, and I watched as the city passed by my window on the way to the airport. New York was a city so full of sounds and smells and life. I thought of all the dreamers who had sacrificed everything to be here, the ones who had left family and friends and loved ones. I thought of the ones who had been willing to start over, no matter what the cost, without any promises in return.

That's what hope did: it blinded us to reality.

****

"Mom!"

My heart lifted at that word spoken in a beloved voice.

I ran to him in baggage claim, and Cody threw his arms around me as soon as I was within hugging range. There was no sweeter hug in the entire world. He talked a million miles a minute as Briggs grabbed my bags off the belt. We headed to the car, an inferno of hot air hitting me the instant we walked outside of the Dallas airport. Briggs and I listened and laughed as Cody recapped his favorite moments of soccer camp—again.

What a strange feeling to walk inside my house.

Though the place was familiar, it was unmistakably absent of that homey feeling.

Waiting for us in the living room, Rosie rushed at me as I dropped my purse onto a side table.

"You look so good!" she yelled.

"You look good, too, Rose. I missed you." My voice cracked briefly. She pulled away from our hug to inspect me—like I had a glob of chocolate syrup on my face.

I hadn't told her.

I couldn't tell her. Not on the phone.

Her eyes went from being a focused beam of joy to a dismal understanding—apparently this was my new effect on people. My lip trembled as I turned away to keep Cody from seeing tears splash down my cheeks.

"Cody, can you go check the trunk for your mama—make sure she got everything?" Rosie asked.

"Si!" Cody called.

She laughed. "Gracias, chico."

The second he was gone, she pulled me into the bathroom.

I sat on the side of the tub and brought my hands to my face. She shut the door behind her quietly.

"Oh no…no, no, no," she murmured over and over.

I nodded, grabbing a wad of toilet paper and blowing my nose. I'd managed to hold my tears in all day. Evidently the holding tank had reached its limit.

"It's not over," she said defiantly as she put her hand on her hip.

"It is, Rose. He's fighting to stay at his company; he doesn't want me."

"No, this is not how the story ends."

I rolled my eyes, thinking if she only knew the kind of ending Jackson was capable of writing, she would have a different opinion.

"Sorry Rose. Not everyone gets a happy ending."

She pushed my shoulder back, almost knocking me off balance and into the tub.

"You do."

I smiled weakly as she pulled me in for another hug.

****

I spent the evening catching up with Cody, snuggling with him on the couch. I finally made him go to bed when his head bobbed for the tenth time or so. Grudgingly, he turned off his light and went to sleep. I shut down the house and made my way back to my bedroom. Apparently, Briggs had left my suitcases and garment bags on top of my bed.

I glanced at the clock. It was almost eleven, which meant it felt like midnight to my body. I knew myself too well though. I would not want to spend tomorrow unpacking and organizing. Better just to rip the band-aid off now.

I unlocked and unzipped the larger of the two suitcases and then stood back...blinking.

There was a wrapped, light blue box in the center of my suitcase with a card attached. I bit my lip and shifted my weight back and forth on my feet as a thousand questions filled my mind—the most obvious being, *who had done this?*

My options were limited at best:

1. Walt

2. An airplane bomber with a master luggage key

3. A magical fairy

I deduced it was the first, although I approached the box as if it were indeed a nicely packaged bomb that lay in wait for me and not a gift. My fingers shook as they held the box, the shiny paper was miraculously without a wrinkle as I began the process of unwrapping it. I didn't want to read the card first, somehow I knew whatever words awaited me there would be more painful than the contents of this box.

"Oh my gosh…" I gasped. The lid held a familiar logo, one I'd only seen in magazines or on TV. *Or in New York City.*

As I lifted the lid to peek inside the box a sob broke from my chest.

My necklace.

No, not my old, frail, faded pendant and chain. A *new* one—or rather, an exquisitely expensive replica of the old. One that hadn't been weathered with time or tears.

I sank down to the floor near my bed and laid my head against the comforter, opening the box again to stare at the most beautiful piece of jewelry I'd ever seen—much less been given. I touched the cool silver charm of angel wings surrounded by a heart encrusted with diamonds, and let the sobs roll out until I was short of breath.

I stared at the unopened note, afraid to read the message attached to such an exquisite gift.

Several minutes passed until I was brave enough to pick it up.

I opened the envelope and pulled out a card. Jackson's handwriting was yet another kick to the gut. My breathing faltered as I read his words.

Angela,

I wanted to give this to you in person, but I made Walt do it for me instead. I just couldn't do it. I couldn't watch you leave…and I knew I couldn't beg for you to stay either.

I realize I owe you more than a "five nice things list" for not showing up to the airport to see you off properly, but perhaps this gift can help me make a plea bargain?

I know this necklace can never replace the one you lost—or the memories that were attached to it, but I hope it will bring you many new ones. Happy ones. When your Grandpa first gave your Granny that necklace all those years ago, I'm sure he wanted to protect her, to give her a Guardian Angel that would watch over her when he couldn't be there for her…

But the angel I know is not found inside a necklace.

She's not a pendant made from gold or silver. She's as real as her name depicts. Her beauty is as matchless as her heart.

I'm convinced she is my angel, and I miss her something terrible.

I need you, Ang.

Jackson.

P.S. Don't give up on me yet.

I don't know how long I sat on the floor thinking about Jackson, or when I finally gave in to the pull of sleep, but I woke up with a new revelation and a warm feeling in my chest.

When I was a young girl I believed that romantic love had the power to save. I saw it as the great remedy, the one cure that could fix all wounds and mend all hearts. But I didn't believe that anymore.

Sometimes love was not all we needed.

Sometimes it didn't cure our hurts.

Sometimes it wasn't the eraser of our mistakes.

Love is instead, the bridge that leads the broken to grace, hope, and redemption. Love is the greatest amplifier that God ever gave to us. Our strengths are made stronger with it, and our faults are shown mercy because of it.

As much as I wanted to be with Jackson, to hold his hand, and kiss his lips...I knew *my* love could not heal him. I could no sooner make him fly than I could reach into his soul and make him forgive himself. He had to do it on his own. I knew all about recovery, and Jackson needed to recover from his guilt more than I needed him to love me.

If Jackson needed distance, then I could give him that.

After all, I'd already given him my heart.

I opened my phone and sent him a text:

Thank you for the necklace. It's the most stunning gift I've ever been given.

P.S. I won't give up on you, Jackson.

Chapter Forty-Two

"You ready babe?" I called out.

"Yep! Uncle B's coming tonight, too!" Cody yelled back from his room. I filled his water bottle as he put his cleats on. He was so excited about tonight's game. And I was happy to watch him play.

I'd just finished my book revisions for Sally last night. She would be proud of my efforts. During the last two weeks, I'd stayed up late in order to get them finished since my hours at the flower shop had picked up. Editing had served as a great way to cope with my now quiet evenings. Crazy to think I'd been more than fine with the quiet prior to NYC—prior to Jackson Ross.

I hadn't heard from him in several days. We'd texted brief exchanges back and forth almost daily since I'd been home, but I was careful not to initiate. I wanted him to take the lead. He knew where I stood. I'd already poured out my heart to him in the middle of Central Park.

If there was a next move for us, it would be in *his* timing, and knowing Jackson the way I did...it could be a very, very long wait.

"I'll be in the car, mom!" Cody called as he ran out the door, leaving me with all the soccer loot.

Nice. Thanks.

I followed Cody out the door, trying to balance a duffle bag, mini-cooler, and water bottle and purse, all while locking the deadbolt behind me.

"I need to ask Santa for octopus arms for Christmas!" I yelled out to no one.

I heard a deep, familiar chuckle come from somewhere behind me. I froze in place.

I closed my eyes.

"I only have two arms to offer—but they're yours if you want them."

I turned around slowly, tears already blurring my vision.

"Jackson." The word was like a sweet prayer on my lips.

In that instant, while watching him take my porch steps two at a time and unburdening my arms, my life came full-circle. The man of my dreams had finally replaced the man of my nightmares.

He wrapped his arms around me and nuzzled his face into the crook of my neck as Cody whooped and hollered somewhere nearby.

"You surprised, Mom? I told you I could keep a secret, Jackson!" Cody yelled.

My laugh was giddy, elated even. Jackson's smile was huge as he waved Cody over to the steps. He hugged my son close.

"You did a great job, buddy. Remind me to tell your Uncle B thanks, too, okay?"

Cody gave Jackson a high-five. "You bet…but we should get going so I don't have to run laps." He ran to Jackson's black, shiny rental car.

"You're staying for his game?" I asked, hopeful.

"I'm staying," he said, his eyes intense with meaning.

My heart soared at the infinite possibilities hidden within those two words. He leaned down and scooped up my son's soccer paraphernalia as I followed after him.

****

I leaned into Jackson's shoulder as Cody ran toward his teammates, my heart racing with unbelief. I inhaled, taking in a whiff of his aftershave and cologne—the one that smelled of mint and ocean and cedar.

Jackson laughed. "Did you just smell me?"

I looked up at him. "Sorry, I'm still not sure you're really here."

He glanced over at the field where the practice drills had begun and pulled me toward a large oak tree. As he put his hands on my face his gaze dropped to the necklace I was wearing for the first time. His fingers trailed over my collarbone and lifted the pendant, staring at it for several seconds before fixing his gaze on my eyes once more.

"I'm in love with you, Angela Flores."

A tiny laugh escaped me at the bluntness of his confession. But as he put a finger to my lips I no longer felt like laughing. I stared at his face, his eyes, his lips…

"I thought about something you said at the lake—it was like an anthem in my head every day that I wasn't with you. You know what it was?"

I shook my head, my lips desiring his kiss more and more with each passing second.

"You said, you didn't have time to grow bitter, not when you had someone to love. Remember that?"

I nodded again, dumbfounded at his memory.

"And I remember so much more than that, Ang."

He moved his finger across my lips and dipped his head, claiming my mouth with his own. Even when I tasted the salt of my tears mingling with our lips he was not deterred.

"How long are you here?" I whispered, finding my footing as he laced our fingers together.

"I told you, Ang. I'm staying—as long as you'll let me that is."

"That might be a really long time," I said smiling.

"Deal."

****

"You're so beautiful, Angie," he said, watching me walk across the living room after tucking Cody into bed.

A slow blush crept into my cheeks as he reached his hand out for mine. His mouth curved into a slow smile, and I debated with myself when the last time was that I had felt such infectious joy.

His eyes held steady as he spoke. "I took your advice."

"What advice was that?" I asked.

Jackson lifted my hand to his lips and kissed it. "When the board meeting came down to my vote...I realized I'd been fighting for the wrong thing for far too long. I resigned that day. I'm choosing to move on, and I told Stewart that before I voted him in." He shifted in his seat. "I don't want to be the man I've been anymore, Ang."

My heart pounded in response to him. "Then who do you want to be?"

"The guy who gets the girl in the end."

I squished closer to him on the sofa, wrapping my arms around his neck. "You already have her."

He nuzzled his lips into the sensitive spot beneath my ear. "But I don't deserve her."

"If we based God's goodness to us on what we deserved, then how would any of us ever know happiness, or love?"

His lips found mine, kissing me with such tender passion, my scalp tingled.

Pulling away gently, his breath fluttered across my mouth. "I don't plan on being anywhere that you're not. I hope that works for you and Cody."

Planting my lips on his once more, I showed him my approval.

"And you're going to write again?" I asked eagerly.

He cupped my face, kissing my nose, my cheek, my chin. "Yes, I'm going to write again."

"And you promise to write happy endings?"

"I promise," he said in between kisses. "Happy...endings."

I pulled back slightly, teasing him. "So you've changed your stance, then?"

His eyes crinkled with delight. "What stance is that?"

"That true love is just a dream."

Drawing me close again, his breath tickled my ear as he whispered, "If it is, then let me never wake up."

The End

Epilogue

Almost four years had passed since the first time I visited the Lake House in Connecticut with Cody and Jackson. I'd lost count of how many times we'd been back since, but each time had felt as significant as the first: Jackson and I were engaged there three years ago, Pippy and Caleb were married there two summers ago, and Jacob took his final breaths there this past September.

Which was exactly how he'd wanted it.

Before he passed, Jacob was able to read his brother's most recent work of fiction—a highly acclaimed mystery series based on an expedition near the Nile River. Jackson dedicated the series to Jacob, knowing full well that without him, it would never have been written. And much to Jacob's delight, Jackson also dropped his pen name.

As I packed, Jackson's arms encircled my waist from behind. He planted a kiss at the base of my neck, sending a tingle of pleasure dancing down my spine.

"You about ready, gorgeous? Briggs is here to take us to the airport. Cody's outside loading the suitcases now."

Biting my bottom lip, I checked the contents of the bag one last time. *Did I remember everything?* It'd been so long since—

Jackson spun me around. "Everything will be fine. It's only a three-hour flight." He kissed the tip of my nose. "And I promise to be the one to do a midnight store-run on the off-chance you actually forgot to pack something."

His eyes sparkled when he spoke, and I knew he was just as excited as I was.

Glancing at the bag, he asked, "Can I take this to the van for you?"

He reached for the strap.

"Wait," I said, pulling him back. "I'm not finished yet."

Jackson arched an eyebrow as my lips found his. I'd never grow tired of kissing this man.

"*Now* you can take it."

Chuckling, Jackson hoisted the mini-goliath onto his shoulder and left our bedroom. My stomach fluttered as I walked across the hall and cracked open the nursery door. Waiting for me inside was a sight I once believed I'd never see again, not in my home anyway.

A sleeping baby. *My baby.*

The adoption was finalized just last week, and Lucy, the beautifully spunky nine-month old, was ours. Officially. Tears pricked my eyes as I leaned over her crib. Running my hand over her dark hair and onto her bag, I lifted up a quiet prayer, the same prayer I'd prayed over Cody.

A prayer of protection, one God had answered many times over.

Lucy grunted and stretched as I brought her to my chest. Cradling her sleepy head into my neck, I swayed in the dimly-lit room.

"Are you ready for this, Lucy?" I whispered. "There are some very special people waiting to meet you...your aunt Pippy has been begging to kiss your sweet cheeks." I kiss the top of her head. "There's no place like the lake house. You will love it there. I promise."

I changed her diaper then headed toward the front door, Lucy rubbing her tired brown eyes as we walked into the sunshine.

"There she is! I need to kiss my niece before you whisk her away. I don't want her getting any ideas about the East Coast. She loves Texas—don't you, Lucy?" Briggs took Lucy from my arms as Cody kissed her temple.

"She may not be able to say it yet, but she knows I'm the *cool* Uncle," Briggs said.

I rolled my eyes. "Well, how could she not? You remind her—and us—*every* time you hold her."

Cody laughed. "You are cool, Uncle B."

Briggs slung an arm around Cody's shoulder. "See?"

Lucy giggled as she touched Briggs' animated face. My heart swooned.

"Can I buckle her in the car seat, mom?" Cody asked. He was as smitten with her as I was.

"Sure, Code."

Cody took Lucy from Briggs and walked around the van, talking to her expressively.

"You ready to go?" Briggs asked Jackson and I.

"Yeah, thanks again for taking us Briggs," Jackson said, slapping him on the back.

"No problem. Charlie wanted to come, but the twins aren't feeling well. She didn't want to risk getting Lucy sick before her first big flight."

Getting in the van, I glanced back at our farmhouse. Just north of Dallas, we'd purchased enough land to be considered "country folk". And where Cody finally got his dog, a dog that was currently staying with Auntie Rosie.

Though we thought long and hard about where we would call home, we realized once again that home was comprised of so much more than the property we chose, but of the family we cherished—a family that had grown by one more in the recent months. We decided to stay in Texas—much to my brother's delight—after agreeing to make several trips a year to visit the East Coast.

As Cody sang his sister a song in the backseat and Briggs and Jackson laughed in the front, a thankful tear escaped as I reflected on a poem I'd written nearly a decade ago.

All Who Dream

There's a time and place for dreaming

A melody within life's meaning

You search and seek and pray and pine

Yet in the end its hope you'll find

Some days are bleak while others bare

Some feel rooted in deep despair

But don't lose faith and don't lose sight

For dreams will come to those who fight

If chance is slim and risk is great

Remember the reward at stake

The test is found in how you fail

For joy itself cannot turn stale

This truth and hope act as a team

They light a path for all who dream

Author's Note:

As I reflect on the *Letting Go* series as a whole, my heart is filled with so many emotions. I have loved these characters like friends, laughing with them, crying with them, and at times even learning from them. Though it's difficult to say goodbye, I am overwhelmed with gratefulness for you, my readers.

I am not the same woman I was in January of 2013 when I self-published my debut novel, *All for Anna*. My dream was to write a love story that was dipped in the raw truths of recovery; the ups and downs, the hurts and heartaches, and the hope that comes when we look beyond ourselves. Never in my wildest imagination did I envision how *All for Anna* would so radically change my life.

Writing is my passion, but the beauty of love's transforming power is what stirs my soul.

Thank you for taking a chance on me. *Thank you* for sharing this series with your friends, and *thank you* for your emails, messages, and posts of support and encouragement. Without the inspiration of my faithful readers, my stories would have never come to life.

So, from the deepest corners of my heart, *thank you.*

Acknowledgements:

These are the major ingredients that make up the recipe of an author. Each of you are vital to my writing, to my voice, and to my passion. Thank you is simply not enough.

God, you are my **hope**.

Husband, Tim Deese, you are my **heart**.

Family, you are my **anchor**.

Friends, you are my **sanity**.

Agent, Jessica Kirkland, you are my **encouragement**.

Beta readers, you are my **support**.

Editors, Julie Gwinn and Jill Elizabeth Nelson, you are my **rescue**.

Cover artist, Sarah Hansen @ Okay Creations, you are my **vision**.

Readers, you are my **inspiration**.

Special Thanks:

Jessica Kirkland, Literary Agent at the Blythe Daniel Agency: I could write a book on the phraseology of Jessica Kirkland. Between your southern "might cans, might shoulds, might coulds" and lovely encouragements to "beef-up the romance, Nicole!"—not to mention your flowery revision comments (ahem...cough, cough)—your knowledge of what makes fiction *great,* is truly exceptional. It's borderline superhuman, actually. You are so much more than my agent, Jess. I count you as one of my greatest blessings. I'm so grateful for our divine appointment last fall, and for the friendship we have since established. Thank you for taking a chance on me, and thank you for believing in my voice. I <3 you!

Julie Gwinn, Editor: Thank you for your thoughtful insights, critiques, and suggestions. I feel so blessed to have worked with you on this manuscript. I hope we can have a cup of coffee together at next year's conference (and maybe a plate full of chocolate, too) so we can discuss our love of romance and literature.

Jill Elizabeth Nelson, Editor: When I entered the silent auction last fall, I never could have guessed that the editorial package I won would include an author, mentor, editor and *friend.* Your skillful eye for detail has made me a better writer. You have taught me SO MUCH! (And yes, those caps are just for you! Hahaha!) Truly, I am so blessed to know you, Jill. Thank you the hours you poured into me, and into this novel.

Beta Readers: Amy Matayo, Aimee Thomas, Ashley Thomas, Kim Southwick, Renee Deese, Nicki Davis, Kacy Koffa, Rebekah Zollman, Bethany Deese, Britni Nash, Jenny Knudsen, Kim Crank, Jessica Kirkland, Desi Brown, Lara Brahms, Kristin Avila. Thank your for your hours of devotion and loyalty to these characters. I love each of you!

Author Bio:

Nicole Deese is a lover of fiction. When she's not writing (or listening to the voices in her head), she can be found curled up on the sofa, reading. She often fantasizes about *reading escapes*, which look a lot like kid-free, laundry-free, and cooking-free vacations. A girl can dream, right?

Her debut novel, a contemporary romance, *All for Anna*, was released in January 2013 and has hit multiple milestones, including a 4.6 star rating on Amazon and over 150,000 downloads on Kindle. She has since completed the Letting Go series, and a Christmas novella, *A Cliché Christmas*, which will be released in November 2014.

Nicole lives in Frisco, Texas with her hunk-of-a-husband Tim, and two rowdy boys, Preston and Lincoln.

More From Nicole Deese

All For Anna – Letting Go – Book One:
http://www.amazon.com/All-For-Anna-ebook/dp/B00B4XI0SG

All She Wanted – Letting Go – Book Two:
http://www.amazon.com/All-She-Wanted-Letting-ebook/dp/B00D2IBTCK

Website:
http://www.nicoledeese.com

Facebook:
https://www.facebook.com/nicoledeeseauthor

This author is represented by Jessica Kirkland of the Blythe Daniel Agency.
All media requests should be directed to:
http://www.theblythedanielagency.com

Made in the USA
Columbia, SC
22 September 2020